СКАЗКИ НАРОДОВ СССР

A MOUNTAIN OF GEMS

Fairy-Tales of the Peoples of the Soviet Land

Fredonia Books
Amsterdam, The Netherlands

A Mountain of Gems:
Fairy-Tales of the Peoples of the Soviet Land

Translated by
Irina Zheleznova

ISBN: 1-58963-562-0

Reprinted from the original edition

Fredonia Books
Amsterdam, the Netherlands
http://www.fredoniabooks.com

CONTENTS

5

FROM THE TRANSLATOR

Dear readers!

I am sure you all know that the Soviet Union is a huge country, the largest in the world. Its neighbours are Alaska in the East and Scandinavia in the West. In the south it stretches as far as the Caucasus and Pamir mountain ranges, and in the North reaches out into the Arctic Ocean. And the heart, the pulsating heart of this great country, is Moscow.

When the rays of dawn light up the sky of Khabarovsk in the Far East, the sun is only just beginning to set in Minsk, Kiev and other cities in the west; and while icy winds blow in Yakutia, roses bloom in Tashkent and vacationers enjoy the sun on the pebbly beaches of the Black Sea.

Many different peoples live in this huge country, each with its own habits and traditions, its own language. The Uzbek language, for instance, bears as little resemblance to the Russian or, say, the Moldavian as the Arabic does to the English or the Chinese.

And each of the peoples of the Soviet Union has its own fairy-tales.

The Chukchi and Nenets tales as well as the tales of other peoples of Russia's North transport us into the snowy tundra, a realm of fierce frosts and howling blizzards, where the dog and the reindeer are man's best friends. In the tales of the peoples of Central Asia caravans of camels plod slowly over the scorching sands, and the ceaseless murmur of water comes from the numerous canals that feed the ever thirsty fields. Other scenes and images rise up before us when we read Russian fairy-tales. The stout-hearted young heroes of these tales gallop on horseback over hills and dales which are green in summer and carpeted with snow in winter, while their lovely tsarevnas sit patiently waiting for them in their log towers with windows of mica.

Do you know why I have translated all these fairy-tales for you? It was because I enjoyed reading them so much.

Open the book, and you will find yourselves in a world of magic. None of your old friends will be there—neither Jack the Giant Killer, nor Little Red Riding Hood, nor Cinderella or any of the others. Instead, together with Ivan the Peasant's Son you will cross swords with Chudo-Yudo, the fire-breathing monster; follow Pokati-Goroshek the Rolling Pea into the underground kingdom and return from there on the back of an eagle; marvel at the cleverness of Zarniyar who outwitted the sly and cruel Shah; be filled with admiration at Boroldoi-Mergen, the brave hunter of the Altai Mountains who risked the life of his own son in order to save his people; delight in the resourcefulness of a simple weaver who surpassed in wisdom the wisest councillors of the tsar.

And I know that when you have met them, these and other heroes in this book, you will grow to love them, and they will become your good and faithful friends.

THE FROG TSAREVNA

A Russian Fairy-Tale

Long, long ago there was a Tsar who had three sons. One day, when his sons were grown to manhood, the Tsar called them to him and said:

"My dear sons, while yet I am not old I should like to see you married and to rejoice in the sight of your children and my grandchildren."

And the sons replied:

"If that is your wish, Father, then give us your blessing. Who would you like us to marry?"

"Now then, my sons, you must each of you take an arrow and go out into the open field. You must shoot the arrows, and wherever they fall, there will you find your destined brides."

The sons bowed to their father, and each of them taking an arrow, went out into the open field. There they drew their bows and let fly their arrows.

The eldest son's arrow fell in a boyar's courtyard and was picked up by the boyar's daughter. The middle son's arrow fell in a rich merchant's yard and was picked up by the merchant's daughter. And as for the youngest son, Tsarevich Ivan, his arrow shot up and flew away he knew not where. He went in search of it and he walked on and on till he reached a marsh, and what did he see sitting there but a Frog with the arrow in its mouth.

Said Tsarevich Ivan to the Frog:

"Frog, Frog, give me back my arrow."

But the Frog replied:

"I will if you marry me!"

"What do you mean, how can I marry a frog!"

"You must, for I am your destined bride."

Tsarevich Ivan felt sad and crestfallen. But there was nothing to be done, and he picked up the Frog and carried it home. And the Tsar celebrated three weddings: his eldest son he married to the boyar's daughter, his middle son—to the merchant's daughter, and poor Tsarevich Ivan—to the Frog.

Some little time passed, and the Tsar called his sons to his side.

"I want to see which of your wives is the better needlewoman," said he. "Let them each make me a shirt by tomorrow morning."

The sons bowed to their father and left him.

Tsarevich Ivan came home, sat down and hung his head. And the Frog hopped over the floor and up to him and asked:

"Why do you hang your head, Tsarevich Ivan? What is it that troubles you?"

"Father bids you make him a shirt by tomorrow morning."

Said the Frog:

"Do not grieve, Tsarevich Ivan, but go to bed, for morning is wiser than evening."

Tsarevich Ivan went to bed, and the Frog hopped out on to the porch, cast off its frog skin and turned into Vasilisa the Wise and Clever, a maiden fair beyond compare.

She clapped her hands and cried:

"Come, my women and maids, make haste and set to work! Make me a shirt by tomorrow morning, like those my own father used to wear."

In the morning Tsarevich Ivan awoke, and there was the Frog hopping on the floor again, but the shirt was all ready and lying on the table wrapped in a handsome towel. Tsarevich Ivan was overjoyed. He took the shirt and he went with it to his father who was busy receiving his two elder sons' gifts. The eldest son laid out his shirt, and the Tsar took it and said:

"This shirt will only do for a poor peasant to wear."

The middle son laid out his shirt, and the Tsar said:

"This shirt will only do to go to the baths in."

Then Tsarevich Ivan laid out his shirt, all beautifully embroidered in gold and silver, and the Tsar took one look at it and said:

"Now that is a shirt to wear on holidays!"

The two elder brothers went home and they spoke among themselves and said:

"It seems we were wrong to laugh at Tsarevich Ivan's wife. She is no frog, but a witch."

Now the Tsar again called his sons.

"Let your wives bake me some bread by tomorrow morning," said he. "I want to know which of them is the best cook."

Tsarevich Ivan hung his head and went home. And the Frog asked him:

"Why are you so sad, Tsarevich Ivan?"

Said Tsarevich Ivan:

"You are to bake some bread for my father by tomorrow morning."

"Do not grieve, Tsarevich Ivan, but go to bed. Morning is wiser than evening."

And her two sisters-in-law, who had laughed at the Frog at first, now sent an old woman who worked in the kitchen to see how she baked her bread.

But the Frog was sly and guessed what they were up to. She kneaded some dough, broke off the top of the stove and threw the dough down the hole. The old woman ran to the two sisters-in-law and told them all about it, and they did as the Frog had done.

And the Frog hopped out on to the porch, turned into Vasilisa the Wise and Clever and clapped her hands.

"Come, my women and maids, make haste and set to work!" cried she. "By tomorrow morning bake me some soft white bread, the kind I used to eat at my own father's house."

In the morning Tsarevich Ivan woke up, and there was the bread all ready, lying on the table and prettily decorated with all manner of things: stamped figures on the sides and towns with walls and gates on the top.

Tsarevich Ivan was overjoyed. He wrapped up the bread in a towel and took it to his father who was just receiving the loaves his elder sons had brought. Their wives had dropped the dough into the stove as the old woman had told them to do, and the loaves came out charred and lumpy.

The Tsar took the bread from his eldest son, he looked at it and he sent it to the servants' hall. He took the bread from his middle son, and he did the same with it. But when Tsarevich Ivan handed him his bread, the Tsar said:

"Now that is bread to be eaten only on holidays!"

And the Tsar bade his three sons come and feast with him on the morrow together with their wives.

Once again Tsarevich Ivan came home sad and sorrowful, and he hung his head very low. And the Frog hopped over the floor and up to him and said:

"Croak, croak, why are you so sad, Tsarevich Ivan? Is it that your father has grieved you by an unkind word?"

"Oh, Frog, Frog!" cried Tsarevich Ivan. "How can I help being sad? The Tsar has ordered me to bring you to his feast, and how can I show you to people!"

Said the Frog in reply:

"Do not grieve, Tsarevich Ivan, but go to the feast alone, and I will follow later. When you hear a great tramping and thundering, do not be afraid, but if they ask you what it is, say: 'That is my Frog riding in her box.'"

So Tsarevich Ivan went to the feast alone, and his elder brothers came with their wives who were all dressed up in their finest clothes and had their brows blackened and roses painted on their cheeks. They stood there, and they made fun of Tsarevich Ivan.

"Why have you come without your wife?" asked they. "You could have brought her in a handkerchief. Wherever did you find such a beauty? You must have searched all the swamps for her."

Now the Tsar with his sons and his daughters-in-law and all the guests sat down to feast at the oaken tables covered with embroidered cloths. Suddenly there came a great tramping and thundering, and the whole palace shook and trembled. The guests were frightened and jumped up from their seats. But Tsarevich Ivan said:

"Do not fear, honest folk. That is only my Frog riding in her box."

And there dashed up to the porch of the Tsar's palace a gilded carriage drawn by six white horses, and out of it stepped Vasilisa the Wise and Clever. Her gown of sky-blue silk was studded with stars, and on her head she wore the bright crescent moon, and so beautiful was she that it cannot be pictured and cannot be told, but was a true wonder and joy to behold! She took Tsarevich Ivan by the hand and led him to the oaken tables covered with embroidered cloths.

The guests began eating and drinking and making merry. Vasilisa the Wise and Clever drank from her glass and poured the dregs into her left sleeve. She ate some swan meat and threw the bones into her right sleeve.

And the wives of the elder sons saw what she did and they did the same. They ate and drank and then the time came to dance. Vasilisa the Wise and Clever caught Tsarevich Ivan by the hand and began to dance. She danced and she whirled and she circled round and round, and everyone watched and marvelled. She waved her left sleeve, and a lake appeared; she waved her right sleeve, and white swans began to swim upon the lake. The Tsar and his guests were filled with wonder.

Then the wives of the two elder sons began dancing. They waved their left sleeves, and only splashed mead over the guests; they waved their right sleeves, and bones flew about on all sides, and one bone hit the Tsar in the eye. And the Tsar was very angry and drove out both his daughters-in-law.

In the meantime, Tsarevich Ivan slipped out, ran home, and finding the frog skin, threw it in the stove and burnt it.

Now Vasilisa the Wise and Clever came home, and she at once saw that her frog skin was gone. She sat down on a bench, very sad and sorrowful, and she said to Tsarevich Ivan:

"Ah, Tsarevich Ivan, what have you done! Had you but waited just three more days, I would have been yours for ever. But now farewell. Seek me beyond the Thrice-Nine Lands in the Thrice-Ten Tsardom where lives Koshchei the Deathless."

And Vasilisa the Wise and Clever turned into a grey cuckoo-bird and flew out of the window. Tsarevich Ivan cried and wept for a long time and then he bowed in four directions and went off he knew not where to seek his wife, Vasilisa the Wise and Clever. Whether he walked a distance short or long, for a time that was short or long no one knows, but his boots were worn, his caftan frayed and torn, and his cap battered by the rain. After a while he met a little old man who was as old as old can be.

"Good morrow, good youth!" quoth he. "What do you seek and whither are you bound?"

Tsarevich Ivan told him of his trouble, and the little old man who was as old as old can be, said:

15

"Ah, Tsarevich Ivan, why did you burn the frog skin? It was not yours to wear or to do away with. Vasilisa the Wise and Clever was born wiser and cleverer than her father, and this so angered him that he turned her into a frog for three years. Ah, well, it can't be helped now. Here is a ball of thread for you. Follow it without fear wherever it rolls."

Tsarevich Ivan thanked the little old man who was as old as old can be, he went after the ball of thread, and he followed it wherever it rolled. In an open field he met a bear. Tsarevich Ivan took aim and was about to kill it, but the bear spoke up in a human voice and said:

"Do not kill me, Tsarevich Ivan, who knows but you may have need of me some day."

Tsarevich Ivan took pity on the bear and went on without killing it. He looked, and lo!—there was a drake flying overhead. Tsarevich Ivan took aim, but the drake said to him in a human voice:

"Do not kill me, Tsarevich Ivan, who knows but you may have need of me some day!"

And Tsarevich Ivan spared the drake and went on. Just then a hare came running. Tsarevich Ivan took aim quickly and was about to shoot it, but the hare said in a human voice:

"Do not kill me, Tsarevich Ivan, who knows but you may have need of me some day!"

And Tsarevich Ivan spared the hare and went farther. He came to the blue sea and he saw a pike lying on the sandy shore and gasping for breath.

"Take pity on me, Tsarevich Ivan," said the pike. "Throw me back into the blue sea!"

So Tsarevich Ivan threw the pike into the sea and walked on along the shore. Whether a long time passed by or a short time no one knows, but by and by the ball of thread rolled up to a forest, and there in the forest stood a little hut on chicken's feet, spinning round and round.

"Little hut, little hut, stand as once you stood, with your face to me and your back to the wood," said Tsarevich Ivan.

The hut turned its face to him and its back to the forest, and Tsarevich Ivan entered, and there, on the edge of the stove ledge, lay Baba-Yaga the Witch with the Switch, in a pose she liked best, her crooked nose to the ceiling pressed.

"What brings you here, good youth?" asked Baba-Yaga. "Is there aught you come to seek? Come, good youth, I pray you, speak!"

Said Tsarevich Ivan:

"First give me food and drink, you old hag, and steam me in the bath, and then ask your questions."

So Baba-Yaga steamed him in the bath, gave him food and drink and put him to bed, and then Tsarevich Ivan told her that he was seeking his wife, Vasilisa the Wise and Clever.

"I know where she is," said Baba-Yaga. "Koshchei the Deathless has her in his power. It will be hard getting her back, for it is not easy to get the better of Koshchei. His death is at the point of a needle, the needle is in an egg, the egg in a duck, the duck in a hare, the hare in a stone chest and the chest at the top of a tall oak-tree which Koshchei the Deathless guards as the apple of his own eye."

Tsarevich Ivan spent the night in Baba-Yaga's hut, and in the morning she told him where the tall oak-tree was to be found. Whether he was long on the way or not no one knows,

2—824   17

but by and by he came to the tall oak-tree. It stood there and it rustled and swayed, and the stone chest was at the top of it and very hard to reach.

All of a sudden, lo and behold! the bear came running and it pulled out the oak-tree, roots and all. Down fell the chest, and it broke open. Out of the chest bounded a hare and away it tore as fast as it could. But another hare appeared and gave it chase. It caught up the first hare and tore it to bits. Out of the hare flew a duck, and it soared up to the very sky. But in a trice the drake was upon it and it struck the duck so hard that it dropped the egg, and down the egg fell into the blue sea.

At this Tsaverich Ivan began weeping bitter tears, for how could he find the egg in the sea! But all at once the pike came swimming to the shore with the egg in its mouth. Tsarevich Ivan cracked the egg, took out the needle and began trying to break off the point. The more he bent it, the more Koshchei the Deathless writhed and twisted. But all in vain. For Tsarevich Ivan broke off the point of the needle, and Koshchei fell down dead.

Tsarevich Ivan then went to Koshchei's palace of white stone. And Vasilisa the Wise and Clever ran out to him and kissed him on his honey-sweet mouth. And Tsarevich Ivan and Vasilisa the Wise and Clever went back to their own home and lived together long and happily till they were quite, quite old.

AXE PORRIDGE

A Russian Fairy-Tale

An old soldier was once on his way home for his leave, and he was tired and hungry. He reached a village and he rapped at the first hut.

"Let a traveller in for the night," said he.

The door was opened by an old woman.

"Come in, soldier," she offered.

"Have you a bite of food for a hungry man, good dame?" the soldier asked.

Now the old woman had plenty of everything, but she was stingy and pretended to be very poor.

"Ah, me, I've had nothing to eat myself today, dear heart, there is nothing in the house," she wailed.

"Well, if you've nothing, you've nothing," the soldier said. Then, noticing an axe without a handle under the bench: "If there's nothing else, we could make porridge out of that axe."

The old woman raised both hands in astonishment.

"Axe porridge? Who ever heard the like!"

"I'll show you how to make it. Just give me a pot."

The old woman brought a pot, and the soldier washed the axe, put it in the pot, and filling the pot with water, placed it on the fire.

The old woman stared at the soldier, never taking her eyes off him.

The soldier got out a spoon and stirred the water and then tasted it.

"It will soon be ready," said he. "A pity there's no salt."

"Oh, I have salt. Here, take some."

The soldier put some salt in the pot and then tried the water again.

"If we could just add a handful of groats to it," said he.

The old woman brought a small bag of groats from the pantry.

"Here, add as much as you need," said she.

The soldier went on with his cooking, stirring the meal from time to time and tasting it. And the old woman watched, and could not tear her eyes away.

"Oh, how tasty this porridge is!" the soldier said, trying a spoonful. "With a bit of butter there would be nothing more delicious."

The old woman found some butter too, and they buttered the porridge.

"Now get a spoon, good dame, and let us eat!" the soldier said.

They began eating the porridge and praising it.

"I never thought axe porridge could taste so good!" the old woman marvelled.

And the soldier ate, and laughed up his sleeve.

CHESTNUT-GREY

A Russian Fairy-Tale

Once upon a time there lived an old man who had three sons. The two elder sons were well-favoured young men who liked to wear fine clothes and were thrifty husbandmen, but the youngest, Ivan the Fool, was none of those things. He spent most of his time at home sitting on the stove ledge and only going out to gather mushrooms in the forest.

When the time came for the old man to die, he called his three sons to his side and said to them:

"When I die, you must come to my grave every night for three nights and bring me some bread to eat."

The old man died and was buried, and that night the time came for the eldest brother to go to his grave. But he was too lazy or else too frightened to go, and he said to Ivan the Fool:

"If you will only go in my stead to our father's grave to-night, Ivan, I will buy you a honey-cake."

Ivan readily agreed, took some bread and went to his father's grave. He sat down by the grave and waited to see what would happen. On the stroke of midnight the earth crumbled apart and the old father rose out of his grave and said:

"Who is there? Is it you, my first-born? Tell me how everything fares in Rus: are the dogs barking, the wolves howling or my child weeping?"

And Ivan replied:

"It is I, your son, Father. And all is quiet in Rus."

Then the father ate his fill of the bread Ivan had brought and lay down in his grave again. As for Ivan, he went home, stopping to gather some mushrooms on the way.

When he reached home, his eldest brother asked:

"Did you see our father?"

"Yes, I did," Ivan replied.

"Did he eat of the bread you brought?"

"Yes. He ate till he could eat no more."

Another day passed by, and it was the second brother's turn to go to the grave. But he was too lazy or else too frightened to go, and he said to Ivan:

"If only you will go in my stead, Ivan, I shall make you a pair of bast shoes."

"Very well," said Ivan, "I shall go."

He took some bread, went to his father's grave and sat there waiting. On the stroke of midnight the earth crumbled apart, the old father rose out of the grave and said:

"Who is there? Is it you, my second-born? Tell me how everything fares in Rus: are the dogs barking, the wolves howling or my child weeping?"

And Ivan replied:

"It is I, your son, Father. And all is quiet in Rus."

Then the father ate his fill of the bread Ivan had brought and went back to his grave. And Ivan went home, stopping to gather some mushrooms on the way. He reached home and his second brother asked him:

"Did our father eat of the bread you brought?"

"Yes," Ivan replied. "He ate till he could eat no more."

On the third night it was Ivan's turn to go to the grave and he said to his brothers:

"For two nights I have gone to our father's grave. Now it is your turn to go and I will stay home and rest."

"Oh, no," the brothers replied. "You must go again, Ivan, for you are used to it."

"Very well," Ivan agreed, "I shall go."

He took some bread and went to the grave, and on the stroke of midnight the earth crumbled apart and the old father rose out of the grave.

"Who is there?" said he. "Is it you, Ivan, my third-born? Tell me how everything fares in Rus: are the dogs barking, the wolves howling or my child weeping?"

And Ivan replied:

"It is I, your son Ivan, Father. And all is quiet in Rus."

The father ate his fill of the bread Ivan had brought and said to him:

"You were the only one to obey my command, Ivan. You were not afraid to come to my grave for three nights. Now you must go out into the open field and shout: 'Chestnut-Grey, hear and obey! I call thee nigh to do or die!' When the horse appears before you, climb into his right ear and come out of his left, and you will turn into as comely a lad as ever was seen. Then mount the horse and go where you will."

Ivan took the bridle his father gave him, thanked him and went home, stopping to gather some mushrooms on the way. He reached home and his brothers asked him:

"Did you see our father, Ivan?"

"Yes, I did," Ivan replied.

"Did he eat of the bread you brought?"

"Yes, he ate till he could eat no more and he bade me not to go to his grave any more."

Now, at this very time the Tsar had a call sounded abroad for all handsome, unmarried young men to gather at court. The Tsar's daughter, Tsarevna Lovely, had ordered a castle of twelve pillars and twelve rows of oak logs to be built for herself. And there she meant to sit at the window of the top chamber and await the one who would leap on his steed as high as her window and place a kiss on her lips. To him who succeeded, whether of high or of low birth, the Tsar would give Tsarevna Lovely, his daughter, in marriage and half his tsardom besides.

News of this came to the ears of Ivan's brothers, who agreed between them to try their luck.

They gave a feed of oats to their goodly steeds and led them from the stables, and themselves put on their best apparel and combed down their curly locks. And Ivan, who was sitting on the stove ledge behind the chimney, said to them:

"Take me with you, my brothers, and let me try my luck, too."

"You silly sit-by-the-stove!" laughed they. "You will only be mocked at if you go with us. Better go and hunt for mushrooms in the forest."

The brothers mounted their goodly steeds, cocked their hats, gave a whistle and a whoop and galloped off down the road in a cloud of dust. Ivan took the bridle his father had given him, went out into the open field and shouted as his father had taught him:

"Chestnut-Grey, hear and obey! I call thee nigh to do or die!"

And lo and behold! a charger came running towards him. The earth shook under his hoofs, his nostrils spurted flame, and clouds of smoke poured from his ears. The charger galloped up to Ivan, stood stock-still and said:

"What is your wish, Ivan?"

Ivan stroked the steed's neck, bridled him, climbed into his right ear and came out through his left. And lo! he was turned into a youth as fair as the sky at dawn, the handsomest youth that ever was born. He got up on Chestnut-Grey's back and set off for the Tsar's palace. On went Chestnut-Grey for a week or a day, passing mountain and dale with a swish of his tail, skirting houses and trees as quick as the breeze.

When at last Ivan arrived at court, the palace grounds were teeming with people. There stood the castle of twelve pillars and twelve rows of oak logs, and in its highest attic, at the window of her chamber, sat Tsarevna Lovely.

The Tsar stepped out on the porch and said:

"He from amongst you, good youths, who leaps up on his steed as high as yon window and places a kiss upon my daughter's lips, shall have her in marriage and half my tsardom besides."

One after another the wooers of Tsarevna Lovely rode up and pranced and galloped, but, alas, the window was out of their reach. Ivan's two brothers tried with the rest, but with no better success.

When Ivan's turn came, he sent Chestnut-Grey at a gallop and with a whoop and a shout leapt up as high as the highest row of logs but two. On he came again and leapt up as high as the highest row but one. One more chance was left him, and he pranced and whirled Chestnut-Grey round and round till the steed chafed and fumed. Then, bounding like fire past her window, he took a great leap and placed a kiss on the honey-sweet lips of Tsarevna Lovely. And the Tsarevna struck his brow with her signet-ring and left her seal there.

The people roared: "Hold him! Stop him!" but Ivan and his steed were gone in a cloud of dust.

Off they galloped to the open field, and Ivan climbed into Chestnut-Grey's left ear and came out through his right, and lo! he was transformed to his proper shape again. Then he let Chestnut-Grey run free and himself went home, stopping to gather some mushrooms on the way. He entered the house, bound his forehead with a rag, climbed up on the stove ledge and lay there as before.

By and by his brothers arrived and began telling him where they had been and what they had seen.

"Many were the wooers of the Tsarevna, and handsome,

too," they said. "But one there was who outshone them all. He leapt up on his fiery steed to the Tsarevna's window and he kissed her lips. We saw him come, but we did not see him go."

Said Ivan from his perch behind the chimney:

"Perhaps it was me you saw."

His brothers flew into a temper and said:

"Stop your silly talk, fool! Sit there on your stove and eat your mushrooms."

Then Ivan untied the rag that covered the seal from the Tsarevna's signet-ring and at once a bright glow lit up the hut. The brothers were frightened and cried:

"What are you doing, fool? You'll burn down the house!"

The next day the Tsar held a feast to which he summoned all his subjects, boyars and nobles and common folk, rich and poor, young and old.

Ivan's brothers, too, prepared to attend the feast.

"Take me with you, my brothers," Ivan begged.

"What?" they laughed. "You will only be mocked at by all. Stay here on your stove and eat your mushrooms."

The brothers then mounted their goodly steeds and rode away, and Ivan followed them on foot. He came to the Tsar's palace and seated himself in a far corner. Tsarevna Lovely now began to make the round of all the guests. She offered each a drink from the cup of mead she carried and she looked at their brows to see if her seal were there.

She made the round of all the guests except Ivan, and when she approached him her heart sank. He was all smutted with soot and his hair stood on end.

Said Tsarevna Lovely:

"Who are you? Where do you come from? And why is your brow bound with a rag?"

"I hurt myself in falling," Ivan replied.

The Tsarevna unwound the rag and a bright glow at once lit up the palace.

"That is my seal!" she cried. "Here is my betrothed!"

The Tsar came up to Ivan, looked at him and said:

"Oh, no, Tsarevna Lovely! This cannot be your betrothed! He is all sooty and very plain."

Said Ivan to the Tsar:

"Allow me to wash my face, Tsar."

The Tsar gave him leave to do so, and Ivan came out into the courtyard and shouted as his father had taught him to:

"Chestnut-Grey, hear and obey! I call thee nigh to do or die!"

And lo and behold! Chestnut-Grey came galloping towards him. The earth shook under his hoofs, his nostrils spurted flame, and clouds of smoke poured from his ears. Ivan climbed into his right ear and came out through his left and was turned into a youth as fair as the sky at dawn, the handsomest youth that ever was born. All the people in the palace gave a great gasp when they saw him.

No words were wasted after that.

Ivan married Tsarevna Lovely, and a merry feast was held to celebrate their wedding.

IVAN THE PEASANT'S SON
AND THE THREE CHUDO-YUDOS

A Russian Fairy-Tale

Long, long ago, in a certain tsardom, in a certain realm there lived an old man and an old woman who had three sons, the youngest of whom was called Ivan. They lived not idly, they loved to toil: from morn till night they tilled the soil.

One day the evil tidings spread through the realm that Chudo-Yudo the Monster of Monsters was planning to fall upon the land, to kill all the people and to burn down all the towns and villages. The old man and the old woman began to grieve and to sorrow, and their two elder sons said, trying to comfort them:

"Do not grieve, Mother, do not grieve, Father! We will go against Chudo-Yudo the Monster of Monsters, and we will fight him to the death! And that you may not be lonely, Ivan will stay with you. He is too young to go with us to do battle."

"No," said Ivan, "I do not want to stay at home and wait for you. I, too, will go out to fight Chudo-Yudo!"

And the old man and the old woman did not try to stop him from going, nor did they say a word against it. They got their three sons ready for their journey, and the brothers took their heavy cudgels, filled their wallets with bread and like simple fare, and jumping on their goodly horses, rode off.

Whether they were long on the way or not no one knows, but by and by they met an old man.

"Good morrow, good youths!" said the old man.

"Good morrow, grandfather!"

"Whither are you bound?"

"We are on our way to do battle with Chudo-Yudo the Monster of Monsters, and to defend our native land!"

"Yours is a worthy cause! Only it is not cudgels you need to fight Chudo-Yudo, but swords of Damascus steel."

"Where are we to get them, grandfather?"

"That I will tell you. Ride straight ahead, good youths, till you reach a tall mountain. Now in that mountain there is a deep cave, the entrance to which is blocked by a large rock. Roll the rock aside, enter the cave, and there you will find the swords."

The brothers thanked the old man and rode straight ahead as he had told them to. They looked, and they saw a tall mountain with a large grey rock resting against one side of it. The brothers pushed the rock away and entered the cave, and what did they see inside but weapons of all kinds without count or number! They each took a sword and then rode on again.

"The old man has done us a great kindness and many thanks to him," said they. "It will be far easier for us to fight with these swords!"

On and on they rode until they came to a village. They looked, and there was not a soul in sight. Everything was burnt out and lay in ruins, except for one small hut. The brothers entered the hut, and they saw an old woman lying on the stove ledge and groaning.

"Good morrow, grandmother!" the brothers said.

"Good morrow, good youths! Whither are you bound?"

"We are going to the Cranberry Bridge that's on the Currant River. We want to do battle with Chudo-Yudo the Monster of Monsters that he may not invade our land."

"Ah, my good youths, yours is a worthy cause! The black-hearted monster plunders and kills and lays waste wherever he appears. And that is what he has done in our parts. I alone am left alive...."

The brothers spent the night at the old woman's house, and early in the morning they rose and set off again on their journey.

They rode up to the Currant River and the Cranberry Bridge, and they saw that the river-bank was strewn with broken swords, broken bows and the bones of men. An empty hut stood near, and it was there they decided to stop.

"Listen to me, my brothers," said Ivan. "We have come to a far and a strange land, and we must be wary and hearken for every sound. Let us take turns watching so that

Chudo-Yudo the Monster of Monsters will not cross the Cranberry Bridge."

On the first night the eldest brother went out to watch. He walked along the bank and he looked out across the Currant River. All was quiet, no one was to be seen, and nothing to be heard. So he lay down under a broom bush and at once fell asleep and began snoring loudly.

As for Ivan, he lay in the hut and could not sleep, nor even so much as doze. And when midnight had passed, he took his sword of Damascus steel and went to the Currant River. He looked, and there under a bush lay his elder brother, fast asleep, snoring mightily. But Ivan did not wake him. Instead, he hid under the Cranberry Bridge and stood there guarding the crossing.

Suddenly the waters of the river began to seethe and to boil, and the eagles began screaming in the oak-trees, and Chudo-Yudo the Monster of Monsters, he of the six heads, came riding up. He rode out to the middle of the Cranberry Bridge, and his horse stumbled under him, the black raven on his shoulder flapped its wings and the black dog behind him bristled.

Said Chudo-Yudo, he of the six heads:

"Why do you stumble, my steed? Why do you flap your wings, black raven? Why do you bristle, black dog? Do you sense the presence of Ivan the Peasant's Son? But he has not yet been born, and even if he has, he is as nothing beside me. I will take him up in one hand and crush him with the other!"

At this Ivan the Peasant's Son stepped out from under the bridge.

"Do not boast, Chudo-Yudo, you black-hearted monster!" cried he. "You have not shot the bright falcon, so attempt not to pluck his feathers! You know me not for the goodly youth I am, so sneer not at me! Rather match your strength with mine, and let him who overcomes the other boast to his heart's content."

They closed then, and their swords clashed, so that the earth around them trembled and droned, and Chudo-Yudo had the worst of it, for Ivan the Peasant's Son cut off three of his heads at one blow.

"Stay, Ivan the Peasant's Son!" cried Chudo-Yudo. "Let me rest!"

"Nay, there can be no talk of resting now! You, Chudo-Yudo, have three heads, and I have only one. When you have but one head left to you, then shall we rest."

And they closed again and measured swords, and Ivan the Peasant's Son smote off Chudo-Yudo's three remaining heads. Then he hacked his body into small pieces, threw them into the Currant River, laid the six heads beneath the Cranberry Bridge and himself returned to the hut and went to bed.

In the morning his eldest brother came in, and Ivan saw him and asked:

"Well, did you see anything?"

"No," replied the other, "not even a fly flew past me."

And to this Ivan said not a word.

On the second night the middle brother went out to watch. He walked here and he walked there, he looked to all sides of him and decided that all was quiet. So he crawled into a clump of bushes, curled up on the ground and fell asleep.

But Ivan relied no more on him than on his eldest brother. When midnight had passed, he at once got ready, and taking his sharp sword, went down to the Currant River. He hid himself underneath the Cranberry Bridge and waited.

Suddenly the waters began to seethe and to boil, the eagles began screaming in the oak-trees, and Chudo-Yudo the Monster of Monsters, he of the nine heads, came riding up. He rode out on to the Cranberry Bridge, and the horse under him stumbled, the black raven on his shoulder flapped its wings and the black dog behind him bristled. Chudo-Yudo raised his whip and brought it down on the horse's flanks, the raven's feathers and the dog's ears.

"Why do you stumble, my steed?" cried he. "Why do you flap your wings, black raven? Why do you bristle, black dog? Do you sense the presence of Ivan the Peasant's Son? But he has not yet been born, and even if he has, fight the good fight he cannot, for I will crush him with one finger!"

At this Ivan the Peasant's Son leaped out from under the Cranberry Bridge.

"Stay, Chudo-Yudo!" cried he. "Boast not before we have crossed swords. We shall see who will vanquish whom!"

And Ivan fell on Chudo-Yudo and he flourished his sword of Damascus steel, once and then again, and he smote off six of the monster's heads. Then Chudo-Yudo struck Ivan a blow and drove him knee-deep in the damp soil. But Ivan the Peasant's Son scooped up a fistful of sand and dashed it into his foe's fiery eyes, and while the monster, blinded, was rubbing the sand out, Ivan chopped off his three remaining heads. Then he hacked his body into small pieces, threw them into the Currant River, and putting the monster's nine heads underneath the Cranberry Bridge, returned to the hut, lay down and fell asleep just as if nothing had happened.

In the morning the middle brother came back.

"Well, did you see anything during the night?" Ivan asked him.

"No," the other replied. "Not a fly flew past me, nor a gnat."

"Well, if that is so, then come with me, my dear brothers," said Ivan, "and I will show you both the gnat and the fly."

And Ivan led his brothers under the Cranberry Bridge and showed them the two monsters' heads.

"Those," said he, "are the flies and gnats that fly about here at night. And you, my brothers, are not made to fight battles but to warm your bones on a stove ledge."

The two brothers dropped their heads in shame.

"We were overpowered by sleep," said they.

On the third night Ivan himself prepared to go out to watch.

"A fearful battle have I before me," said he. "You, my brothers, must not sleep, but listen for my whistle. As soon as you hear it, send my horse to me and hasten to my aid."

So saying, Ivan the Peasant's Son went to the Currant River, stood underneath the Cranberry Bridge and waited.

No sooner had midnight passed than the earth began trembling and rocking, the river waters seething and boiling, the wild winds howling, and the eagles in the oak-trees screaming. Chudo-Yudo the Monster of Monsters, he of the twelve heads, rode out to the Currant River. All Chudo-Yudo's twelve heads were whistling and all twelve were spurting fire and flame. Twelve wings had Chudo-Yudo's steed, and his hair was of copper and his mane and his tail of iron. Chudo-Yudo rode on to the Cranberry Bridge, and at once his horse stumbled under him and the black raven on his shoulder flapped its wings and the black dog that came behind him bristled. And

Chudo-Yudo brought down his whip on the horse's flanks, the raven's feathers and the dog's ears.

"Why do you stumble, my steed?" cried he. "Why do you flap your wings, black raven? Why do you bristle, black dog? Do you sense the presence of Ivan the Peasant's Son here? But he has not yet been born, and even if he has, he cannot stand up against me. I have only to blow once, and not so much as a handful of dust will be left of him."

At this Ivan the Peasant's Son stepped out from under the Cranberry Bridge.

"Wait, and do not boast, Chudo-Yudo," cried he, "else will you be sorely shamed!"

"Ah, it's you, Ivan the Peasant's Son! What brings you here?"

"I have come to feast my eyes on you, you villanous monster, and to test your courage!"

"Test my courage indeed! You are as a fly beside me!"

Said Ivan the Peasant's Son:

"I have not come here to beguile you with tales, nor indeed to listen to yours. I have come to fight you to the death, cursed monster, and to deliver good folk from your presence!"

And Ivan the Peasant's Son brandished his sharp sword, and he smote off three of Chudo-Yudo's heads. But Chudo-Yudo caught them up, and swishing his fiery finger over them, set them back on their necks, and at once they grew fast to them, just as if they had never been cut off at all.

By then Ivan was in a sorry state, for Chudo-Yudo deafened him with his whistling, burned him with his fiery tongues, showered him with sparks and drove him knee-deep into the damp soil.

"Perhaps you would rest a while, Ivan the Peasant's Son?" he jeered.

"Speak not of rest," Ivan replied. "To cut and to thrust unsparingly—that is my way!"

Thereupon, he gave a loud whistle and flung his right glove at the hut where his brothers were. And the glove smashed all the windows, but the brothers slept on and heard nothing.

Then Ivan the Peasant's Son summoned all his strength, brandished his sword more fiercely than ever, and chopped off six of Chudo-Yudo's heads. But Chudo-Yudo caught them up, and swishing his fiery finger over them, set them back on their necks, and they grew fast to them, and it was as if they had been there all the time. Then he fell upon Ivan the Peasant's Son and drove him waist-deep into the damp soil.

Ivan now realised that he was in desperate straits. He took off his left glove and flung it at the hut, and it broke through the roof, but the two brothers slept on and heard nothing.

Then Ivan the Peasant's Son brandished his sword a third time, and he smote off nine of Chudo-Yudo's heads. But Chudo-Yudo caught them up, and swishing his fiery finger over them, set them back on their necks, and they grew fast to them again. After that he hurled himself upon Ivan the Peasant's Son and drove him shoulder-deep into the damp soil.

But Ivan pulled off his hat and threw it at the hut, and the hut shook and swayed at the blow and almost crashed to the ground. Only then did the brothers wake, and they heard Ivan's horse neighing loudly and trying to break loose from the chains with which he was tethered.

They rushed to the stable and untied the horse and themselves ran after him.

Ivan's horse galloped up to his master and began kicking out at Chudo-Yudo with his hoofs. And Chudo-Yudo let out a whistle and a hiss and he showered the horse with sparks.

And Ivan the Peasant's Son heaved himself out from the ground and swiftly cut off Chudo-Yudo's fiery finger and then began chopping off his heads till there was not one left! After that he cut up his body into small pieces and threw them into the Currant River.

Just then the two elder brothers came running up.

"What a sorry pair you are!" Ivan said. "I nearly paid with my head for your loving sleep so much."

And the two brothers led him to the hut and washed him, and they gave him food and drink and then put him to bed.

In the morning Ivan rose early and began to dress.

"Why are you up so early?" his brothers asked. "You are in need of rest after so fierce a combat."

"Nay, I cannot rest," said Ivan. "I lost my belt by the Currant River and must go there to look for it."

"What's the need!" the brothers replied. "We can go in to town, and you'll buy yourself a new belt."

"No, I want my old belt back!"

And Ivan made off alone for the Currant River. But he did not stop to look for his belt. He went across to the opposite bank by way of the Cranberry Bridge and stole unnoticed to the stone palace of the Chudo-Yudos. He crept to an open window and he crouched under it, listening, for he wanted to hear if any evil plan were being hatched there.

He looked, and he saw, sitting inside, the three wives of the Chudo-Yudos and the old she-dragon, their mother. They sat there and they talked among themselves.

Said the first wife:

"I will wreak vengeance on Ivan the Peasant's Son for my husband! I will run ahead of them when he and his brothers are returning home, I will make the heat of day insufferable and turn myself into a well. They will thirst for a drink of water and will drop dead at the first sip!"

"That is rightly said," quoth the old she-dragon.

Said the second wife:

"And I will run ahead of them and turn into an apple-tree. They will each want an apple, but will drop dead at the first bite!"

"That is rightly said, too," quoth the old she-dragon again.

Said the third wife:

"As for me, I will put a sleep spell on them; I will run ahead of them and turn into a soft carpet with silken cushions. The brothers will want to lie down and rest, and they will be burnt to cinders!"

"And that too is no less rightly said," quoth the she-dragon. "But if you three fail to do them to death, then I will turn myself into a huge sow, and catching them up, will devour all three!"

Ivan the Peasant's Son heard their talk and hurried back to his brothers.

"Well, have you found your belt?" they asked him.

"I have."

"And was it worth while wasting your time?"

"It was, my brothers, it was."

Thereupon, the three brothers got ready and set off homewards. They rode across steppes and they rode across meadows, and the day was so parching hot that they felt they must have a drink of water or perish. They looked about them and saw a well nearby, with a silver dipper floating on the top. Said the two elder brothers to Ivan:

"Let us stop, Ivan, and have some cool water to drink and water our horses too."

"Who knows but that the water in that well is foul," Ivan replied.

And jumping down from his horse, he lay about him with his sword, hacking down and chopping up the well. At this a terrible howling and shrieking arose from the well, a sudden fog came down, the heat abated, and they were thirsty no longer.

"Now you see, my brothers, what kind of water was in the well," said Ivan.

They rode on, and no one knows whether a long time passed by or a little time, but by and by they saw an apple-tree laden with large, rosy apples.

The two elder brothers sprang from their horses and were about to pluck the apples. But Ivan was quicker than they, and he lay about him with his sword and began chopping at the very roots of the apple-tree; and the apple-tree began shrieking and howling.

"Now, my brothers, do you see what kind of apple-tree this is? The apples on it are not for our palates!" said Ivan.

And the three of them mounted their horses again and rode on.

They rode a long time, and they felt very tired. They looked about them, and there on the field lay a soft, bright carpet, with silken cushions on it.

"Let us lie down on the carpet and rest our weary bones," the two elder brothers said.

"No, my brothers, you will not find that carpet soft," Ivan told them.

At this the two elder brothers became very angry.

"Why do you preach to us?" they asked. "We are not to do this and not to do that!"

But Ivan said not a word in reply. He took off his belt and threw it on the carpet, and the belt flared up and was burnt to a cinder.

"That is what would have happened to you, too," said Ivan to his brothers. He went closer and began hacking up the carpet and the cushions with his sword. He cut them up into shreds and flung them away and said:

"You should not have grumbled at me, my brothers. For the well, the apple-tree and the carpet were none of them what they seemed, but the wives of the three Chudo-Yudos. They wanted to do us to death, but they failed, and perished themselves, instead!"

The brothers rode on, and whether they rode a long way or a little way no one knows, but all of a sudden the sky grew very dark, the wind began howling and the earth trembling and droning, and they saw a huge sow running after them. She opened wide her jaws and was about to swallow Ivan and his brothers. But the three, not being simple, snatched from their wallets a pood of salt apiece and threw it straight into the sow's gaping maw.

The sow was overjoyed, for she thought that she had caught Ivan the Peasant's Son and his two brothers, and she stopped and began chewing the salt. But feeling by the taste of it that it was salt, she rushed off again after them.

She ran, her bristles standing on end, and she gnashed her teeth, and she was soon at their heels and about to catch them up.

Seeing her, Ivan told his brothers to ride in different directions, and one of them rode to the right, and the other to the left, and Ivan himself—straight ahead.

The sow ran up and then stopped short, for she did not know which of them to go after first.

While she stood hesitating and waggling her snout from side to side, Ivan rushed at her, lifted her up and dashed her to the ground with all his might. The sow crumbled to dust, and the dust was scattered by the wind.

From then onwards no monsters, dragons or serpents were ever again seen in those parts, and the people knew no more fear.

As for Ivan the Peasant's Son and his two brothers, they went back home to their mother and father, and they all lived happily ever after, ploughing their fields, sowing their wheat and having plenty of good things to eat.

A TRIAL LIKE NO OTHER

A Russian Fairy-Tale

Once there lived two brothers. One of them was poor and the other rich.

Now one day the poor brother's wood came to an end, and he had nothing with which to heat his stove. It was very cold in his hut.

He went to the forest and chopped some wood, but he had no horse to bring the wood home.

"I'll go to my brother and ask him for a horse," he thought to himself.

He went to his brother, but it was a cold welcome his brother gave him.

"You can take the horse this once, but see that you don't make the load too heavy," said he. "And don't think you can come to me for anything of the sort again. It's always one thing today and another tomorrow, and you'll have me out begging in the streets before I know where I am."

The poor brother led the horse home, and only then remembered that he had forgotten to ask for a horse-collar.

"And it's no use going back for it now, my brother will not give it to me," said he to himself.

So he tied the sledge as tight as he could to the horse's tail and drove to the forest.

On the way back the sledge got wedged in a tree-stump, but the poor man did not notice it and gave the horse a touch of the whip.

The horse was a fiery one; it plunged ahead, and lo! its tail came off.

When the rich brother saw that his horse had no tail, he began cursing and scolding the poor brother.

"You've ruined my horse!" he cried. "Don't think I will leave it at that!"

And he brought an action against him.

A short time passed by and a long time, and the brothers were summoned to court.

They set off for town, they walked and they walked, and the poor brother said to himself:

"A poor man fighting a rich man's lawsuit is like a weak man wrestling with a strong man: neither can win. They're sure to find me guilty."

Just then they were crossing a bridge, and as the bridge had no handrail, the poor brother slipped and fell off. It so chanced that at that very moment a merchant was driving over the icebound river below, taking his old father to a doctor, and the poor brother dropped straight on to the old man in the merchant's sledge, killing him outright without sustaining the slightest injury himself.

The merchant seized the poor brother and held him.

"Come with me to the judge!" he cried.

And so now the three of them proceeded to the town together, the two brothers and the merchant.

The poor brother felt more sad and crestfallen than ever.

"They'll be sure to find me guilty now," he said to himself.

Suddenly he saw a heavy stone on the road. He picked it up, wrapped it in a rag and thrust it inside his coat.

"As well be hanged for a sheep as for a lamb," said he to himself. "If the judge judges unfairly and I am found guilty, I'll kill him as well."

They came before the judge, and now there were two cases instead of one against the poor brother. And the judge set about the business of judging and began asking questions.

And the poor brother would glance at the judge now and again, take out the stone wrapped in the rag and whisper:

"Judge away, Judge, judge away, but see what I've brought to court today!"

He said it once, and he said it again, and he said it a third time, and the judge watched him and thought to himself:

"Could the muzhik be showing me a nugget of gold?"

And he looked once again and was tempted.

"Even if it's only silver," thought he to himself, "it will still bring in quite a handsome sum of money."

And he passed sentence and ruled that the tailless horse be given to the poor brother to keep till such time as its tail would grow again.

And to the merchant he said:

"As punishment for having killed your father this man must stand on the ice under the very same bridge, and you must leap on him from the bridge and kill him in just the same way as he killed your father."

And with that the trial ended.

Said the rich brother to the poor brother:

"Oh, well, so be it, I'll take the tailless horse from you."

"Oh, no, brother," the poor man replied. "Let it be as the judge decreed. I'll keep your horse until its tail grows again."

Then the rich brother began pleading with the poor one.

"I'll give you thirty rubles, only give me back my horse," said he.

"Very well, let it be as you wish," the poor brother agreed.

The rich brother counted out the money, and the matter was settled between them.

Now the merchant, too, spoke in pleading tones.

"Let's forget the whole affair, my good man," said he. "I forgive you. It will not bring back my father if I don't, anyway."

"No, no, come along and do as the judge said. Drop down on me from the bridge."

"I don't want to kill you. Let us be friends and I will give you a hundred rubles," the merchant begged.

The poor man took the hundred rubles and was about to leave, when the judge called him to his side.

"Now give me what you promised," said he.

And the poor man drew the bundle from his coat, turned back the rag and showed the judge the stone.

"That is what I showed you when I said: 'Judge away, Judge, judge away, but see what I've brought to court today!' Had you judged differently, I would have killed you with this stone."

"It's a good thing I judged the way I did," said the judge to himself, "or I would not have been alive now."

As for the poor man, he went home in high spirits, singing a song at the top of his voice.

POKATI-GOROSHEK

A Ukrainian Fairy-Tale

There once lived a man who had six sons and one daughter, Alyonka by name. One day the sons went out to plough the field and they told their sister to bring them their dinner there.

"Tell me where you will be, so I'll know where to come," she said.

Said the brothers:

"We shall dig a furrow from the hut to the patch where we will be ploughing. You can find us if you follow the furrow."

And with that they drove away.

Now in the forest by that field there lived a Dragon, and he came and filled up the furrow the brothers had dug and made his own, leading to the door of his house. And Alyonka, when she took her brothers' dinner to them, followed the false trail and walked straight into the Dragon's courtyard where he at once seized her.

The sons came home in the evening, and they said to their mother:

"We were ploughing all day. Why didn't you send us anything to eat?"

"But I did," the mother replied. "I sent Alyonka to the field with your dinner, and I thought she would be coming back with you. Could she have lost her way?"

"We must go and look for her," the brothers said.

And so the six of them followed the Dragon's furrow till they came to his courtyard. They entered, they looked, and there was their sister before them!

"My sweet brothers, where will I hide you when the Dragon comes? He will eat you up!" Alyonka cried.

And lo!—there was the Dragon flying toward them and hissing like the serpent that he was.

"I smell a man, I smell many men!" cried he. "Well, now, my fine fellows, are we going to do battle or are we going to make peace?"

"We will do battle!" cried they.

"Let us go to the iron threshing-floor, then."

So they went to the iron threshing-floor, but they did not fight long. For the Dragon struck one blow at them and drove them into the floor. Then he pulled them out, barely alive, and threw them into a deep dungeon.

The mother and father waited for their sons to return, but, alas! they waited in vain.

One day the mother went with some washing to the river; she looked, and there, rolling toward her along the road, she saw a tiny pea. She picked it up and ate it, and in due time a son was born to her and they called him Pokati-Goroshek or Rolling Pea.

Pokati-Goroshek began to grow; he grew and grew, and though young in years, he grew to be big and strong.

One day his father and he began digging a well, and they dug till their spades struck a huge rock. The father then went to fetch people to help him lift the rock, but before he returned Pokati-Goroshek had lifted and thrown it out himself. The people came and looked and were amazed and frightened too, for they saw that Pokati-Goroshek was so much stronger than any of them. Indeed, so frightened were they, that they decided to kill Pokati-Goroshek. But Pokati-Goroshek tossed the rock up into the air and then caught it, and seeing this feat of strength, the people fled.

The father and son went on digging. They dug till they found a huge piece of iron, and Pokati-Goroshek lifted it out and hid it.

One day Pokati-Goroshek asked his mother and father:

"Did I not have brothers or sisters?"

"Indeed, you had, son," they answered. "You had one sister and six brothers, but...." And they went on to tell him the whole story.

"I will go in search of them," Pokati-Goroshek said.

The mother and father pleaded with him not to go.

"Do not go, son," they said. "Your brothers went, and all six of them perished, and you, all alone as you are, will surely perish."

"No, go I will!" said Pokati-Goroshek. "For I must free my own flesh and blood!"

And he took the piece of iron that he had found and went with it to the blacksmith.

"Forge me a sword, the bigger the better!" said he to the blacksmith.

And the blacksmith forged him a sword so large and heavy that it was as much as anyone could do to carry it out of the smithy. But Pokati-Goroshek took the sword and brandished it and tossed it up to the sky.

"I shall now have a long sleep," said he to his father. "Wake me in twelve days' time, when the sword comes flying back."

He went to bed and slept for twelve days, and on the thirteenth day the sword came flying back, making a humming sound as it flew. The father woke Pokati-Goroshek, and Pokati-Goroshek sprang up and raised his fist; the sword struck it and fell to the ground, split in two.

"I cannot go to seek my sister and brothers with this sword," said Pokati-Goroshek. "I must have another."

And taking the broken sword, he went to the blacksmith again.

"Forge me a new sword out of this one," said he. "Make one that is worthy of my strength."

The blacksmith made him a sword that was even bigger than the first, and Pokati-Goroshek flung it up to the sky and went to bed and slept for another twelve days. On the thirteenth day the sword came flying back, droning and humming so that the earth shook. The mother and father woke Pokati-Goroshek who at once sprang to his feet. He held up his fist, and the sword struck it, but did not break and only bent a little.

"Here is a good sword indeed," said Pokati-Goroshek. "Now I can seek my sister and brothers. Bake me some bread, Mother, and dry me some rusks, and I will start on my way."

And he took his sword and a bagful of rusks, and taking leave of his mother and father, set out.

He followed the Dragon's old furrow that was now barely visible, and entered a forest. On and on he walked through the forest till he reached a large, fenced-in courtyard. He walked into the yard and on into the rich house that stood there, and he found Alyonka, his own sister, but there was no sight or sound of the Dragon.

"Good morrow, fair maiden!" said Pokati-Goroshek.

"Good morrow to you, gallant youth! Why have you come? The Dragon will soon be here and he will eat you up."

"We shall see! Perhaps he won't. But who are you, fair one?"

"I used to live with my mother and father, and I was their only daughter, but the Dragon carried me off, and though my six brothers tried to free me, they did not succeed."

"Where are your brothers?"

"The Dragon threw them in a dungeon, and I do not know if they are alive or not."

"Perhaps I can free you," said Pokati-Goroshek.

"How can you! My brothers could not do it, and there were six of them, while you are all alone!"

"That's nothing," Pokati-Goroshek replied.

And he sat down by a window to wait.

Just then the Dragon came flying back. He flew into the house and he twitched his nose.

"I smell a man!" cried he.

"Of course you smell a man," Pokati-Goroshek replied. "For here he is!"

"Aha, my young fellow! What do you want—to do battle or to make peace?"

"To do battle, of course!" Pokati-Goroshek replied.

"Then let us go to the iron threshing-floor."

"Very well."

They went to the iron threshing-floor, and the Dragon said: "You strike first."

"No, you!" Pokati-Goroshek replied.

They crossed swords, and the Dragon struck Pokati-Goroshek a heavy blow and drove him ankle-deep into the iron threshing-floor. But Pokati-Goroshek pulled himself free and brandished his sword and he fetched the Dragon an answering blow that drove him to his knees into the iron threshing-floor. But the Dragon heaved himself out and struck Pokati-Goroshek again and drove him knee-deep into the floor. Then Pokati-Goroshek struck a second blow which drove the Dragon waist-deep into the floor, and followed with a third that killed him on the spot.

He then made his way to the dungeon, and it was deep and dark; he freed his brothers who were more dead than alive, and taking them and Alyonka and all the gold and silver in the Dragon's house, set off homewards. But he never once mentioned that he was their brother.

Whether they were long on the way or not no one knows, but by and by they sat down to rest under a young oak-tree. And Pokati-Goroshek was so weary after his battle that he fell fast asleep. And his six brothers took counsel with one another and said:

"People will laugh at us when they learn that the six of us could not do away with the Dragon while this young lad did it all by himself. Besides, all the Dragon's riches will now go to him."

They talked together in this wise and decided, while Pokati-Goroshek was asleep and could feel nothing, to bind him to the oak-tree with ropes of bast and leave him there to be devoured by wild beasts. No sooner said than done. They tied him to the tree and left him and themselves went away.

Meanwhile Pokati-Goroshek slept on and felt nothing. He slept for a day and he slept for a night and he woke to find himself bound to the tree. But he gave a sudden jerk, pulled out the oak by its roots, and hoisting it on to his shoulder, went home. He approached the hut and overheard his brothers talking to their mother.

"Did you have any more children, Mother?" they asked her.

And the mother replied:

"Yes, indeed! I had another son, Pokati-Goroshek by name, who went off to free you."

Said the brothers:

"Then it must have been Pokati-Goroshek we tied to the oak-tree! We had better go and release him."

But Pokati-Goroshek brandished the oak he was carrying and struck the roof of the hut so hard with it that the hut nearly crumbled to the ground.

"Stay where you are since you are what you are!" cried he. "And I will go and roam the wide world."

And shouldering his sword, he strode off.

On and on he walked until he spied two mountains, one on the left side and one on the right; and between them stood a man who had set his hands and his feet against them and was moving them apart.

"Good morrow, friend!" said Pokati-Goroshek.

"Good morrow to you!"

"What are you doing?"

"Moving the mountains apart to make a road."

"Where are you going?"

"Wherever I can make my fortune."

"That's where I am going too! What is your name?"

"Sverni-Gora, Mover of Mountains. What's yours?"

"Pokati-Goroshek the Rolling Pea. Let us go together!"

"Let's!"

So they went along together; they walked and they walked, until they met a man in the forest. He was tearing up oaks by the roots and he had only to move his hand once for an oak to be uprooted.

"Good morrow, friend!" called Pokati-Goroshek and Sverni-Gora.

"Good morrow to you!"

"What are you doing?"

"Uprooting trees to have room for walking."

"Where are you going?"

"Wherever I can make my fortune."

"That's where we are going too. What's your name?"

"Verti-Dub, Uprooter of Oaks. What are yours?"

"Pokati-Goroshek the Rolling Pea and Sverni-Gora, Mover of Mountains. Let us go together!"

"Let's!"

So the three of them went along together. They walked and they walked, and by and by they saw a man with the longest of long whiskers standing over the river, and he had only to twirl one whisker for the waters to part and roll away, leaving a passage for one to walk on over the dry river-bed.

"Good morrow, friend!" they called to him.

"Good morrow to you!"

"What are you doing?"

"Parting the waters to cross the river."

"Where are you going?"

"Wherever I can make my fortune."

"That's where we are going too. What is your name?"

"Kruti-Yus, Parter of Waters. And what are yours?"

"Pokati-Goroshek the Rolling Pea, Sverni-Gora, Mover of Mountains and Verti-Dub, Uprooter of Oaks. Let us go together!"

"Let's!"

So they went along together, and very easy they found it, for Sverni-Gora moved aside every mountain, Verti-Dub uprooted every forest and Kruti-Yus parted the waters of every river that lay in their way.

By and by they entered a large forest and saw a small hut there. They went inside and found the hut empty.

"We can spend the night in this hut," Pokati-Goroshek said.

So they spent the night in the hut, and on the following morning Pokati-Goroshek said:

"You stay at home, Sverni-Gora, and cook our dinner for us, and we three will go hunting."

So off they went, and Sverni-Gora boiled and roasted and cooked a good many things and then lay down for a sleep. . . . Suddenly there came a rap at the door.

"Open the door!" someone called.

"I'm no servant of yours to open doors!" Sverni-Gora called back.

The door opened, and the same voice cried again:

"Carry me over the threshold!"

"You're no lord of mine, so don't you whine!" Sverni-Gora replied.

And suddenly there climbed over the threshold the tiniest old man that ever was seen, with a beard so long that it trailed all of five feet over the ground. The little old man caught Sverni-Gora by his forelock and hung him on a nail in the wall. Then he ate up all there was to eat and drank up all there was to drink, and after flaying a long strip of skin from Sverni-Gora's back, went away.

Sverni-Gora twisted and turned on the nail till he succeeded, not without the loss of a lock of hair, in releasing himself; then he set to work to cook the dinner anew. He was still busy over it when his friends returned.

"Why are you so late getting dinner?" they asked in surprise.

"I dozed off and forgot all about it," Sverni-Gora replied.

They ate their fill and went to bed, and the following morning Pokati-Goroshek said:

"Now you stay at home, Verti-Dub, and the rest of us will go hunting."

They went away, and Verti-Dub boiled and roasted and cooked a good many things and then he lay down for a sleep. Suddenly there came a rap at the door.

"Open the door!" cried a voice.

"I'm no servant of yours to open doors!" Verti-Dub called back.

"Carry me over the threshold!" the same voice cried again.

"You're no lord of mine, so don't you whine!" Verti-Dub replied.

And lo!—there climbed into the hut the tiniest old man that ever was seen, with a beard so long that it trailed all of five feet over the ground. He caught Verti-Dub by his forelock and hung him on a nail, and then he ate up all there was to eat and drank up all there was to drink, and after flaying a long strip of skin from Verti-Dub's back, went away.

Verti-Dub twisted and turned this way and that, and he floundered like a fish out of water, and at last he succeeded in breaking loose and dropping to the ground. At once he set to work to make dinner anew.

His friends came and were surprised.

"Why are you so late getting dinner?" they asked.

"I must have dozed off," said he.

But Sverni-Gora said nothing, for he knew the truth of the matter.

On the third day Kruti-Yus was the one to remain at home, and the same thing happened to him.

Said Pokati-Goroshek:

"You are indeed slow getting dinner, all of you! But never mind. Tomorrow you'll go hunting, and I'll stay at home."

And that was just what they did. The following morning his three friends went hunting, and Pokati-Goroshek remained at home. He boiled and he roasted and he cooked a good many things and then he lay down for a sleep. Suddenly there came a rap at the door.

"Open the door!" cried a voice.

"Bide a while, I'm coming!" Pokati-Goroshek replied.

He opened the door, and there before him was the tiniest old man that ever lived, with a beard so long that it trailed all of five feet over the ground.

"Carry me over the threshold!" said the little old man.

Pokati-Goroshek picked up the old man and carried him into the hut, the old man kept taking little flying jumps at him.

"What do you want?" Pokati-Goroshek asked.

"You'll soon see what I want," said the little old man, and reaching for Pokati-Goroshek's forelock, he was about to grasp it, when Pokati-Goroshek cried out: "Ah, that's the sort you are!" and caught him by the beard!

Then, taking an axe, he dragged the little old man to an oak-tree, split the oak-tree in two and thrust the little old man's beard into the cleft so that it was held fast there.

"Since you were mean enough to try and catch me by the hair," said he to the little old man, "you'll have to sit here until I come again."

He returned to the hut, and there were his friends come back from hunting.

"Is dinner ready?" asked they.

"Oh yes, it's been ready a long time," Pokati-Goroshek replied.

They ate the dinner, and Pokati-Goroshek said:

"Come with me and I will show you the most marvellous sight!"

He led them to the oak-tree, but lo! there was no oak-tree to be seen, and no little old man, either: for the little old man had pulled out the oak by its roots and dragged it away with him.

Pokati-Goroshek then told his friends of all that had happened to him, and they, for their part, confessed that the little old man had set them hanging by their forelocks and had flayed strips of skin from their backs.

"If that's the sort he is," said Pokati-Goroshek, "then we had better go and find him."

Now the little old man had left a trail on the ground where he had dragged the oak-tree, and so the four friends followed this trail.

They walked along till they reached a deep hollow in the ground so deep that the bottom could not be seen.

"Climb down the hole, Sverni-Gora!" Pokati-Goroshek said.

"Not I!"

"Well, then you do it, Verti-Dub!"

But neither Verti-Dub nor Kruti-Yus would agree.

"Very well, then I will climb down myself," said Pokati-Goroshek. "Let us plait a rope!"

They plaited a rope, and Pokati-Goroshek wound one end of it round his hand.

"Let me down now!" said he.

They began lowering him, and it took them a long time, for the hollow was so deep that to reach the bottom was like reaching the nether world. But at last they set him down, and Pokati-Goroshek began walking about and looking to all sides of him until he saw a large palace. He entered the palace, and everything in it sparkled and shone, for it was all made of gold and precious stones. He passed from chamber to chamber, and suddenly there ran towards him a princess so beautiful that no pen could describe her and no tongue sing her praises.

"Oh, and why have you come here, good youth?" asked she.

"I am looking for a tiny old man with a long bushy beard," Pokati-Goroshek replied.

"Ah," said she, "the little old man is trying to pull out his beard from the oak-tree. Don't go to him, for he will kill you! He has killed many men."

"He won't kill me," said Pokati-Goroshek. "It was I that pinched his beard for him. But who are you and what are you doing here?"

"I am a princess, and the little old man carried me off from my home and is keeping me captive."

"Have no fear, I will free you. And now take me to him!"

She led him to the little old man, and Pokati-Goroshek looked and saw that she had spoken truly, for there sat the little old man, but he had already pulled out his beard from the oak-tree. Seeing Pokati-Goroshek, he cried out angrily:

"Why have you come? To do battle or to make peace?"

"I want no peace with you," Pokati-Goroshek replied. "Let us do battle!"

They crossed swords then, and fought fiercely and long until at last, with one thrust from Pokati-Goroshek, the little old man was pierced through and dropped dead.

Then Pokati-Goroshek and the princess took all the gold and precious stones, and filling three sacks full of the treasure, made for the hollow down which Pokati-Goroshek had climbed.

They came to the hollow, and Pokati-Goroshek called up to his friends:

"Ho, my brothers, are you there?"

"We are!" his friends called back.

Then Pokati-Goroshek tied one of the sacks to the rope and called to his friends to hoist it up.

"This is yours!" he cried.

They pulled up the sack and let the rope down again, and Pokati-Goroshek tied the second sack to it.

"This is yours too!" he cried again.

And the third sack, too, he gave them. He gave them everything he had taken from the little old man.

After that he tied the princess to the rope.

"Now this is mine!" he cried.

The three friends pulled up the princess, and now there was only Pokati-Goroshek left at the bottom. This set them thinking.

"Why should we pull him up?" said they. "If we leave him there we'll get the princess for ourselves too. Let us hoist him up a little way and then let go, and he will fall and be killed."

But Pokati-Goroshek guessed what they were up to, and tying a large stone to the rope, cried:

"Pull me up now!"

And they hoisted up the stone a little and then released the rope, so that the stone crashed down with a b-o-o-o-m!

"So that's the kind of friends I have!" said Pokati-Goroshek to himself, and away he went to roam the world at the bottom of the hollow. He walked and he walked, and lo! the sky became overcast by storm-clouds, and the rain came down, and hail, too. Pokati-Goroshek hid under an oak-tree, and all of a sudden he heard the peep-peeping of baby eagles coming from a nest in the top of the tree. So he climbed the oak-tree and covered the eaglets with his warm jacket. By now the rain was coming down in torrents, and a huge eagle flew up, the parent of the fledgelings in the nest. He saw that his children were covered and asked:

"Who covered you, my children?"

And the eaglets replied:

"We'll tell you if you don't eat him up."

"Never fear, I won't."

"Well, do you see that man sitting under the tree? It was he that did it."

At that the eagle flew down to Pokati-Goroshek.

"Ask whatever you will of me, and I will do it," said he. "This is the first time that any of my children have not been drowned in such a downpour, with me away."

"Carry me out of here to my own world," Pokati-Goroshek asked.

"This is no easy task you set me," the eagle replied. "But there's no help for it. I shall try to do what you ask. We shall take with us six kegs of meat and six casks of water. Every time I turn my head to the right you will throw a piece of meat into my mouth, and every time I turn my head to the left you will give me a sip of water to drink. If you don't do what I say, I shall never get there, but drop to the ground on the way."

They took six kegs of meat and six casks of water, Pokati-Goroshek climbed on to the eagle's back, and away they flew! They flew and they flew, and whenever the eagle turned his head to the right, Pokati-Goroshek thrust some meat into his mouth, and whenever he turned his head to the left, he gave him a sip of water.

A long time passed by and they were still flying, but they now had only a little way to go before reaching the world of men. The eagle turned his head to the right for the meat, but there was not a piece of meat left. So Pokati-Goroshek cut off a piece of his own leg and threw it in the eagle's mouth. They soared up again, and the eagle asked:

"What is it you have given me to eat? It's very good."

"A piece of my own flesh," Pokati-Goroshek replied, pointing to his leg.

Then the eagle spat out the piece of meat and he flew off a way and brought back some magic water. And no sooner had they put the piece that had been cut off against the wound in Pokati-Goroshek's leg and sprinkled some of the water over it, than lo! the leg was whole again.

After that the eagle flew home, and Pokati-Goroshek went to look for his three friends.

But the three friends had made their way to the palace of the princess' father and were now living there and quarrelling among themselves, for each wanted to marry the princess and would not give her up to the other.

It was in the palace that Pokati-Goroshek found them, and seeing him, they were badly frightened, for they had good reason to think that he would kill them.

Said Pokati-Goroshek:

"My own brothers betrayed me, so what can I demand of you! Nothing remains but to forgive you."

And forgive them he did, and himself married the princess and has lived with her in love and cheer ever since.

GOOD AND EVIL

A Ukrainian Fairy-Tale

Once upon a time there lived two brothers, one of whom was rich and the other poor. One day they came together and fell to talking, and the poor brother said:

"Cruel as life is, still it's better to do good than evil."

"What an idea!" cried the rich brother. "There's no such thing as good in the world now, but only evil. To do good will get you nowhere."

But the poor brother stood his ground.

"No, brother," said he, "I still think it pays to do good."

"Very well, then," said the rich brother. "Let's lay a wager and go and ask the first three people we meet what they think. If they say that you are right, then everything I have will be yours. But if they say that I am right, then I will take all you have for myself."

"So be it!" agreed the poor man.

They went along the road, they walked and they walked, and they met a man who was coming back from a place where he had spent the season working.

"Greetings, friend!" said they, coming up to him.

"Greetings to you!"

"There's something we want to ask you."

"Go ahead!"

"Which do you think is the better way to live: by doing good or evil?"

"Where can you find good these days, kind folk!" the man replied. "Look at me. I worked long and I worked hard, but my earnings amount next to nothing, and even so the master managed to fleece me of a part of them. No, there's no living honestly. Better to do evil than good!"

"Well, what did I tell you, brother!" said the rich man. "I am right, and you are wrong."

The poor man's spirits fell, but there was nothing to be done, and the two of them went on. By and by they met a merchant.

"Greetings, honest merchant!" said they.

"Greetings to you!" the merchant replied.

"There is something we want to ask you."

"Go ahead!"

"Which do you think is the better way to live: by doing good or evil?"

"What a question, kind folk! To do good doesn't pay! If you want to sell something, you have to lie and cheat a hundred times over. There is no selling anything otherwise."

And with that he rode on.

"There, I am right the second time!" the rich man said.

The poor man became sadder than ever, but there was nothing to be done, and so they went on again. They walked and they walked, and they met a lord.

"Greetings, Your Lordship!" said they.

"Greetings to you!"

"There is something we want to ask you."

"Go ahead then!"

"Which do you think is the better way to live: by doing good or evil?"

"What a question, kind folk! There is no such thing as good in the world these days, and there's no living honestly. If I were to follow the ways of righteousness, why, I—" And without finishing what he had to say, the lord rode on.

"Well, now, brother," the rich man said. "Let us go home. You must turn over to me all you have!"

The poor man went home, and he was deeply grieved. And the rich man took away all his humble belongings and only left him his hut.

"You can stay here for the time being," said he. "I don't need it now. But you'll have to look for another place to live in soon."

The poor man sat in the hut with his family, and there was not a piece of bread or anything else for them to eat and nowhere to earn any money, for it was a bad year for crops. The poor man tried to bear it, and so he did for a time, but his children began crying from hunger, and he took a sack and went to the rich brother to ask for flour.

"Give me a measure of flour or of grain, any you can spare," said he. "There is nothing to eat in the house, the children have grown swollen with hunger!"

Said the rich brother:

"You can have a measure of flour if you let me put out your eye."

The poor man thought it over, and he knew there was no way out but to agree.

"So be it," said he. "Put it out, and may God be with you, only give me some flour, for Christ's sake!"

So the rich man put out the poor man's eye and gave him a measure of mouldy flour. The poor man brought it home, and his wife took one look at him and gasped.

"What has happened to you, where is your eye?" she asked.

"My brother put it out," said he.

And he told her all about it. They cried and they sorrowed for a time, but they had to eat the flour, for it was all the food they had.

A week passed or, perhaps, a little over a week, and the flour was all gone. So the poor man took his sack and went to his brother again.

"Do please give me some flour, my dear brother," said he. "The flour you gave me last time is all gone."

"I'll give you a measure if you let me put out your eye," the rich brother replied.

"How can I live without both my eyes, brother! You have put one out already. Be merciful and give me the flour without blinding me."

"Oh, no, I won't, not unless you let me put out your other eye."

The poor man had no choice.

"Go ahead and put it out, then, and may God be with you," said he.

So the rich brother took a knife, put out his poor brother's second eye and filled his sack with flour. And the blind man took it and went home.

He walked with the greatest difficulty, stumbling and groping his way from one wattle fence to another, but he finally reached his house, bringing the flour with him. His wife looked at him and her blood froze in horror. "How will you live without your eyes, you poor, unhappy man!" cried she. "Who knows but we might have got some flour elsewhere, and now...."

And she wept so, poor woman, that she could not utter another word.

Said the blind man:

"Do not cry, wife! I am not the only blind man in the world. There are many like me, and they manage to live without their eyes."

But a measure of flour is not much for a family, and soon the last of it was gone.

"I won't go to my brother any more, wife," the blind man said. "Take me to the large poplar on the road beyond the village and leave me there for the day. And in the evening you can come for me and take me home. Many people pass that way on foot and on horseback; surely someone will give me a piece of bread."

So his wife led the blind man where he had asked her, seated him under the poplar and returned home.

The blind man sat there, and some gave him a penny or two, but soon it was getting on towards evening, and yet his wife did not come. The blind man was tired and he decided to go home by himself, but he turned off in the wrong direction and instead of getting to his house walked on and on without knowing where he was going. Suddenly he heard the trees rustling all around him, and he knew that he was in a forest and would have to spend the night there. But, fearing the wild beasts, he climbed a tree, a feat he managed with difficulty, and there he sat motionless.

Midnight struck, and all of a sudden, to the selfsame spot under the selfsame tree, the evil spirits came flying, and the chief one among them began to ask them what they had been doing.

"I made one brother blind another for two measures of flour," said one.

"You did well, but not as well as could be," the chief of the evil spirits told him.

"Why not?"

"Because the blind brother has only to rub his eyes with the dew that is under this tree, and he will see again."

"But no one knows or has heard of that, so blind he will remain."

Said the chief of the evil spirits, turning to another of them:

"Now you tell me what you did."

"I dried up all the water in a village, leaving not a drop, so now they have to carry water from forty versts away, and there's many that drop dead on the way."

"You did well, but not so well as could be."

"Why not?"

"If the large rock lying in the town nearest the village is moved, enough water will gush from under it to satisfy everyone."

"But no one knows or has heard of that, so the water will stay where it is."

"And what of you, what did you do?" the chief of the evil spirits asked yet another of them.

"I blinded the only daughter of the tsar of a certain tsardom, and the doctors and physicians can do nothing."

"You did well, but not so well as could be."

"Why not?"

"One has only to rub her eyes with the dew that is under this tree, and she will see again."

"But no one knows or has heard of that, so blind she will remain."

And the blind man sat in the tree and heard everything that was being said, and when the evil spirits had flown away, he climbed down from the tree, rubbed his eyes with the dew and lo! he could see again.

"Now I will go and help other people," said he to himself.

And gathering some dew into a small flask he had with him, he set off on his way.

He came to the village where there was no water, and he saw an old woman carrying two pails on a yoke.

"Give me a drink of water, grandmother," said he, bowing to her.

"Ah, my son," the old woman replied, "I am carrying this water from forty versts away, and I have spilled a good half already. And mine is a big family, they will die without water!"

"When I come to your village there will be enough water for all," he told her.

The old woman gave him a drink of water, and so happy was she to hear the good news that she rushed to the village and told the villagers about him. And the villagers did not know whether to believe her or not, but they came forth to meet him and they bowed to him, saying:

"Save us from the cruel death that awaits us, kind stranger."

"I'll do that," said he. "But if you want to help me you must take me to the town nearest your village."

They took him to the town, and he looked here and he looked there and at last he found the rock the evil spirits had spoken about.

Then the people set to, in a body, and they lifted the rock and moved it. And that same moment the water gushed from under it! It ran in a wide stream and filled all the springs and made all the ponds and rivers very full and deep.

The people were overjoyed, and they thanked the man and gave him lots of money and many, many gifts.

The man got on a horse and rode off, and of everyone he met he asked the way to the tsardom the evil spirits had spoken about.

Whether he was long on the way or not no one knows, but he reached it at last, and riding up to the tsar's palace, said to the servants:

"I have heard that the daughter of your tsar is very ill. Perhaps I can cure her."

"Not you!" said they. "The best doctors could do nothing to help her, so you needn't even try."

"Still, you had better tell the tsar about me."

They did not want to do it, but so insistent was he that they yielded at last and went to the tsar and told him. The tsar at once called him to the palace.

"Can you really cure my daughter?" he asked.

"I can," the man replied.

"If you cure her, I will give you whatever you ask for."

They took the man to the chamber where the Tsarevna lay, and he rubbed her eyes with the dew he had brought, and lo! she could see again.

The tsar's joy was such that no words could describe it, and he gave the man so many riches that a whole caravan of carts had to carry them all away.

Meanwhile, the wife was grieving and sorrowing, not knowing where her husband was. She was beginning to think him dead when lo! there he was, knocking at the window and calling out:

"Open the door, wife!"

She recognised his voice and was overjoyed. She ran out and opened the door for him and made to lead him into the hut, for she thought that he was blind.

"Bring a lighted splinter!" said he.

She brought the splinter, she looked at him and she lifted her hands in surprise, for there he stood, with his sight regained!

"God be thanked!" cried she. "How did it all happen, tell me?"

"Wait a bit, wife, let us first carry in what I have brought with me."

They carried in what he had brought, and he was now so rich that the rich brother's riches were as nothing to his.

And so now they had a full house and began living in style, and .the rich brother heard about it and came running to them.

"How did it happen, brother, that you got back your sight and became rich?" asked he.

And the other made no secret of it and told him everything there was to tell.

And now the rich brother was eager to become richer still, so when night came, he stole into the forest, climbed the selfsame tree and sat there very quietly.

Suddenly, on the stroke of midnight, the evil spirits came flying with the chief one among them at their head.

Said the evil spirits:

"What can it mean! No one knew anything and no one heard anything, and yet the blind brother has regained his sight and the water has been let out from under the rock and the Tsarevna has been cured. Perhaps someone eavesdrops on us? Let us go and see!"

They rushed to look, they climbed the tree, and lo! there sat the rich man. . . . And they pounced on him and tore him to bits.

THE WOLF, THE DOG AND THE CAT

A Ukrainian Fairy-Tale

Once upon a time there lived a Peasant who had a Dog. While the Dog was young, he guarded his master's house, but when he grew old, his master chased him away. The Dog roamed through the steppe, caught mice and what other little animals he could find there and ate them.

One night the Dog saw a Wolf coming towards him.

"Hello, Dog!" the Wolf said.

The Dog made a polite reply, and the Wolf asked:

"Where are you going, Dog?"

"While I was young," the Dog explained, "my master was quite fond of me, for I watched over his house, you see. But when I grew old, he chased me away."

"You must be hungry, Dog," said the Wolf.

"I am, very," replied the Dog.

"Then come with me, and I shall feed you."

So off the Dog went with the Wolf. Now their way lay through the steppe, and by and by the Wolf saw a herd of sheep at pasture and said to the Dog:

"Go and see who those creatures are, grazing there."

The Dog went and looked and he soon came running back.

"Those are sheep," he said.

"A plague on them! If we try to eat them, we'll have our teeth full of wool and nothing but empty bellies to show for it. Let us go further, Dog!"

So on they went, and by and by the Wolf saw a flock of geese in the steppe.

"Go and see who those creatures are, browsing there," he said to the Dog.

The Dog went and looked and he soon came running back.

"Those are geese," he said.

"A plague on them! If we try to eat them, we'll have our teeth full of feathers and nothing but empty bellies to show for it. Let us go further!"

So on they went, and by and by the Wolf saw a horse at pasture.

"Go and see who that creature is, feeding there," he said.

The Dog went and looked and he soon came running back.

"That is a horse," he said.

"Well, he will be ours!" said the Wolf.

So they ran towards the horse, and the Wolf pawed at the ground and gnashed his teeth, all to make himself very angry.

Said he to the Dog:

"Tell me, Dog, is my tail quivering?"

And the Dog looked and said that indeed it was.

"And now," said the Wolf, "see if my eyes have grown bleary."

"Indeed they have," the Dog replied.

Then the Wolf sprang up and he seized the horse by the

mane, dashed him to the ground and tore him to pieces. And he and the Dog began to feast on the horse's flesh. The Wolf was young and soon filled his belly, but the Dog was old and he gnawed and gnawed and still ate hardly anything. Other dogs ran up and drove him away.

The Dog set off down the road again and, coming towards him, he saw a Cat as old as himself, who was roaming the steppe in search of mice.

"Hello, there, Brother Puss!" said the Dog. "Where are you going?"

"I am going wherever the road takes me. When I was young, I served my master by catching mice. But when I grew old and slow and my sight dimmed, my master stopped feeding me, and he turned me out of the house. So now here I am knocking about the world."

"Then come along with me, Brother Puss," said the Dog, "and I shall feed you." For the Dog had decided to do just what the Wolf had done.

So the Dog and the Cat set off down the road together.

By and by the Dog saw a herd of sheep at pasture and he said to the Cat:

"Go and see who those creatures are, grazing there, Brother Puss."

The Cat went and looked and he soon came running back.

"Those are sheep," he said.

"A plague on them! We'll have our teeth full of wool and nothing but empty bellies to show for it. Let us go further!"

So, on they went, and by and by the Dog saw a flock of geese in the steppe.

Said he to the Cat:

"Run and see who those creatures are, browsing there, Brother Puss!"

The Cat went and looked and he soon came running back.

"Those are geese," he said.

"A plague on them! We'll have our teeth full of feathers and nothing but empty bellies to show for it."

And so the two of them went on their way. They walked and they walked, and by and by the Dog saw a horse at pasture.

Said the Dog:

"Run and see who that creature is, feeding there, Brother Puss."

The Cat went and looked and he soon came running back.

"That is a horse," he said.

"Well," said the Dog, "we'll kill him and then we'll have enough food and to spare."

So the Dog began to paw at the ground and to gnash his teeth, all to make himself very angry.

Said he to the Cat:

"See if my tail is quivering, Brother Puss."

"No," the Cat replied, "it isn't."

Then the Dog began to paw at the ground again to make himself very angry indeed.

Said he to the Cat:

"Isn't my tail quivering now, Brother Puss? Say that it is!"

The Cat looked and he said:

"Well, yes, it is, just a wee bit."

"Watch and see, we'll soon get the better of the horse!" said the Dog.

And he began to paw at the ground again.

"See if my eyes have grown bleary, Brother Puss," said he after a while.

"No, they haven't," the Cat replied.

"That's a lie! You must say that they have."

"Very well, they have grown bleary if you say so, I don't mind," said the Cat.

Then the Dog flew into a temper and he fell on the horse. But the horse kicked out with his hoofs and he struck the Dog on the head! And the Dog fell to the ground and his eyes popped out. And the Cat ran up to him and said:

"Ah, Brother Dog, now your eyes have indeed grown bleary!"

HOW A MUZHIK DINED
WITH THE HAUGHTY LORD

A Ukrainian Fairy-Tale

Once upon a time there lived a lord who was both rich and haughty. There were few people with whom he would have anything to do. And as for the muzhiks, he refused altogether to consider them human beings, saying that an evil smell, the smell of earth, came from them, and he ordered his servants to chase them away if any of them ventured near.

One day the muzhiks got together and began talking about the lord.

"I saw the lord quite close, I met him in the field," said one.

"And I looked over the fence yesterday and saw the lord having coffee on the balcony," said another.

Just then a third muzhik, the poorest of the poor, came up, and hearing them, laughed.

"Pooh, that's nothing," said he. "Anyone could peek at the lord over the fence. If I so wish, I will dine with him!"

"What do you mean! Dine with him, indeed!" laughed the

first two muzhiks. "Why, the moment he sees you he'll have you thrown out. He won't let you near the house!"

And the two muzhiks began jeering at the third and calling him names.

"You're a liar and a braggart!" cried they.

"I am not!"

"Well, if you dine with the lord, you'll get three sacks of wheat and two bullocks from us, but if you don't, you'll do everything we tell you to do."

"Very well," the muzhik replied.

He came into the lord's courtyard, and when the lord's servants saw him they rushed out of the house and made to drive him out.

"Wait!" the muzhik said. "I have good tidings for the lord."

"What are they?"

"That I will tell to no one but the lord himself."

So the lord's servants went to the lord and told him what the muzhik had said.

The lord felt curious, for the muzhik had come not to ask for anything, but to bring news. Perhaps it was something that might prove useful. . . .

"Show in the muzhik!" said he to his servants.

The servants let the muzhik into the house, and the lord came out to him and asked:

"What are the tidings you bring?"

The muzhik glanced at the servants.

"I should like to talk with you in private, my lord," said he.

By now the lord's curiosity was thoroughly aroused (for what could the muzhik have to tell him?), and he ordered the servants to leave them.

Said the muzhik in an undertone as soon as they were alone:

"Tell me, gracious lord, what might be the cost of a piece of gold as big as a horse's head?"

"What do you want to know that for?" asked the lord.

"I have my reason."

The lord's eyes gleamed and his hands began to shake.

"It's not for nothing that the muzhik asks me such a question," said he to himself. "He must have found some treasure."

And he began trying to worm out an answer from the muzhik.

"Tell me, my good man, why do you want to know about it?" he asked again.

Said the muzhik with a sigh:

"Well, if you don't wish to tell me, you needn't. And now I must be going, for my dinner is waiting for me."

The lord forgot to be haughty. He was fairly trembling with greed.

"I'll outwit this muzhik," thought he to himself, "and get the gold out of him." And to the muzhik: "Look here, my good man, why should you hurry home? You can have dinner with me if you are hungry. Come, servants, make haste and set the table, and don't forget the vodka!"

The servants at once set the table and served the vodka and cold dishes, and the lord began to regale the muzhik and offer him this and that.

"Drink, my good man, and eat your fill! Don't stand on ceremony!" said he.

And the muzhik did not refuse and ate and drank heartily, while the lord kept heaping his plate and refilling his glass.

Said the lord when the muzhik had eaten till he could eat no more:

"And now go quickly and bring me your piece of gold the size of a horse's head! I shall know much better than you how to dispose of it. And as a reward I'll give you a ruble."

"No, my lord, I won't bring you the gold," the muzhik said.

"Why ever not?"

"Because I haven't got it."

"What?! Then why did you want to know the cost of it?"

"Just out of curiosity!"

The lord fell into a great passion. He went purple in the face and he stamped his feet.

"Get out of here, fool!" cried he.

Said the muzhik in reply:

"I am not the fool you think me, O most gracious lord! I had my bit of fun at your expense, and I have won into the bargain my wager of three sacks of wheat and two round-horned bullocks. It takes brains to do that!"

And with that he went away.

THE MAGIC FIDDLE
A Byelorussian Fairy-Tale

Once upon a time there lived a boy who from his earliest years began playing on a pipe. While tending bullocks, he would cut himself a reed, make a pipe out of it and begin to play, and the bullocks would stop nibbling the grass, prick up their ears and listen. Hearing him, the birds in the forest would grow quiet, and even the frogs in the swamps would stop croaking.

He would go off to tend the horses at night, and it would be all gay and merry in the meadows, with the lads and lasses singing and joking, as young people should. The night would be beautiful and warm, and the ground fairly steaming.

And the boy would up and start playing on his pipe, and all the lads and lasses would grow quiet at once. And to each it seemed that a kind of balm had soothed the aching heart, and that an unknown force were raising him up and up to the bright stars in the deep blue sky.

The night herdsmen would sit there without stirring, forgetful of their aching, weary limbs and empty stomachs.

They would sit there and listen.

And each felt he could spend a whole lifetime sitting on and on and listening to the enchanting melody.

The music would stop, but no one dared so much as move from his place lest he frighten away the magical voice that poured out songs like the nightingale through the groves and forests and far into the sky.

Then the pipe would play again, a sorrowful tune this time, and sadness and melancholy would descend on all. . . . Peasant men and women, on their way late at night from their master's fields, would stop and listen on hearing it, and they never seemed to have their fill. Their lives would rise before their eyes, the poverty and the suffering, the cruel lord and the judge and stewards. And their hearts would be so heavy that they longed to give voice to their sadness in loud lamentations as they would have done for a dear departed soul, or for a son sent off to the wars.

But the sad tune would change to a gay one, and the listeners would throw down their scythes, rakes and pitchforks, and with arms akimbo begin to dance.

The men and women, the horses, the trees, the stars and clouds in the sky would dance—all the world would dance and make merry.

So great was the piper's magic power that he could do with the heart whatever he wished.

When he grew to manhood, the piper made himself a fiddle and with it roamed the land. Wherever he went, he would play his fiddle; and he dined and wined and was treated as the most welcome of guests and had good things heaped on him when he went on his way.

For many a long day the fiddler wandered over the land, a joy to good folk, a plague to cruel lords. A thorn in the side was he to the masters, for wherever he went the bondsmen no longer obeyed their lords.

So the lords decided to do away with him, and first one, then another man did they try to send forth to kill or drown the fiddler. But no one was willing, for the peasants loved the fiddler, and the stewards thought him a sorcerer and were afraid.

Then the lords called up the demons from the nether world, and together they plotted against him. For, of course, everyone knows that lords and demons are tarred with the same brush.

One day, when the fiddler was walking in the forest, the demons sent twelve hungry wolves against him. The wolves stood in the fiddler's path, they gnashed their teeth and their eyes gleamed like coals. And the fiddler had no weapon in his hand save the bag with his fiddle in it.

"My end has come," thought he.

So he took his fiddle from the bag, for he wished to make music just once more before dying. He leaned against a tree and drew his bow across the strings.

The fiddle spoke out like a living thing, and peals of music resounded in the forest. The bushes and trees became suddenly stilled, not a single leaf stirred; the wolves, jaws gaping, their hunger forgotten, stood frozen to the spot, listening intently.

And when the music stopped, the wolves moved off as in a dream to the depths of the forest.

The fiddler walked on. The sun was setting beyond the forest, its golden rays flecking the tops of the trees. It was so quiet that not a breath of sound could be heard.

The fiddler sat down on a river-bank, took out his fiddle and began to play. So well did he play that earth and sky gave ear to him, seeming ready to listen for ever. Then he struck up a gay polka, and all around began to dance: the stars whirled and twisted like the blizzard snow in winter, the clouds floated across the sky, and the fish leapt up and thrashed about until the river seethed like boiling water.

Even the king of the water-sprites lost control and joined the dancing too, and such capers did he cut that the river overflowed its banks.

The demons were frightened and bounded out of their backwaters, but though they gnashed their teeth in fury, there was nothing they could do to the fiddler.

And the fiddler, seeing that the king of the water-sprites was flooding the people's fields and gardens, stopped playing, put the fiddle into his bag and went on his way.

He walked and he walked, and all of a sudden two young lords ran up to him.

"We have a ball tonight," said they. "Come and play for us, fiddler, we shall pay you well."

The fiddler thought it over, and what was he to do! The night was dark, and he had nowhere to sleep, and no money, either.

"Very well," said he, "I'll play for you."

The young lords brought the fiddler to a palace, where were

so many young lords and ladies that there was no counting them.

Now on the table stood a large bowl, and one by one the lords and ladies were continually running to it. Each in turn thrust a finger into the bowl and then passed it across his eyes.

The fiddler, too, went up to the bowl, dipped in his finger and passed it across his eyes. No sooner had he done so than he saw that this was no palace at all, but the nether world itself, and these were no lords and ladies, but devils and witches.

"Oh, so that's the kind of ball it is!" said the fiddler to himself. "But just you wait, I'll play you a fine tune!"

So he tuned up his fiddle and his bow struck its living strings, and all around him was shattered to dust, and the devils and witches were scattered afar and were never seen again!

WHY THE BADGER AND THE FOX LIVE IN HOLES

A Byelorussian Fairy-Tale

It is said that long, long ago neither wild nor tame animals had any tails. Only the Lion, tsar of the beasts, had one.

It was a poor life the animals led without tails. They got along somehow in winter, but when summer came, the flies and midges gave them no peace at all. For what could they chase them off with? Many were the animals bitten to death by gadflies and breezes. Once they fell on you there was just nothing you could do to save yourself.

Now the Lion, tsar of the beasts, learning of this and wishing to help them in their misfortune, sent out an order for all the animals to come to him that he might present them with tails.

The tsar's messengers rushed to all ends of the realm to call the animals. Like the wind they flew, on the trumpets they blew, and they beat on a drum with a ra-ta-ta-tum! They saw the Wolf, and they told him of the tsar's order. They saw the Bull and the Badger, and they told them too. And they called the Fox, the Marten, the Hare, the Elk, the Wild Boar and all the rest. All but the Bear. For him they searched for a long time till at last they found him in his lair, fast asleep. They shook him awake and they told him to make haste and go for his tail.

But who ever heard of the Bear hurrying!... He strolled along slowly, tramp-a-tramp, a single step at a time; he let his gaze stray to all sides of him, and kept sniffing the air for a breath of honey. All of a sudden he looked, and there before him, in the hollow of a lime-tree, he saw a beehive.

"The road to the tsar's palace is long," said the Bear to himself. "I had better have something to eat to help me along."

And he climbed the tree and found the hollow was as full of honey as could be! With a growl of delight he began scraping out the hollow, scooping up the honey and cramming himself full. By and by, feeling that he had had enough, he looked at himself and found that his coat was all sticky with honey and pieces of honeycomb.

"How can I show myself in the tsar's presence, looking the way I do?" the Bear asked himself.

He went to the river, washed his coat and lay down on the hillside to dry. And the sun was so warm that before the Bear knew where he was he was fast asleep and gently snoring.

Meanwhile the animals were beginning to gather at the tsar's palace. The first to come was the Fox. She looked around her, and there, in front of the palace, she saw a whole heap of tails: long tails and short ones, bushy and hairless ones.

The Fox bowed to the tsar.

"O most radiant majesty!" said she. "I was the first to come at your call, and so I beg you to allow me to choose for myself the tail I like best."

Now the tsar, of course, cared not a whit which tail the Fox would get.

"Very well," said he, "you may choose a tail to your liking."

So the sly Fox went through the whole heap of tails, and choosing the most beautiful tail which was long and bushy, rushed away with it before the tsar had time to think better of his generosity.

After the Fox, the Squirrel came hopping up, and she picked herself a tail that was quite as fine as the Fox's, but smaller. The next to come was the Marten, and he too made off with a handsome, bushy tail.

The Elk chose the longest of the tails with a thick brush at the end to wave away the gadflies and breezes. And the Badger pounced upon a tail that was broad and thick.

The Horse took a tail that was all hair and nothing much else. He stuck it on, swept it over his right flank and then over his left, and seeing that the flies were now an easy target for him, whinnied with pleasure.

"This'll mean the death of all flies!" said he, and he galloped off to his meadow.

The last to come running up was the Hare.

"Where have you been?" the tsar asked him. "All I have left is a tiny little tail."

"It will do for me nicely, thank you," said the Hare happily. "A little tail is as good as any other. It won't be in the way when I'm running from a wolf or a dog!"

And the Hare stuck his little blob of a tail to the place where it belonged; he gave one hop and then another, and ran home very happily indeed.

And the Lion, having now given out all the tails, went to bed.

As for the Bear, he awoke only towards evening, and it was then that he remembered that he had to hurry to the tsar's palace for his tail. He looked, and there was the sun rolling down the sky beyond the forest. So he lumbered off on all fours for all he was worth. He ran so hard, poor soul, that he was soon in a sweat. He rushed up to the tsar's palace, and lo! not a tail did he see: there was nothing and no one there.

"What am I going to do now?" the Bear asked himself. "Everyone will have a tail except me."

And the Bear turned back and tramped off again to his own forest as angry as could be! He lumbered along slowly, and by and by what did he see but the Badger twisting and turning on a tree-stump and admiring his handsome tail.

"Listen, Badger," the Bear said, "what do you want with a tail? Give it to me!"

"What strange notions you do have, Bear!" the Badger returned, taken aback. "Who would want to part with such a beautiful tail?"

"Well, if you won't give it to me of your own free will, I'll take it away by force!" the Bear roared, laying his heavy paw on the Badger's tail.

"You shan't have it!" the Badger cried, and with all the strength he had in him, he wrenched himself free from the Bear's grasp and broke into a run.

The Bear looked, and there, clinging to his claws, was a piece of the Badger's coat and the very tip of his tail. He threw the piece of coat away, and sticking on the bit of tail, went off to finish the honey in the tree hollow.

As for the Badger, he was so frightened that he did not know what to do with himself. No matter where he hid, it always seemed to him that the Bear would come at any moment and take the rest of his tail away. So he dug out a large hole in the ground and made his home there. The wound on his back healed, and only a long dark stripe was left to show where it had been. And it has never grown any lighter since.

One day the Fox came scuttling near, she looked, and she saw a hole in the ground from which came loud snores, just as though someone had had too much to drink. She got into the hole, and lo! there was the Badger, fast asleep.

"Isn't there enough room for you up above, neighbour," asked the Fox in surprise, "that you have hidden yourself here, under the ground?"

"No, Foxy dear, there isn't," sighed the Badger. "If it weren't for food that I must hunt, I would never leave this hole, not even at night."

And the Badger told the Fox why it was there was no room for him above ground.

"Hm," said the Fox to herself, "if the Bear has tried to steal the Badger's tail, then I am in danger of losing mine, for it is a hundred times more handsome."

And she ran off in search of a place in which to hide from the Bear. She ran around searching all through the night, but no such place could she find. At last, towards morning, she dug herself a hole just like the Badger's, scrambled into it, covered herself with her bushy tail and went peacefully to sleep.

So the Badger and the Fox have lived in holes ever since, while the Bear to this day has nothing but a poor little button of a tail.

HOW VASIL VANQUISHED THE DRAGON

A Byelorussian Fairy-Tale

Whether it was so or not, whether it is true or false, let us hear what the tale has to tell.

And so here it is.

To a certain land there once came a most fearful and terrible Dragon. He dug himself out a deep hole by a mountain in the midst of a forest, and lay down to rest.

Whether he rested long or not no one now recalls, but the moment he rose he shouted loudly for all to hear:

"Come, folk, men and wives, old and young, you must each of you bring me a tribute every day: one of you can bring me a cow, another—a lamb, and a third—a pig! He who obeys, will live. But he who does not, will die, for him I will devour!"

The people were frightened, and they began paying the Dragon the tribute he asked for. This went on for a long time till at last there came a day when there was nothing left to bring, for they were all reduced to the direst need. But the Dragon was of the kind that could not let a day pass without gorging himself. So he began flying from village to village, seizing people and carrying them off to his den.

The people went about wailing like lost souls, vainly trying to find a way to deliver themselves from the cruel Dragon.

Now at that very time a man named Vasil came to those parts, and he found that the people went about sad and crestfallen, wringing their hands and weeping loudly.

"What is the trouble?" asked he. "Why are you all weeping?"

The people told him of their trouble, and Vasil tried to comfort them.

"Calm yourselves," said he. "I will try to save you from the Dragon."

And taking a heavy cudgel, he went to the forest where the Dragon lived.

The Dragon saw him, and rolling his great green eyes, asked:

"Why have you come here with that cudgel?"

"To give you a beating!" Vasil replied.

"My, how brave you are!" said the Dragon. "You had better run away while you still can. For I only have to blow once, and you will be blown clean away from here, a full three versts!"

Vasil smiled.

"Don't you boast, you old scarecrow," said he. "I've seen worse monsters than you! We'll see which of us can blow the harder. Go on, blow!"

And the Dragon blew so hard that the leaves rained down from the trees, and Vasil was thrown to his knees.

"Ha, that's nothing!" said he, springing to his feet. "Why, it's enough to make a cat laugh! Now let me try. Only first you must bandage your eyes if you don't want them to jump out of their sockets."

The Dragon tied a kerchief over his eyes, and Vasil came up and struck him such a blow on the head with his cudgel that sparks poured from the Dragon's eyes.

"Can it be that you are stronger than I?" the Dragon asked. "Let's try again and see which of us is fastest at crushing a rock."

And the Dragon seized a rock weighing all of a hundred poods and squeezed it with his claws so hard that the dust rose up in clouds.

"There's nothing to that!" laughed Vasil. "Let's see you squeeze it so that the water will run from it."

The Dragon was frightened. He was beginning to feel that Vasil was the stronger of the two, and glancing at Vasil's cudgel, said:

"Ask of me what you will, and you shall have it."

"I don't need anything," Vasil replied. "I have plenty of everything in the house, more than you have."

"Can that be true?" asked the Dragon in disbelief.

"If you don't believe me, come and see for yourself!"

So they got into a cart and drove off.

By now the Dragon was becoming very hungry. He saw a herd of bullocks on the edge of a forest and he said to Vasil:

"Go and catch a bullock and we'll have a bite to eat."

And Vasil went to the forest and began stripping bast from

the lime-trees. The Dragon waited and waited, and at last went to look for him.

"What is taking you so long?" he asked him.

"Can't you see I am stripping bast from the lime-trees," Vasil replied.

"What do you need bast for?"

"To make some rope so as to catch us five bullocks for dinner."

"What do we need five bullocks for? One is enough."

And the Dragon caught a bullock by the nape of its neck and dragged it to the cart.

"Now go and bring us some wood to roast the bullock," said he to Vasil.

And Vasil sat down under an oak-tree in the forest, rolled himself a cigarette and began to smoke.

The Dragon waited for him for a long time, and at last, losing patience, went to look for him.

"What is taking you so long?" he asked him.

"I want to take a dozen oaks or so, so I'm trying to pick the thickest among them."

"What do we want with a dozen oaks? One is enough," said the Dragon, and giving one wrench, he pulled out the thickest of the oaks.

He roasted the bullock and invited Vasil to join him.

"Go ahead and eat it yourself," said Vasil. "I'll have something at home. What's one bullock for me—just a bite!"

The Dragon ate the bullock and licked his lips. They rode on and soon came to Vasil's house. The children saw their father coming from a distance, and they cried out joyously:

"Father's coming! Father's coming!"

But the Dragon did not catch the words and asked:

"What are the children shouting?"

"They are pleased that I am bringing you home for their dinner. They're very hungry."

By now the Dragon was badly frightened, so he jumped from the cart and took to his heels. But he missed the road and landed in a bog. The bog was very deep, so deep indeed that the bottom could not be reached, and the Dragon sank in and was drowned. And so that was the end of him.

PILIPKA

A Byelorussian Fairy-Tale

Once there lived a man and his wife. They had no children, and the wife was always sorrowing and grieving that she had no one to rock in the cradle and to kiss and fondle.

One day the husband went to the forest, chopped out a log from an alder-tree and brought it home to his wife.

"Here," said he, "rock this."

The wife put the log in a cradle and she began rocking it and singing as she rocked:

"Little son, rock-a-bye, you are white of body and dark of eye. . . ."

She rocked the log one day, and she rocked it the next, and on the third day she looked, and there was a little baby boy lying in the cradle!

The husband and wife were overjoyed. They called their little son Pilipka and began caring for him tenderly.

·When Pilipka grew up he said to his father:

"Make me a golden boat, Father, and a silver paddle. I want to go fishing."

And the father made him a golden boat and a silver paddle and sent him to the lake to catch fish.

Pilipka set to fishing in earnest, and he fished whole days and nights on end. Indeed, so well were the fish biting that he would not even go home, and his mother brought his dinner to him. She would come to the lake and call:

"Pilipka, my son, the day is half done, and here is a pie for you to try!"

And Pilipka would make for the shore, throw the fish he had caught out on to it, and having eaten his mother's pie, paddle to the middle of the lake again.

Now Baba-Yaga the Witch with the Switch, hearing how his mother called to Pilipka, decided to put him to death.

She took a sack and a poker, came to the lake and began calling:

"Pilipka, my son, the day is half done, and here is a pie for you to try!"

Pilipka thought that it was his mother calling and paddled to the shore, and Baba-Yaga hooked his boat with her poker, dragged it up the bank, and seizing Pilipka, thrust him into the sack.

"Aha!" cried she. "You won't be catching fish any more!"

And throwing the sack over her shoulder, she carried it off with her into the forest thicket. But the way to her house being long, she soon grew tired, sat down to rest and fell asleep. And Pilipka crawled out of the sack, filled it full of heavy stones and went back to the lake again.

When Baba-Yaga woke up, she caught up the sack and carried it home with many moans and groans.

She brought it home and she said to her daughter:

"Roast this fisherman for my dinner!"

She shook the sack out on the floor, and lo! nothing but stones dropped out of it.

Baba-Yaga flew into a temper.

"I'll show you how to fool me!" she cried at the top of her voice, and running to the lake shore again, she began calling to Pilipka:

"Pilipka, my son, the day is half done, and here is a pie for you to try!"

Pilipka heard her and called back:

"I know you well! You are not my mother, but Baba-Yaga. My mother's voice is ever so much thinner."

And though Baba-Yaga kept calling to him, Pilipka did not heed her.

"Never you mind," said Baba-Yaga to herself, "I'll make me a thin little voice."

And she ran to a blacksmith.

"Blacksmith, blacksmith, sharpen my tongue and make it thinner," said she.

"Very well," replied the blacksmith. "Just put it on my anvil."

So Baba-Yaga stuck out her long tongue and laid it on the anvil, and the blacksmith took his hammer and pounded away at it till it became quite thin.

After that Baba-Yaga ran to the lake, and she called to Pilipka in a thin little voice:

"Pilipka, my son, the day is half done, and here is a pie for you to try!"

Pilipka heard her and thought it was his mother calling. He paddled in to shore, and Baba-Yaga snatched him up and thrust him into her sack.

"You won't fool me any more!" Baba-Yaga cried, overjoyed, and without stopping to rest, she took him straight home. She shook him out of the sack and said to her daughter:

"Here he is, the cheat! Light the stove and roast him for dinner."

And with these words she went out.

And her daughter lit the stove, and bringing a spade, said to Pilipka:

"Lie down on the spade, I'll put you in the stove."

And Pilipka lay down on the spade, with his legs sticking up in the air.

"Not that way!" Baba-Yaga's daughter cried. "I shan't be able to put you in the stove if you hold your legs up."

Pilipka dropped his legs, letting them hang down over the spade.

"Not that way!" Baba-Yaga's daughter cried again.

"Then how?" Pilipka asked. "Show me!"

"How stupid you are!" exclaimed Baba-Yaga's daughter. "This is the way it's done. Look!"

And she stretched herself out on the spade. And Pilipka snatched up the spade and shoved it into the burning stove. After that he closed the stove and put Baba-Yaga's poker against it so that her daughter could not jump out.

He ran out of the hut, and lo! there was Baba-Yaga walking towards it. Pilipka leaped up into a tall and leafy sycamore-tree and hid himself in the branches.

Baba-Yaga came into the hut, she sniffed and she smelt the smell of roasting meat. She took the roast out of the stove, ate up the meat. and throwing the bones out into the yard, began rolling over them, saying:

"On these bones I did fall-fall, o'er these bones I will roll-roll, for I have eaten of Pilipka's flesh and I have drunk of his blood."

And Pilipka called to her from his hiding-place:

"On these bones you may fall-fall, o'er these bones you may roll-roll, for you have eaten of your daughter's flesh and drunk of your daughter's blood."

Baba-Yaga heard him and she grew black with rage. She ran to the sycamore-tree and began gnawing at it with her teeth. She gnawed and she gnawed, and she broke her teeth, but the tree stood there as tough and strong as ever.

Baba-Yaga ran to the blacksmith.

"Blacksmith, blacksmith," cried she, "forge me a steel axe! If you don't, I will eat up your children."

And the blacksmith was frightened and forged her an axe.

Baba-Yaga rushed with it to the sycamore-tree and began chopping it down.

Said Pilipka:

"Strike no tree, but strike a rock!"

Said Baba-Yaga:

"Strike no rock, but strike the tree!"

Said Pilipka again:

"Strike no tree, but strike a rock!"

Here the axe suddenly struck a rock and became all chipped and blunted.

Baba-Yaga gave a howl of rage, snatched up the axe and returned to the blacksmith to have it sharpened.

Pilipka looked, and he saw that the sycamore-tree was beginning to lean over to one side. Baba-Yaga had chopped it nearly through, and he had to hurry to save himself before it was too late.

Just then a flock of geese flew over.

"Geese, geese, do not screech, drop me down a feather each," he called to them. "To my mother and father I will fly with you, and there I will pay you for your service true!"

The geese dropped him a feather each, and of these feathers Pilipka fashioned himself half a wing.

Then a second flock of geese came flying. And Pilipka called to them and said:

"Geese, geese, do not screech, drop me down a feather each. To my mother and father I will fly with you, and there I will pay you for your service true!"

And the second flock dropped him a feather each.

After that came a third and a fourth flock, and all the geese dropped Pilipka a feather each.

Pilipka fashioned himself a pair of wings and flew after the geese.

Just then Baba-Yaga came running from the blacksmith's shop, and she began chopping down the sycamore-tree again. She chopped so hard that the chips flew.

She chopped and she chopped, and the sycamore-tree fell on her with one great cr-r-r-ash! and killed her.

And Pilipka came flying home with the geese. When his mother and father saw him they were overjoyed. They seated him at the table and began regaling him with all sorts of delicacies.

And to the geese they gave oats and ale, and that is the end of this long-short tale.

OLD FROST AND YOUNG FROST

A Lithuanian Fairy-Tale

Once there lived Old Father Frost, and he had a son—Young Frost. And such a braggart was this young one that you would be hard put to it even to tell about it. To hear him, you would think there was no one in all the world more clever and stronger than he.

One day Young Frost said to himself:

"My father has grown old, and he does his work badly. I am young and I am strong, and I can freeze people far better. No one can hide from me, no one can get the better of me. I can lick anyone!"

And Young Frost set off in search of someone to freeze. He flew out on to a road, and he saw a lord riding in a buggy drawn by a sleek, well-fed horse. The lord himself was big and fat, he had on a warm fur coat and his legs were covered with a rug.

Young Frost looked the lord over and laughed.

"Ha!" said he. "You can wrap yourself in furs all you will, but it isn't going to save you. The old man, my father, may not have been able to cope with you, but I can: I'll chill you to the marrow. So hold tight! Neither your fur coat, nor the rug will help."

And Young Frost flew up to the lord and began plaguing and worrying him: getting under the rug, and creeping into his sleeves, and stealing under his collar, and nipping his nose.

At that the lord ordered his coachman to whip up the horse.

"I shall freeze to death!" cried he.

And Young Frost continued to plague the lord more and more. He nipped his nose till it hurt, chilled his hands and feet and took his breath away.

The lord moved this way and that, he fidgeted on his seat and he shivered and shrank with cold.

"Drive faster!" cried he to the coachman. "Faster!"

But after a while he stopped shouting, for he had lost his voice.

When he reached his house, he was carried half-dead out of the buggy.

Young Frost now flew to Old Frost, his father, and began boasting and bragging.

"Look at me, Father!" he cried. "Look at me! I am very strong! You'll never be able to keep up with me! Just see what a big, fat lord I froze! And what a warm coat I crept under! You could never do it! You could never freeze anyone so big and strong!"

Old Frost smiled.

"You little braggart!" said he. "Do not be in such a hurry to boast of your strength and daring. It's true you froze that fat lord and crept under his warm coat. But that is nothing. Look over there. See that skinny muzhik in his threadbare coat riding on the scraggy horse?"

"Yes, I see him."

"Well, he is on his way to the forest to chop wood. Just you try and freeze him. If you succeed, then I will believe you when you say that you are strong!"

"Humph! Here is a wonder indeed!" Young Frost cried. "Why, I'll freeze him in a moment!"

And Young Frost rose up into the air and flew off to overtake the muzhik. He caught him up and fell on him and began plaguing and harassing him. He flew at him now from one side and now from the other, but the muzhik rode on and never stopped. Then Young Frost began nipping his feet, but the muzhik jumped from his sledge and ran alongside his horse.

"Just you wait!" thought Young Frost. "I'll freeze you in the forest!"

The muzhik came to the forest, he took out his axe and he began chopping down the spruces and birches so that the chips flew to all sides!

And Young Frost would give him no peace. He caught him by the hands and feet and crept under his collar. . . .

But the harder Young Frost tried to freeze him, the faster the muzhik swung his axe and the more trees he chopped down. In the end, so warm did he get that he even took off his mittens.

Young Frost continued to harass the muzhik until he was quite worn out.

"Never you mind," said he to himself, "I'll get the better of you, anyway. I'll chill you to the bone when you are on your way home."

He ran to the sledge, and seeing the muzhik's mittens, crept into them. He sat there and he laughed, saying to himself:

"I'd just like to see how the muzhik is going to put on his mittens. So stiff have I made them that one can't thrust one's fingers into them!"

There sat Young Frost in the muzhik's mittens, and the muzhik went on chopping the wood and seemed to have no thought for anything else. He chopped till he had a whole cartload ready.

"Now," said the muzhik, "I might just as well go home."

He took his mittens and tried to put them on, but they were as hard and stiff as rock.

"Well, what are you going to do now?" Young Frost said to himself, laughing.

But the muzhik, seeing that he could not put on his mittens, took his axe and began striking them with it again and again.

The muzhik went thump-thump! over the mittens with his axe, and Young Frost went oh-oh! inside them.

And such a trouncing did the muzhik give Young Frost that Young Frost ran from him, barely alive.

The muzhik drove home with his wood, urging on his horse with loud cries. And Young Frost tottered off, groaning, to his father.

Old Frost saw Young Frost and burst out laughing.

"What's the matter, son," asked he, "why are you tottering so?"

"I'm completely knocked out, trying to freeze the muzhik."

"And why are you groaning so piteously?"

"Who wouldn't, in my place! My sides ache from the whipping the muzhik gave me."

"Now let this be a lesson to you, my son. It's easy enough to worst the thumb-twiddling lords, but no one can get the better of a muzhik. And don't you forget it!"

HOW A LORD WAS TURNED INTO A HORSE

A Latvian Fairy-Tale

In olden times there lived a cruel lord. He never spared his workmen and forced them to labour until they were half-dead. Even on holidays he gave them no rest.

One morning, on a big holiday, when most people were resting from their labours, the lord sent his workmen to the barn to thresh grain.

Now the workmen had been threshing all day and all night, and they were so tired they could hardly stand.

They had just set to work when the lord himself rushed into the barn armed with a stick. It seemed to him that his workmen were too slow, and he fell on them with threats and abuse, flourishing his stick.

"You loafers!" he yelled. "You won't leave the barn till you've threshed all the rye!"

The men asked for a horse to hitch to the thresher that the work might be done more quickly.

"What?!" the lord cried. "I'm to give you a horse?... With my own bare hands I'll strangle to death every one of you loafers if you so much as dare suggest such a thing again! You'll get no horse from me! The horse must rest. You can very well do the work yourselves!"

And having shouted himself hoarse, the lord hurried from the threshing-barn, for there is little pleasure in swallowing dust.

He had no sooner gone than the workmen heard someone cry out:

"Whoa, there! Stop! Whoa!..."

Then a horse neighed, and a bridle jingled. It was clear that a horse was being harnessed.

Who could be doing it?

Suddenly an old man entered the threshing-barn. He was very, very old, with a long grey beard and eyes that flashed like lightning. Behind him, led firmly by the reins, came a sturdy bay stallion.

The old man greeted the workmen, saying:

"Here is a horse for you. Hitch him to the thresher and use him for the hardest work. When you go to the forest, don't pile timber on a wagon, but after felling a tree, tie the horse to the crown and let him drag the tree, boughs, twigs and all, to the lord's house. If he balks and refuses to do it, lash him mercilessly, and don't spare the whip! Flog his flanks and back, but mind you don't touch his head. And don't give him anything to eat. When you lead him into his stall in the evening, hoist him up on straps to the ceiling. Let him hang for a night after a day's work. It will only do him good."

With these words, the old man vanished.

The horse neighed loudly, and so closely did the tones of his voice resemble those of the lord that the workmen guessed what sort of horse this was.

"It must have been old Father Perkon himself, lord of thunder and lightning, that brought him here!" said they. "And Perkon's command must be obeyed. What he has told us to do with the horse, that shall we do."

And they hitched the bay stallion to the thresher and at once set to work. Now the stallion was stubborn, and he jibbed and neighed, and stamped his hoofs and twisted his neck: it was all too plain he did not want to work. But they paid no heed and gave him a good lashing that he might not balk any more.

And so it went on from that day. Whenever the hardest work had to be done, they were sure to harness the bay stallion. And if he balked, they flogged him mercilessly with whips and rods.

The stallion would toil all day without resting, and when night came, he would be taken to his stall and hoisted up on straps to the ceiling to hang there till morning.

Nor was he given any food. In all the time he worked he only succeeded in stealing a wisp of straw from a wagon in winter and nibbling at some nettles under the fence in summer, and that was all.

Now on the very day that the bay stallion had made his appearance, the cruel lord had disappeared. His lady searched and searched for him, but she could not find him.

A whole year passed by. In the beginning the stallion had been strong and stately and sleek, but at the end of the year he was wasted away: his eyes had sunk in, his mouth hung loose, his ribs poked through his flanks, his back had caved in and his hair hung down limp and straggly.

One day the lady saw the stallion in the yard, and she said to the groom:

"That wretched old jade there had better be taken to the forest and shot. It makes me sick to look at it!"

But the steward, too, must have guessed what sort of horse it was, and so he did not kill it.

One morning, on a big holiday, when everyone was resting, the bay stallion quietly left his stall. He got into the lord's kitchen garden and began eating the cabbages.

The lady went out for a walk, she strolled into the kitchen garden, and what did she see but the same wretched stallion greedily peeling off cabbage leaves and swallowing them.

The lady flew into a passion.

"You good-for-nothing brute, you!" cried she. "Just wait, I'll teach you a lesson!"

And picking up a thick stick, she caught the horse a blow over the head! And lo! in a trice there stood her lord himself.

Said the lord in a weak and pitiful voice:

"My dear wife, why do you beat me? Do you grudge me a few cabbage leaves?... After a year of starvation they seem sweeter to me than the choicest dishes I ever tasted!"

Now the lady recognised him, and she began oh'ing and ah'ing. The lord did not look like himself at all: he was very thin and dark of face, his beard and his finger-nails had grown very long, his whole body was a mass of cuts and bruises, and of his clothes nothing was left but the seams and tatters.

The lady seized him by the hand and led him quietly into the house, so that no one might see.

And from that time onwards the lord was ever meek and humble.

TO EACH HIS DESERTS

An Estonian Fairy-Tale

Once upon a time a poor old wayfaring man was walking along a road. Dusk had descended, and night was approaching.

The old man decided to ask for shelter, and he knocked at the window of a large house.

"Let me in for the night, good folk!" said he.

Hearing him, the mistress of the house, who was a rich woman, came out and began to scold the stranger and shout at him.

"I will let the dogs loose on you!" cried she. "Then you'll know how to ask me to put you up for the night. Get away from here!"

The old man walked on. He saw a poor little house, and he knocked at the window.

"Won't you give me shelter for the night, good folk?" he asked.

"Come in, come in!" the mistress of the house called to him in friendly tones. "You are welcome to spend the night with us. Only it's noisy and there isn't much room. I hope you don't mind."

The stranger came into the house, and he saw that the family was very poor. There were many children, and the shirts they had on were tattered and worn.

"Why do you let your children go about in such rags?" the stranger asked. "Why don't you make them new shirts?"

"How can I?" the woman replied. "My husband is dead, and I have to bring up the children all alone.... We haven't enough money for bread even, to say nothing of clothing."

The stranger heard her out, and said not a word in reply. And the mistress of the house put the supper on the table and invited him to join them.

"Come and eat with us," said she.

"No, thank you," the old man replied. "I am not hungry. I ate but a short time ago."

And untying his bag, he took out all the food he possessed and treated the children to it. After that he lay down and at once fell asleep.

In the morning the old man rose, thanked the mistress of the house for her hospitality and said in parting:

"That which you do in the morning, you will do until evening."

The woman did not understand the stranger's words and paid no heed to them. She saw him to the gate and then came back into the house.

"If even this poor man says that my children are ragamuffins, what will all the others say!" she thought to herself.

And as there was not enough cloth for more, she decided to

make one shirt out of the last piece of cloth she had in the house. So she went to her rich neighbour's house to borrow a yardstick to measure the cloth and see if there was enough for even that one shirt.

From her neighbour's house the poor woman went at once to her store-room. She took the piece of cloth from the shelf and began to measure it. As she measured, the piece kept growing larger and larger, and there seemed no end to it at all! She spent the whole day measuring it and finished only late in the evening.

She was sure now that there was enough cloth to last her and all her children for the rest of their lives.

"So that was what the stranger meant!" she thought to herself.

That same evening she took the yardstick back to her rich neighbour, and without holding back anything, told her how at the word of the stranger she had acquired a store-room of cloth.

"Dear me, why didn't I let him in for the night!" the rich woman thought to herself, and she called to her workman:

"Come, my man, quickly harness a horse and ride fast after that beggar. Bring him back here at any cost! The poor should be helped without stint. I have always said so."

The workman at once drove off in search of the old man, and he caught him up on the following day. But the old man refused to go back.

The workman was sorely grieved.

"Unhappy man that I am!" said he. "If I don't bring you back, my mistress will drive me out without my wages."

"Don't fret, my lad," the old man said. "So be it! I'll go with you."

And climbing into the cart, he drove off with the workman.

The rich woman stood at her gate, all impatience. She met the old man with bows and smiles, and leading him into the house, gave him food and drink and made up a soft bed for him, saying:

"Lie down, father, and rest!"

The old man lived in the rich woman's house for a day and for another and for a third. He ate and drank and slept and smoked his pipe. The mistress of the house gave him food and drink and she spoke kindly to him, but inwardly she was fuming.

"When will the old good-for-nothing get out of here!" said she to herself.

But she dared not turn the old man out, for then all the trouble she had gone to on his account would be wasted.

To her great joy, on the fourth day, early in the morning, the old man began getting ready to leave. The rich woman went outside to see him off. The old man walked to the gate in silence and in silence he passed out of it. The rich woman could restrain herself no longer.

"What am I to do today, tell me?" she asked.

The old man looked at her.

"That which you do in the morning, you will do until evening," said he.

The rich woman rushed into the house and she snatched up her yardstick to measure her cloth.

But suddenly she sneezed loudly, so loudly that the chickens in the yard were frightened and fluttered off in all directions.

And she kept on sneezing all day, without a stop:

"A-tishoo! A-tishoo! A-tishoo!"

She could neither eat, nor drink, nor answer any questions. All that came from her was:

"A-tishoo! A-tishoo! A-tishoo!"

And only when the sun had set and darkness fallen did she stop sneezing.

HIYSI'S MILLSTONE

A Karelian Fairy-Tale

Once there lived two brothers, one of whom was poor and the other rich. With his neighbours the rich brother was friendly and ready to please, but with his own brother he acted as if he did not know him, for he feared that the other might come to him a-begging.

Not that the poor brother ever asked anything of the rich one; he never did, if he could help it.

But once a holiday came along, he had nothing in the house, and his wife said to him:

"How are we going to celebrate the holiday? Go to your brother and borrow a little meat of him. He slaughtered a cow yesterday, I saw him."

The poor man did not like to go to his brother and he told his wife so, but there was nowhere else he could go to.

So he came to his rich brother and said:

"Lend me a little meat, brother, we have nothing in the house for the holiday."

And the rich brother threw him a cow's hoof, crying:

"Here, take it and go to Hiysi!"

The poor brother left the rich brother's house, and he said to himself:

"He has given the hoof not to me, but to Hiysi the Wood-Goblin, so to Hiysi I had better take it."

And he started off for the forest.

Whether he walked long in the forest or not no one knows; but by and by he met some woodcutters.

"Where are you going?" asked the woodcutters.

"To Hiysi the Wood-Goblin, to give him this cow's hoof," the poor man replied. "Can you tell me where I can find his hut?"

Said the woodcutters:

"Go straight ahead, never swerving from the road, and you'll come to it. But first listen to us. If Hiysi tries to repay you in silver for the cow's hoof, don't take it. If he tries to give you gold, don't take the gold either. Ask for his millstone and for nothing else."

The poor man thanked the woodcutters for their kind advice, said good-bye to them and went on.

Whether he walked long or not nobody knows, but by and by he saw a hut. He went inside, and whom did he see there but Hiysi himself!

Hiysi looked at him and said:

"People often promise to bring me gifts, but they rarely do so. What have you brought me?"

"A cow's hoof."

Hiysi was overjoyed.

"For thirty years I have eaten no meat," said he. "Give me the hoof quickly!"

And he took the hoof and ate it.

"Now I should like to pay you for it," said he. "Do you want much for it? Here, take these two handfuls of silver."

"I don't want any silver," said the poor man.

Then Hiysi took out some gold, and he offered the poor man two handfuls.

"I don't want any gold, either," said the poor man.

"What do you want, then?"

"Your millstone."

"Oh, no, you can't have that! But I can give you as much money as you like."

But the poor man would not agree and kept asking for the millstone.

"I have eaten the cow's hoof," Hiysi said, "and I suppose I shall have to pay for it. So be it, take my millstone. But do you know what to do with it?"

"No, I don't. Tell me."

"Well," said Hiysi, "this is no simple millstone. It will give you whatever you tell it to give you, only say: 'Grind, my millstone!' And if you want it to stop, just say: 'Enough and have done!' and it will stop. And now go!"

The poor man thanked Hiysi and set off homewards.

For a long time he walked in the forest. It grew dark, rain fell in torrents, the wind whistled, and the branches of trees struck him in the face. It was morning by the time the poor man came home.

"Where were you wandering all day and all night?" his wife asked. "I was beginning to think that I should never see you again."

"I was at the house of Hiysi the Wood-Goblin himself," the poor man replied. "See what he has given me!"

And he took the millstone out of his bag.

"Grind, my millstone!" said he. "Give us nice things to eat for the holiday."

And the millstone began of itself to turn round and round, and on to the table there poured flour and grain and sugar and meat and fish and everything else one could wish for. The poor man's wife brought sacks and bowls, and she filled them full of food, and the poor man tapped the millstone with his finger and said: "Enough and have done!" and the millstone at once stopped grinding and came to a standstill.

The poor man's family had as good a holiday as anyone in the village, and their life from that time changed for the better. There was enough and to spare in the house, the wife and children had fine new clothes and shoes, and they wanted for nothing.

One day the poor man ordered his millstone to grind him a good measure of oats for his horse. The millstone did so, and the horse stood by the house and ate the oats.

Just then the rich brother sent his workman to the lake to water his horses.

The workman drove the horses to the lake, but as they were passing the poor brother's house, they stopped and began eating oats together with the poor man's horse.

The rich brother saw them from his house and he came out on to the porch.

"Hey, there!" cried he to the workman. "Lead the horses away at once! They are picking up sweepings."

The workman brought back the horses.

"You were wrong, master," said he. "Those were not sweepings, but the choicest oats. Your brother has oats and everything else in plenty."

The rich brother's curiosity was aroused.

"I think I shall go and see how such a miracle could have come to pass that my brother has suddenly become rich," said he.

And he went to see his brother.

"How have you become rich all of a sudden?" he asked. "Where do all these good things come from?"

The poor brother did not keep anything back.

"Hiysi helped me," said he.

"What do you mean?" the rich brother asked.

"Just what I say. You gave me a cow's hoof on the eve of the holiday and told me to go to Hiysi with it. And that was just what I did. I gave Hiysi the hoof, and, in return, he made me a present of a magic millstone. It is this millstone that gives me everything I ask for."

"Show it to me!"

"As you wish."

And the poor brother ordered his millstone to give them delicacies of all sorts to eat. The millstone at once began turning, and it loaded the table with pies and roasted meats and other good things.

The rich brother's eyes popped out of his head.

"Sell me the millstone," he begged.

"Oh, no," replied the poor brother, "I need it myself."

But the rich brother was not so easily put off.

"Name your own price, only sell it to me!" he urged.

"It's not for sale."

Realising he would gain nothing by badgering, the rich brother tried a different approach.

"Was there ever anyone as ungrateful as you!" he cried. "Wasn't it I that gave you the cow's hoof?"

"It was."

"There you are, then! And you grudge me your millstone. Well, if you won't sell it, then lend it me for a while."

The poor brother thought this over.

"Have it your own way," said he. "You can have it for a spell."

The rich brother was delighted. He seized the millstone and ran home with it, without so much as asking how, when required, to make it stop turning.

The following morning, he put out to sea in a boat, taking the millstone with him.

"They are salting fish just now," thought he to himself, "and salt is dear. I'm going to trade in salt."

He was well out at sea by now, and he said to the millstone:

"Grind, my millstone! I need salt, and the more the better."

The millstone started spinning and turning, and the purest, whitest salt poured from it.

The rich man looked on in glee, calculating his profits. It was high time to tell the millstone to stop, but all he did was to repeat from time to time:

"Grind, my millstone, grind, don't stop!"

So heavy was the salt that the boat settled deeper and deeper in the water. But the rich brother seemed to have taken leave of his senses, for he did nothing but repeat the words:

"Grind, my millstone, grind!"

By now the water was gushing over the sides, and the boat was near to sinking. This brought the rich brother to his senses.

"Stop grinding, millstone!" he shouted.

But the millstone went on grinding as before.

"Stop grinding, millstone! Stop grinding!" the rich man shouted again, but the millstone went on grinding interminably.

The rich brother tried to snatch up the millstone and throw it overboard, but it seemed to have grown fast to the deck, for he could not lift it.

"Help!" cried the rich brother. "Save me!"

But there was no one there to save him and no one there to help him.

The boat sank, taking the rich brother with it into the watery deep, and the sea closed over him.

And what of the millstone? They say that even at the bottom of the sea it never stopped grinding, and kept making more and more salt. And that, believe it or not, is why sea water is salty.

HOW THREE BROTHERS FOUND THEIR FATHER'S TREASURE

A Moldavian Fairy-Tale

Once upon a time there lived a man who had three sons. He was a hard-working man. He never idled, but laboured from early morn to late at night. He seemed never to be tired and always did everything well and on time.

As for his sons, tall, handsome and strong lads all three, they did not like work.

The father worked in the field, in the garden and in the house, but his sons sat idly chatting in the shade under the trees, or went to fish in the Dniester.

"Why do you never work and help your father?" their neighbours asked.

"Why should we work?" the sons replied. "Father takes good care of us, and does all the work very well by himself."

And so it went on from year to year.

The sons grew to manhood, and the father aged, became weak·and could no longer work as before. The garden round the house was allowed to run wild and the field was overgrown with weeds. The sons saw this, but disliked work so much that they would do nothing about it.

"Why do you sit there, my sons, idling the hours away?" their father would ask them. "I worked when I was young, and now your time has come."

"Oh, it'll never be too late to work," the sons replied.

The old man, deeply troubled that his sons were such loafers, fell ill with grief and took to his bed.

By now the family was in the direst straits. Nettles and thistles stood so high in the garden that the house was barely visible.

One day the old man called his sons to his bedside.

"My sons," said he to them, "my end has come. How are you going to live without me? You don't like work, and don't know how to work."

The sons' hearts were filled with anguish, and they burst into tears.

"Speak to us, Father, give us your dying counsel," begged the eldest son.

"Very well!" the father replied. "I'll tell you a secret. You know that your mother and I toiled hard, and unsparingly. Over many long years, bit by bit, we saved for you a treasure —a pot of gold. I buried the pot near the house, only I don't remember just where. Find my treasure, and you will live without poverty, and never know need."

With that he bade his sons good-bye and breathed his last.

The sons buried their old father and mourned his death. Then one day the eldest brother said:

"Well, brothers, we are poor indeed, we haven't even

money to buy bread. You remember what father said before he died. Let us look for the pot of gold."

They took their spades and began digging little holes near the house. They dug and they dug, but they could not find the pot of gold.

Said the middle brother:

"If we dig in this way, my brothers, we shall never find father's treasure. Let us dig up all the ground round the house!"

The brothers agreed. Again they took their spades, they dug up all the ground round the house, but they still found no pot of gold.

"Let us dig once more, but deeper," said the youngest brother. "Perhaps father buried the pot of gold deep down."

Once again the brothers agreed: they were very eager to find their father's treasure.

They set to work, and the eldest brother, who had been digging a long time, suddenly felt his spade strike something big and hard. His heart beat in excitement, and he called to his brothers:

"Come quickly! I have found father's treasure!"

The middle brother and the youngest brother came running up, and they turned to and helped their elder brother.

They worked very, very hard, but what they dug up from the ground was not a pot of gold, but a large stone.

The brothers were deeply disappointed.

"What shall we do with the stone?" said they. "It's no use leaving it here. Let us carry it away and throw it in a gully."

No sooner said than done. They got rid of the stone and began digging again. They worked all day long, never stopping to eat or rest, and they dug up all the garden. The soil under their spades became soft and friable, but no pot of gold did they find.

"Well," said the eldest brother, "now that we have dug up the soil, it's no use leaving it barren. Let us plant vines here!"

"That's a good idea!" the two younger brothers agreed. "At least our labours will not have been wasted."

So they planted some grapevines and began tending them carefully.

A short time passed by, and they had a fine, large vineyard where ripened sweet, juicy bunches of grapes.

The brothers gathered in a rich harvest. They put aside the grapes they needed for themselves and sold the rest at a profit.

Said the eldest brother:

"It was not in vain, after all, that we dug up our land, for we found the treasure of which father spoke before he died."

BASIL FET-FRUMOS
AND ILANA COSINZANA,
SISTER OF THE SUN

A Moldavian Fairy-Tale

A fact is a fact, and a tale is
a tale,
But where no one passed,
there runs no trail;
What was not planted,
bears no seeds;
What did not happen,
no rumours breeds.

Once upon a time there lived a man and wife, and they had a daughter as beautiful as the morning is bright. She was quick too and skilful with her hands, and as playful and spirited as the spring breeze. Anyone chancing to see her nimble fingers, her sparkling eyes, her flushed and rosy cheeks, could not forget her for the rest of his life, and the sight of her made the lads' hearts beat faster.

One fine day the lovely lass took two pitchers and went to the well to fetch water. Her pitchers filled, she was minded to sit a while by the well. As she sat, she gazed down the well and saw a basil plant growing there. Without another thought she plucked the plant and sniffed at it, and from the smell of it she conceived a child.

When they learned of this, the girl's parents fell to scolding and abusing her. The world seemed no longer a sweet place to live in, and the girl resolved to run away, she knew not where.

Secretly, she made ready and stole quietly out of the house, and soon no sign or trace of her was to be found.

For what with fear and her bitter sense of injury, the girl had gone on and on without stopping until she had reached a dense forest and had there stumbled on a cave. She thought she would rest there and had just stepped inside when towards her, coughing and sighing, there came a very, very old man with a hump on his back, bandy legs, a beard so long that it reached to his knees, whiskers that reached to his shoulders and hair that reached to his heels.

"Who are you and how did you get here?" the old man asked, using his crutch to push up the bushy eyebrows that quite concealed his eyes.

At this, the girl began sobbing and weeping, and finally told him what had happened and how she came to be in his cave.

The old man listened to her tale in silence. He seated the girl on a stone bench and began to comfort her with kind words.

It often happens that just as the rain cools the earth after the burning heat of the sun, so the speeches of old people are a balm to the spirits of the young in times of adversity. The old man's warm sympathy soothed the girl's downcast spirits, and she agreed to stay a while with him in his cave.

So the two shared a home, the girl finding solace for her grief in the old man's company, and the old man—comfort in his old age.

Every morning, three goats would come to the cave, the old man milked them, and the girl and the old man drank the milk and were satisfied.

The time passed swiftly, and the girl gave birth to a little boy so plump and pretty that the sun smiled when it gazed on him. And the old man, poor soul, how happy he was! His feet seemed to dance of themselves, and his heart grew as light as ever it was in his youth.

The moment the child was born, they bathed him in the morning dew so that no evil would cling to him, and they passed over him a flaming torch and a sword of steel that he might pass unharmed through pain and hardship and always be pure and radiant as the sun. Then the mother spoke magic words over him to make him brave and fearless, and the old man rummaged in the darkest corners of the cave and found a club and a broadsword left from the days of his youth. These he presented to the infant that they might do him good service.

Little was eaten or drunk at the christening, but to make up for it there was much joy and laughter. They wished the boy health and happiness and the old man christened him Basil, after the plant his mother had plucked from the well. To this his mother added a second name—Fet-Frumos, or Handsome Youth, for her darling son seemed very handsome to her.

Time flew by, the old man died, and the boy grew up. He would now go out to hunt and he would bring back to his mother everything her heart desired. The older he grew, the happier became his mother's life, for he brought her joy and comfort both by his words and by his deeds.

When Basil Fet-Frumos reached manhood he began to hunt far from home, in distant cedar groves and leafy forests, and he wandered farther and farther away, as far as the eye could see.

One day Basil came to the mouth of a valley, and when he looked into the distance he seemed to see a large green lake in which the sun was bathing. But when he came nearer he saw that the lake was no lake but a palace of pure gold and pearls that shone and sparkled in the midst of the boundless green forest.

Never in his life had he seen beauty such as this, and setting to rights the club and broadsword at his belt, he made straight for the palace. He had not far to go and was soon there. The palace windows and doors stood open, but neither in the palace nor anywhere near it was a living soul to be seen. Basil Fet-Frumos went from chamber to chamber and so through the whole palace. He came out into the courtyard and looked round him again but saw no one. Then, suddenly, he heard a great humming and droning and crackling of twigs, and lo! from the forest came seven fearful-looking dragons, each

> with the head
> of a goat,
> the hoofs
> of an ass,
> the jaws
> of a wolf
> and eyes
> full of venom.

They moved with a kind of hop, skip and jump, and they carried across their shoulders three men, bound hand and foot. They burst into the palace, made up a fire under a great cauldron, and when the water began to boil, threw one of their three captives into the pot. They cooked and ate him up quickly, bones and all, and then did the same with the other two men, eating them up so greedily that their jaws could be heard champing as they ate.

From behind the door where he had hidden himself Basil Fet-Frumos watched them, unable to believe his eyes. The fierce dragons swallowed everything to the last morsel, and then one of them turned, caught sight of Basil and leapt up as if stung.

"Into the yard, into the yard!" cried he. "There's another out there, waiting to be thrown into the cauldron!"

At this, the dragons all jumped up and rushed to the door. But Basil unsheathed his broadsword, and as each of the dragons stepped over the threshold, his sword came down whack! on the dragon's head. Like cut cabbages the heads rolled over the floor, and so one after the other Basil Fet-Frumos killed six of the dragons. But with the seventh he could do nothing, for his broadsword proved powerless against him: he struck him on the neck with the blade of it, he dealt him a blow on the head with the flat of it, he tried piercing him through the heart, but all to no avail. Then, without thinking twice, Basil Fet-Frumos caught up his club, swung it over his head and struck the dragon so hard on the temple that the world went black before his eyes. The dragon spun round and round and began backing away, at every step bumping his head against the walls. Finally, he reached the end room of the palace, opened a trapdoor in the floor and stumbled down a staircase covered with moss and cobwebs. And Basil gave him no quarter and followed after him. They passed through twelve iron doors and at last they reached the bottom. The dragon squeezed himself against the wall, rolling his eyes and baring his teeth, and his heart seemed about to burst with fright.

But Basil left him untouched, shut the door on him, bolted and barred it and went up the stairs again. He barred all twelve doors as he passed through them, locked the last of them and put the key inside his coat. After that, pleased that he had done a good deed, he went home.

He returned to the cave in the highest of spirits and he said to his mother:

"I have found a large and beautiful palace, Mother. From now on we are going to live there."

The mother was overjoyed. She and Basil left the cave, went to the palace of gold and pearls and made their home there.

Said Basil Fet-Frumos:

"All this is ours. But never, on any condition, open the door of the end room, for one last dragon is still there."

"You can depend on me, my son," the mother replied. "The dragon tried to eat you up, so I will know how to keep the door locked."

And taking the key, the mother wrapped it in a kerchief, tied the kerchief with ten knots and put it away so far that no one could find it even if he looked for an eternity.

As though from a horn of plenty all life's boons and blessings now showered on mother and son. The palace they lived in was magnificent, the beauty of the surroundings unsurpassed, and the hunting rich and rewarding.

Thus did they live not for a year and not for two years, but for many years.

But just as spring can suddenly bring with it all the mellow warmth of summer, so may storms descend upon the earth, ready to shatter and destroy everything upon it.

The seven dragons had come from another tsardom. They had been reared by Cloantsa, an old witch with a face as black as pitch and with a heart so mean that a glance from her could reduce the earth to ashes. Now Cloantsa had been waiting for the dragons to visit her and, when after a longer time than usual they failed to come, she was filled with forebodings of evil so great that they scorched her heart. Cloantsa began writhing and twisting like a snake in a fire, and rushed in frenzy to the palace to see what was wrong.

When she learned of the sorry fate that had befallen the dragons, she clutched her head and stood for a while moaning and shaking. Then, beside herself with rage, she threw herself on Basil's mother, forced the key from her and pushed her with all her might into the dungeon where the dragon was kept. The dragon she freed and told him to follow her. And she locked and barred all twelve doors behind them.

Cloantsa and the dragon sat down and held counsel as to how to wreak vengeance on Basil and put him to death.

"You must challenge him to battle," said the witch to the dragon.

"No, I'm afraid of him," the dragon replied. "The strength of his arm far surpasses mine. I think we had better go away while there is still time, and not let him set eyes on us, for it will be the worse for us, otherwise."

"If that is how you feel, then you must put your trust in me," said Cloantsa. "I will goad him until he is in such a state that he will willingly crawl into a snake's hiding-place and seek death there as a deliverance."

And so saying, she concealed the dragon and then began spinning like a top until she had assumed the guise of Basil Fet-Frumos' mother. She pretended to be seriously ill and in great pain and sat down to wait for Basil Fet-Frumos.

One day passed and then another, and Basil Fet-Frumos came back from hunting. No sooner had he crossed the threshold than Cloantsa began moaning and sighing.

"My boy, my boy," said she, between sobs, "I am indeed unhappy, for you went away without so much as thinking that I might need you. And I became seriously ill, and there was no one to help me. Ah, if only I had a drop of bird's milk, just one little drop! . . . My illness would pass then, and I would be back on my feet again."

With heavy heart, Basil Fet-Frumos listened to the tale. He took a pitcher, and telling Cloantsa she could trust him to be back soon, went off in search of bird's milk.

On and on he walked over hills and dales and at last came to a house surrounded by a high fence. He knocked at the gate, and a girl's voice called to him, saying:

"If you are a good man, come in. But if you are a bad man, pass by, or else my dogs will tear you to pieces."

"It is a good man that is knocking at your gate, sweet maiden," Basil Fet-Frumos replied.

The gate opened before him and Basil Fet-Frumos saw a fine house, its doors and windows flung open.

"Good evening," said he, entering.

"Good evening," the girl replied. And what a lovely girl she was! The sun, the moon, the bright rays of dawn grew dim beside her beauty.

Said Basil Fet-Frumos, bowing to her:

"I have walked a long way, and as long a way lies before me. Will you not let me spend the night here?"

"With all my heart," the girl replied, and like the kind and hospitable hostess that she was, seated him on a rug of brocade and put before him every kind of delicacy.

As they sat at table they talked together and Basil Fet-Frumos told the girl of what had brought him so far from his home.

"Do you know where I can find bird's milk?" asked he.

"For as long as I have lived on earth I have heard of no such food and no such remedy," the girl replied. "But you are a good man, and I will do you a kindness and try to find out what you wish to know. A little later I will go to my brother the Bright Sun, and ask him about it, for he knows, if no one else does, what things and where are found on the earth."

So that was how Basil Fet-Frumos came to meet Ilana Cosinzana, sister of the Sun.

A little while later, when her guest, overpowered by fatigue, had fallen asleep, Ilana Cosinzana went to her brother and asked him if he knew where bird's milk was to be found.

"Far away, little sister, far away," the Bright Sun replied. It will take many weeks to get there; the way is to the east all the time, beyond the Copper Mountain. But the bird that gives milk cannot be caught for it is a monster the like of which has never been seen: each of its wings is as large as a cloud, and if anyone approaches, he is carried off to its nest and given to its fledgelings to tear to pieces."

Ilana Cosinzana, sister of the Sun, was filled with compassion and fear at the thought of the terrible fate that awaited Basil Fet-Frumos, who would be going forth to a certain death. And she had promised to help him! The following morning, she led a twelve-winged horse from her stables and presented him to Basil.

"Take this horse, good youth," said she. "He will serve you well and keep you safe. But whether fortune favours you or not, you must stop at my house again on the way back."

Basil Fet-Frumos, who dearly wanted to lay his heart at the feet of this kind and beautiful maiden, thanked her warmly, jumped on his horse and rode away.

> He rode and he rode
> over hill and dale,
> over field and vale,
> over wood, over lea,
> over steppeland free

till he saw something in the distance that looked like a wall of copper. As he came nearer, the wall grew taller and taller till it became a hill and then a huge mountain, and when he reached the foot of the Copper Mountain he saw that its peak held up the sky. Mountains so tall are rare indeed! Basil Fet-Frumos examined it carefully, his eyes swept over it from the foot to the peak, and only then did he spy, high up in the sky, a huge bird with wings as large and as dark as storm-clouds.

141

The bird wheeled round and round, veered off sideways and vanished from sight.

Basil Fet-Frumos pulled tight on the reins and sent his horse up the mountain. Clippety-clop! The horse broke into a gallop, leaping from one jutting rock to another, and carried Basil Fet-Frumos to the highest peak. Basil Fet-Frumos looked around him, and he saw the most wonderful sight! In their nests of copper sat the monster bird's offspring, each, though still unfledged, the size of an ox, and shrieking their heads off with hunger. Basil Fet-Frumos looked around him, and seeing a crevice in the copper cliff, hid in it with his horse. In a little while the mother bird came flying back. It flew from nest to nest, feeding milk to the nestlings. As it flew to the nest near which Basil Fet-Frumos was hiding, he summoned all the courage he had and held out his pitcher, and the bird all unawares let fall some milk into it. Then he jumped on his horse and rode away for dear life! Just then a nestling shrieked again, and the mother bird, looking round, caught sight of Basil. Like a demon from hell it flew after him, but could not overtake him, for it had only one pair of wings, while Basil's horse had six, and so could fly much faster.

On the way back Basil Fet-Frumos again went

> over hill and dale,
> over field and vale,
> over wood, over lea,
> over steppeland free

till he reached the house of Ilana Cosinzana. Ilana received him kindly and invited him to tarry a while and rest.

Basil Fet-Frumos ate and drank and he went to bed; but Ilana, who knew so much more about what was to be than she would ever say, hid the bird's milk and filled Basil Fet-Frumos' pitcher with ordinary cow's milk.

After a while, Basil Fet-Frumos awoke and took up his pitcher.

"You have been kind to me indeed, my sister," said he, "and it is good for me to rest in your house; but I must be on my way, for my sick mother is waiting for me."

And Ilana said in reply:

"Then, brave youth, a happy journey to you, and do not forget to visit me again."

Basil Fet-Frumos bowed to her, bade her good-bye and rode away.

He rode up to his palace, and Cloantsa, sensing his approach, twisted and writhed as though pierced with fiery arrows. On to her bed she threw herself and moaned and sighed as if she were dying.

"Woe is me! Woe is me!" she cried.

But when Basil Fet-Frumos stepped over the threshold, she said to him:

"How glad I am you are back, sweet son. I have waited for you for such a long time! Have you brought me the milk?"

"I have," Basil Fet-Frumos replied, and he held out the pitcher.

Cloantsa put her lips to the pitcher and drank off all the milk.

"Thank you, dearest son, I seem to feel better already," said she.

She lay back and made as if she were asleep, but she could not sleep a wink for wondering where to send Basil Fet-Frumos so that even the memory of him might be erased. She lay there thinking, and then she suddenly began turning and twisting and moaning and pretending to be in greater torment than ever.

"Oh, my dear, dear son!" she cried. "I am again overpowered by sickness. But I dreamt I would recover if I ate of the meat of a young wild boar."

"Then I will go and bring you the meat of a wild boar, for my one wish is that you should be well," said Basil Fet-Frumos.

And jumping on his horse, he rode away. He rode a long time till he came again to the house of Ilana Cosinzana.

"Am I welcome here?" he asked of her.

"You are indeed," Ilana replied. "With a warm heart do I greet you."

Then Basil Fet-Frumos sat down to rest, and he began telling Ilana of the new misfortune that had overtaken him.

"Do you know where I can find a young wild boar?" he asked her. "My mother is again ill. She says only the meat of a young wild boar can save her."

"No, that I do not know, but stay here a while and rest, and in the evening I will discover all from my brother, the Sun," Ilana replied. "He will surely know, for from his seat in the sky he can see all and nothing is hidden from him."

Basil Fet-Frumos spent the night in Ilana's house, and at eventide, having put away his rays, Ilana's brother, too, came in to rest.

Said Ilana to her brother:

"I have heard someone speak of wild boars. Do you know in what part of the world they are found?"

"Far away, my sister, far away to the north," replied the Sun, "beyond wide fields and flowering leas, in a great, shady forest of cedar-trees."

"And how can a young boar be obtained to roast?"

"It cannot be done, sister. So thick are the cedars in the forest that even my rays cannot penetrate it, let alone a man. Even I only see the boars at midday when they come out to the forest edge to wallow in the swamp. Their teeth are sharp, and to venture near is to be torn to shreds."

Ilana Cosinzana told Basil Fet-Frumos what her brother had said, and Basil Fet-Frumos, who now knew where to go as well as the danger that awaited him, mounted his horse and set off on his way. He rode over hills and he rode over dales, he rode over rivers and over ravines, he crossed wide fields and flowering leas, and he came to a great, shady forest of cedar-trees. He rode into the forest, and it was as dark as in the nether world. His twelve-winged horse soared up to the sky, lifting him higher than the tallest of the cedars, and Basil saw the swamp of which Ilana had told him. It was almost midday, and there came from the forest a loud grunting, and the boars began running out to wallow in the mud.

Basil Fet-Frumos spied out a fine young boar, seized him, hoisted him on to his horse's back and rode away for dear life! But the boars had already seen him, and chased after him to catch him, nosing at the ground with their snouts. Basil Fet-Frumos' horse was swift, or it would have been the end of him. As it was, the swiftness of the horse saved him from the sharp tusks of the ferocious beasts. From then onwards the horse pranced and tossed his mane and Basil Fet-Frumos hummed a tune and was as happy as happy can be that this adventure, too, had ended successfully.

On the way back he stopped at Ilana Cosinzana's house as before. While he was eating and drinking and dreaming idly, Ilana Cosinzana replaced the baby boar by an ordinary sucking-pig and, without as much as a sign to Basil Fet-Frumos of what she had done, she saw him off on his way in the friendliest manner possible.

When Cloantsa saw Basil Fet-Frumos returning home she gnashed her teeth so that sparks rained from her mouth. But she had to control her temper and pretend to be mortally ill, so she said to him as he entered her chamber:

"Ah, my son, my dear son, Heaven be praised that you are here and I see you once more! Had you tarried in the slightest, you would not have found me alive. Kill the boar quickly and let me taste of his flesh."

Basil Fet-Frumos slaughtered the pig, roasted him on coals till he was well browned and then gave Cloantsa a taste of the meat.

"I am feeling better now," the witch said, seemingly revived, "and my eyes are no longer dim."

But when she had eaten all the meat, she fell to moaning and sighing more loudly than ever, saying mournfully:

"Oh, my sweet son, my poor boy, you have had enough pain and grief in your journeys to distant parts, but if you truly want me to be cured, you must set out once more. For again I feel worse, and unless you bring me some dead and living water, I shall die."

"Then I shall certainly go, Mother," Basil Fet-Frumos replied, and he set out on his journey.

He rode hard and long and he felt sick at heart and was filled with bitterness, for where could he get what his mother had asked for! Despondent and sad, he reached Ilana Cosinzana's house and complained of his lot in bitter tones.

"My sweet sister," said he to Ilana, "I am driven of necessity to follow untrodden paths. No drugs or potions help my mother, and she has now bade me bring her dead and living water. Do you know where it is to be found and how I am to get it?"

"Bide here a while and rest. Perhaps, this time I can help you too," Ilana replied.

It was almost dusk when she went to her brother, the Sun. who had just returned and was sitting down after his long wanderings.

"O Bright Sun, my brother," said she, "from your seat high in the sky all the earth lies open to your gaze. Do you know in what land dead and living water is found?"

"Far away, my sister, far, far away," replied the Sun, "beyond thrice-nine lands and thrice-nine seas, in the land of the Mistress of the Fields. But of the many who have ever gone to bring back dead and living water, not one has returned alive. For on the border of that land a fierce dragon stands guard. He lets people into the land, but he does not let them out: he drinks the dead and living water and kills the brave men who come to seek it. For a long time now have I been drying their bones."

Basil Fet-Frumos now knew where he was to go and what lay ahead, but he did not fall victim to fear. He set to rights the broadsword and club at his belt, took leave of Ilana Cosinzana, jumped on his horse and rode away. The way was long and he rode without stopping, crossing fields and frontiers, skirting rivers and seas. So, he journeyed beyond thrice-nine seas and thrice-nine lands and reached the most splendid tsardom he had ever seen, where the beauties of nature far surpassed those of any other. Here was no dry twig nor shrivelled blade of grass. All the plants grew rapidly, blossomed luxuriantly and bore rich fruit.

Basil Fet-Frumos roamed the land, and his heart rejoiced at all that he saw. By and by he reached two rocks out of which gushed two springs.

"This must be the dead and living water," thought Basil Fet-Frumos, and, to make sure, he caught a butterfly, tore it to bits and dipped them in the water of one of the springs. The bits at once fitted together and the butterfly became whole again, and when he had dipped it in the water of the second spring, it came to life.

Basil Fet-Frumos was overjoyed. He filled his two leather flasks with water from the springs and set off homewards. But he had hardly reached the border of the tsardom when the trees around him began creaking and crackling like they do during a storm, the sky became overcast, and before him, angrily flourishing his tail, rose a ten-headed dragon.

Basil Fet-Frumos seized his club in one hand and his broadsword in the other, and when the dragon craned one of his necks toward him, struck the head with his club and smote it off with his sword. He did the same with the second head and with the third, and feeling his end was near, the dragon soared up to the sky. But Basil Fet-Frumos' horse flew higher still, and Basil Fet-Frumos chopped off all the dragon's ten heads and knocked him to the ground.

He then rode on unhindered until he came to the house of Ilana Cosinzana. He lay down to rest after the hard battle and long journey, and Ilana Cosinzana replaced the flasks he had brought by two of her own, filled with ordinary water. And, of course, it never for a moment entered Basil Fet-Frumos' head that Ilana Cosinzana, who had helped him so many times, could do anything of the kind. He had a good rest, saddled his horse and rode home.

When Cloantsa saw him she turned black with rage and her heart became filled with venom. She sipped a little water, and recovering her senses a little, fell to pondering over ways and means of disposing of Basil Fet-Frumos.

She allowed him to rest a while after his travels and later called him to her, kissed him tenderly and said:

"My dear son, my own Basil, long have you journeyed and many have been the roads and paths you have followed. You have exhausted all your strength, I'll wager. Come, let me see, can you tear this silken rope?"

And taking out a silken rope, she bound it round him.

"Come, sweet son," said she, "try your hardest, and we shall see if you have exhausted all your strength roaming the wide world and tramping over untrodden paths."

Basil Fet-Frumos braced himself, strained at the rope and broke it in several places.

"And now let me see if you can burst two ropes," the witch said, and she bound him with two ropes.

But Basil burst the two ropes just as he had the first.

"You still have a true hero's strength, but we shall see, perhaps you have spent some of it," said the witch, and she bound him with three silken ropes.

Basil Fet-Frumos tensed his muscles, and strained at the ropes, but burst them he could not. He tried again, and he strained and struggled, but the ropes only bit into his flesh and bound him more tightly. For the third time he tried, putting all his strength into the effort, but the silken ropes cut his flesh to the bone and refused to be broken.

In her joy Cloantsa began hopping on one leg and spinning like a top, crying:

"Come, dragon, where are you hiding? Make haste and do away with Basil Fet-Frumos!"

The dragon snorted joyfully, came out from his hiding-place, snatched up a broadsword and chopped up Fet-Frumos like a head of cabbage. Then, gathering up the pieces and stuffing them into two ragged saddle-bags, he slung the bags over the saddle, lashed the horse and cried out exultantly:

"Hie and away, evil steed! Where you bore him living, there do you bear him dead!"

And the horse raced away, flying like a phantom, the earth humming under his hoofs. He made for the house of Ilana Cosinzana, for there he had been born and bred, tended and cared for, and he came to a halt at the front door.

Ilana Cosinzana came out to the doorstep, but she saw no horseman asking for rest and shelter after his long ride; instead, she saw her very own horse all in lather and spattered with blood. Stricken with grief, she rushed to the horse, pulled down the saddle-bags, and opening them, saw the remains of Basil Fet-Frumos.

"Poor, poor Basil Fet-Frumos!" cried she. "So that is what they have done to you!"

And she began fitting his body together, piece by piece, till he became as he had been before.

This done, she ran to her pantry and brought out the dead and living water, the young boar and the bird's milk. Where pieces of flesh were missing, she fitted in pieces of boar's flesh; and she sprinkled the dead water over him, and the separate pieces grew together. After that she bathed him with the living water, and the youthful hero came back to life. He sighed heavily, did Basil Fet-Frumos, and said:

"Oh, what a long sleep I've had!"

"You would have slept and never wakened had I not been here, dear heart," Ilana Cosinzana told him as she raised the earthen pitcher of bird's milk to his lips.

Basil Fet-Frumos began drinking the milk, and gained new strength at every sip. And when all had been drunk, he was stronger than ever he had been before, for with a blow from his club he could crush to dust a rock of flint.

He rose from the ground, shook off his weakness, and remembering how the dragon had dealt with him, caught up his club and hastened with it to the palace.

Like the rain falling in torrents from the sky was the thirst for vengeance in Basil's breast. He strode on and on, not sparing his feet, until he came to the palace; and there sat the witch and the dragon feasting merrily at table, while his own mother stood by serving them.

When they saw Basil Fet-Frumos entering the dining-hall, the floor seemed to fall away beneath the feet of the two evil ones. But Basil gave them no time for fear. He seized the witch with one hand and the dragon with the other, dragged them out into the courtyard, and cut them into pieces. Then he lit a copper stove and burnt them, so that not a trace of them was left on the ground or in the water, in the meadows free or in the pearly sea, or anywhere else under the blue-grey sky where the eagles fly.

This done, Basil Fet-Frumos embraced his mother tenderly and kissed and comforted her.

Very soon theirs was even a greater joy, for Basil Fet-Frumos asked for the hand of Ilana Cosinzana and she agreed to wed him.

Without count or number, came the wedding guests and a right merry feast they had. And at the top of the table sat the Bright Sun himself, drinking up kegs of wine, wishing joy and cheer to all he held dear and sharing his glee with you and with me!

And after the wedding Basil Fet-Frumos and Ilana Cosinzana began living together in love and peace and, perhaps, are living still if the time has not come for them to die.

THE STORY OF ZARNIYAR WHO HAD
ALL HER WITS ABOUT HER

An Azerbaijan Fairy-Tale

What shall I tell you about? I know. About a merchant named Mamed who lived in the city of Misar, journeyed to strange lands and traded in goods of all kinds.

One day he bethought him to set off to a far-off land. He bought a large number of all kinds of goods, hired servants, and bidding farewell to his family, set off on his way with his caravan.

He went to one place, and then to another, and at last he came to a city he had never heard of before.

Here he decided to rest after his long travels, and he put up with his servants at a caravansary.

As he sat eating and drinking, a stranger came up to him.

"Ho, there, merchant!" said the man. "You must have come

from distant parts if you do not know the customs of this city."

"And what are the customs of this city?" Mamed asked.

"I'll tell you what they are. Every merchant who comes here must present a worthy gift to the Shah. In return, the Shah invites the merchant to his palace and plays a game of *nardi** with him."

What was Mamed to do? He had to go to the Shah whether he wanted to or not. So, choosing the costliest fabrics he had in his possession, he laid them out on a golden tray and set off for the palace.

The Shah received the gifts and began asking the merchant what city he came from, what goods he was trading in and where he had been. Mamed answered him truthfully, and the Shah heard him out and said.

"Come to my palace tonight, and you and I will play *nardi*."

In the evening Mamed came to the palace, and there was the Shah waiting for him, the *nardi* board set up before him.

"Listen to my rules, merchant," said the Shah. "I have a learned cat. It can balance seven lighted lamps on its tail all the night long, from evening to morning. Now if it proves able to balance the lamps all the time we are playing, all your riches and all your wares will be mine, and I will order you to be bound and thrown in a dungeon. But if the cat so much as moves from its place, my whole treasury will be yours and you can do with me whatever you wish."

What was the merchant to do? To run away was not possible, to protest was out of the question. There was no way out

* *Nardi*–draughts.–*Tr.*

154

but to accept the Shah's conditions. So he sat there and cursed himself for having come to that city.

"It's easy enough to lose one's life here, to say nothing of one's possessions!" thought he.

The Shah now called his learned cat, and the cat came and twirled its tail and sat down in front of him.

"Bring the lamps!" the Shah commanded.

At once seven lamps were brought in by the servants and placed on the cat's tail.

The Shah picked up the pieces, and the game began.

The merchant kept glancing at the cat as he moved the figures over the board. And the cat sat there as if turned to stone, not moving, not so much as stirring.

So a day passed, and a night, and then another two days and two nights, and Mamed continued to play *nardi* with the Shah, while the cat sat there as before.

At last Mamed could bear it no longer.

"I cannot play any more!" he cried. "You win, Shah!"

That was all the Shah was waiting for. He called his servants and said to them:

"Bring to me all the merchant's wares and all his gold. And as for the merchant himself, bind him and throw him in a dungeon!"

So the Shah's servants seized Mamed and did all the Shah had ordered them to do.

Mamed, confined in the dungeon, cursed himself for not having had the sense to pass the city by and under his breath berated the Shah and his learned cat.

But now we will leave Mamed where he is and tell you about his wife Zarniyar.

Zarniyar stayed quietly at home waiting for her husband, but he did not come and there was no sight or sign of him.

"Perhaps something has happened to him?" thought she.

For a long time she lived with these anxious thoughts until one day Mamed's servant, his face streaked with dirt and his clothes in tatters, came running to her.

"Mistress, mistress!" cried he. "The Shah of a far-off land has imprisoned the master and has seized all his goods and all his gold. I alone ran away, barely escaping with my life. What are we going to do now?"

Zarniyar asked the servant to tell her everything that had taken place. After that she gave orders for a large number of mice to be caught and a large chest filled full of them. Then, taking a quantity of silver and gold, she dressed herself in man's clothing, hid her long hair under a high fur cap and set off at the head of a caravan to rescue her husband.

She journeyed without halting and without delays of any kind and at last arrived at the city where her husband was languishing in prison.

To some of her servants she gave orders that they should wait at the caravansary for her, to others that they should accompany her to the palace of the Shah.

Then, taking a large tray of chased gold, she laid out on it many valuable gifts and set off for the palace, her servants carrying the chest full of mice behind her.

When they neared the palace, Zarniyar said to her servants:

"While I am playing *nardi* with the Shah, you must let the mice into the chamber, one by one."

The servants remained at the door with the chest, and Zarniyar entered the Shah's chamber.

Said she to the Shah:

"Long years to you, O ruler of rulers! As is the custom of your country, I have brought you a valuable gift."

Taking her for a man, the Shah received Zarniyar with great honours, put the choicest delicacies before her and invited her to join him in a game of *nardi*.

"What will your conditions be, O ruler of rulers?" asked Zarniyar.

Said the Shah:

"We shall play until my learned cat moves from its place."

"And what if your learned cat does move from its place?" Zarniyar asked.

"Then I shall admit that I have lost the game, and you shall do with me what you wish."

"Very well," said Zarniyar. "Let it be as you say."

The Shah called his learned cat, and the cat padded in and sat down very solemnly on the rug in front of him. Then the Shah's servants appeared, bringing seven lamps which they placed on the cat's tail.

The Shah then began playing *nardi* with Zarniyar. He kept smiling as he played, waiting for this young merchant to admit himself the loser.

Zarniyar's servants now opened the chest and let a mouse into the Shah's chamber.

When the cat saw the mouse its eyes began to glitter and it made as if to move from its place. But the Shah looked at it so sternly that it quietened at once and seemed frozen to the spot.

In a little while Zarniyar's servants let several more mice into the chamber. The mice began running up and down the floor and scuttling about near the walls. Now this was too much for the learned cat. It gave one miaow, and jumping up suddenly (whereupon all the seven lamps dropped to the floor), began chasing the mice all over the room.

Shout as the Shah might, his learned cat would not listen to him.

Then only did Zarniyar call her servants, who rushed into the room, tightly bound the Shah hand and foot and began belabouring him with leather thongs, until he called for mercy.

"I will let out all my captives," cried he, "and will give them back all I took away, only spare me!"

Zarniyar's servants continued whipping the Shah, and the Shah screamed at the top of his voice; but although his people heard him they would not come to his aid, for all had long grown weary of his cruelty and greed.

Zarniyar then ordered the release of her husband and all who were with him, and had the Shah thrown into the dungeon.

After that Zarniyar and Mamed returned to their native city of Misar and continued to live there in peace and happiness, eating and drinking of the best in the land. And so must you do, too.

Three apples have fallen from the sky. One is for me, the second for the teller of this tale and the third for him who listened to it.

SHEIDULLAH THE LOAFER

An Azerbaijan Fairy-Tale

Long before our time, in days gone by, there lived a man named Sheidullah who was a loafer and a ne'er-do-well.

His wife and children went hungry most of the time, and they dared not even dream of buying new clothes.

His wife would begin scolding Sheidullah for not wanting to work, and Sheidullah would say:

"Never you mind and don't you grieve! We are poor now, but we shall soon be rich."

"What do you mean!" the wife would exclaim. "How can that be when you lie there day after day without so much as moving a finger!"

But Sheidullah would repeat again:

"Just you wait! The time will come when we shall be rich."

The wife waited and the children waited, but nothing happened, and they remained as poor as ever.

"It's no use waiting," the wife said. "If this goes on we shall starve to death."

So Sheidullah decided to go to a wise man and ask his advice about how he could stop being poor. He prepared himself for the journey and then set off.

Sheidullah walked for three days and three nights, and he met a scraggy, skinny wolf on the road.

"Where are you going, my good fellow?" the wolf asked him.

"To a wise man to ask his advice about how to become rich," Sheidullah replied.

The wolf heard him out and he said to Sheidullah:

"While you are about it, be so kind as to ask him what I am to do. For the third year now I have been suffering from a terrible pain in the stomach. Day and night it gives me no peace. Perhaps the wise man can tell you how I am to find relief."

"Very well," Sheidullah replied, "I'll ask him."

And he went on his way.

He walked for another three days and another three nights, until he saw an apple-tree growing by the roadside.

"Where are you going, my good fellow?" the apple-tree asked him.

"To a wise man to ask his advice about how to live well without having to work."

"Be so kind as to ask the wise man to tell me what to do, too," said the apple-tree. "I bloom every spring, but as soon as my flowers are in blossom, they shrivel and fall off, and I never bear any fruit. Ask the wise man why this is so."

"Very well, I'll ask him," Sheidullah replied, and he went on again.

He continued on his way for another three days and another three nights, until he came to a deep lake.

All of a sudden a large fish thrust its head up out of the water.

"Where are you going, my good fellow?" asked the fish.

"To a wise man, to ask for his advice and help."

"Be so kind as to ask him something on my behalf too. For the seventh year I have been suffering from a sharp pain in the throat. Let the wise man tell you what can cure me."

"Very well, I'll ask him," said Sheidullah, and he went on again.

He walked for three days and three nights, and at last he reached a grove of rose bushes. He looked, and he saw an old man with a long grey beard sitting under one of the bushes.

Said the old man when he saw Sheidullah:

"What do you want, Sheidullah?"

Sheidullah started back in surprise.

"How did you know my name?" asked he. "But perhaps you are the wise man I am on my way to see?"

"Yes, I am," the old man replied. "Tell me quickly what it is you want of me?"

Sheidullah told him why he had come and what he wanted.

"Have you nothing else you want to ask of me?" said the wise man.

"That I have," Sheidullah replied, and he told the wise man what the wolf, the apple-tree and the fish had asked him.

Said the wise man:

"A large gem has stuck in the throat of the fish. The fish will be cured as soon as the gem is removed. Under the apple-tree a large jug of silver is buried. The blossoms of the apple-tree will cease to shrivel and the tree will bear fruit as soon as the jug is taken away. As for the wolf, if he is to be relieved of his pain, he must swallow the first loafer that comes along."

"And what about my request?" Sheidullah asked.

"What you wish for has already been granted. Go!"

Sheidullah was overjoyed, and went home without another question to the wise man.

He walked and he walked till he came to the lake where the big fish was impatiently waiting for him.

"Well, what does the wise man advise me to do?" it asked.

"There is a gem stuck in your throat. When it is taken out you will be cured," said Sheidullah, and he turned to go.

"Have mercy on me, good fellow," the fish cried, "take the gem out of my throat. You will cure me and at the same time get the gem for yourself."

"Oh, no, why should I bother!" said Sheidullah. "I am going to become rich without moving a finger."

With these words he proceeded on his way.

He came to the apple-tree, and at the sight of him all its boughs began fluttering, all its leaves rustling.

"Well," asked the apple-tree, "have you learned from the wise man what my remedy is?"

"Yes, I have," Sheidullah replied. "A large jug of silver lies buried under your roots, and it must be dug out. Then your blossoms will no longer shrivel and you will bear apples."

And with these words Sheidullah turned to go.

Said the apple-tree in pleading tones:

"Please, Sheidullah, dig up the jug of silver from under my roots. You will be helping yourself too, for you will get the silver."

162

"Oh, no, I can't be bothered. The wise man told me I would have everything, anyway," Sheidullah replied, and went on.

He walked and he walked till he met the scraggy wolf, who, seeing Sheidullah, began trembling with impatience.

"Well," asked he, "what advice does the wise man have for me? Don't keep me in suspense, tell me quickly!..."

"You must eat up the first loafer that comes along. That will make you well at once," said Sheidullah.

The wolf thanked Sheidullah and began asking him about all he had seen and heard on the way. Sheidullah told the wolf of his meetings with the fish and the apple-tree and of what they had asked of him.

"But I did not bother with them," he said, "for I will be rich anyway."

The wolf listened and was overjoyed.

"I need not search for a loafer," thought he to himself, "for he has come to me himself. There is no one in the world more stupid and lazy than Sheidullah."

And pouncing upon Sheidullah, he swallowed him whole, on the spot!

And that was the end of Sheidullah the Loafer.

Three apples have fallen from the sky. One is for the teller of the tale, another for the listener and the third for all the rest.

ANAIT

An Armenian Fairy-Tale

I

Once on a morning in spring, young Vachagan, the only
son of Tsar Vache, stood on his balcony. Birds of all kinds
were singing in the garden, but none so beautifully as the
nightingale. As soon as he began his song, all the other birds
fell silent, and listening to him, tried to learn the secret of his
singing: one would imitate his twitter, another his warble, a
third his whistle, and then all three together would repeat the
melodies they had learned. But Vachagan did not listen to
them, for his heart was troubled.

The Tsaritsa Ashkhen, his mother, came up to him and said:

"Dear son, I can see that you are weighed down by sorrow. Do not try to hide it from us, but tell us the reason for
your sadness."

"The joys of life are nothing to me, Mother," Vachagan replied. "Rather would I go off by myself to some lonely place. The village of Atsik, for instance."

"Is that true? You do not, by any chance, wish to go to Atsik because your clever Anait lives there?"

"How did you know her name, Mother?"

"The nightingales living in our garden told me about her. Dear, dear Vachagan, do not forget that you are the son of the Afghan tsar, and the son of a tsar must take as his bride a tsarevna or a princess, and not a simple peasant girl. The tsar of Georgia has three daughters, you can choose from them. The prince of Gugar has a lovely daughter, and she will inherit all her father's rich lands. No less beautiful, too, is the daughter of the prince of Sunik. Then there is Varsenik, the daughter of the commander of our host, reared by the tsar and myself—is she not worthy of your love?"

"I want Anait alone, Mother!"

And with these words Vachagan ran off into the garden.

II

Vachagan had just passed his twentieth birthday. He was a pale youth, and not too strong.

"Vachagan, my son," his father would say to him, "all my hopes are in you. You must marry, for such is the law of life."

But Vachagan would not listen to the tsar. Early in the morning he would go hunting in the mountains and late at night he would return. Many princes tried to court his friendship, but he avoided them and took no one with him on his hunting trips but Vaghinak, his brave and trusty servant, and

Zangi, his faithful sheep-dog. No one meeting them out hunting could have told which was the prince and which the servant, for they were clad alike in simple hunting garb, with a bow and arrow slung over one shoulder and a broad dagger at the belt.

These wanderings over the countryside were good for Vachagan and he grew stronger, healthier and more manly.

One day Vachagan and Vaghinak wandered into the village of Atsik and sat down by a spring to rest. Just then some village girls came to the spring for water. Vachagan was thirsty and he asked the girls for a drink. One of them filled her jug and proffered it to him, but another snatched the jug from her hands and poured out the water. Then she refilled the jug, but only to pour the water out again. Vachagan's throat was parched, so thirsty was he, but the girl seemed to be teasing him, for she filled and emptied the jug alternately. Only when she had filled it for the sixth time did she hold it out to Vachagan.

Vachagan greedily drank the water.

"Why did you not give me the water the first time?" he asked of the girl. "Were you trying to tease or to anger me?"

"It is not our way to tease a stranger," the girl replied. "But you were tired and hot, and the cold water might have harmed you. That was why I waited before giving it to you."

The girl's reply surprised Vachagan and her beauty enchanted him.

"What is your name?" he asked her.

"Anait," the girl replied.

"And who is your father?"

"My father is the village shepherd, and his name is Aran. But why do you ask?"

"Is it a sin to ask?"

"If it is no sin, then you, too, must tell me who you are and where you come from."

"Shall I lie to you or tell you the truth?"

"Do what you think befits you more."

"The truth, of course, and the truth is that I cannot yet tell you who I am. But I give you my word that I shall tell you soon."

"Very well. And now give me back my jug."

And saying good-bye to the prince, Anait took the jug and went away.

The hunters returned home, and Vaghinak, trusty servant that he was, told the tsaritsa all that had taken place. Thus it was that Vachagan's mother learned his secret.

III

Vachagan would not hear of marrying anyone but Anait. Finally, the tsar and tsaritsa agreed to his choice, and they sent Vaghinak and two of their nobles to Atsik to act as matchmakers.

Aran the shepherd welcomed them warmly and spread out a carpet for them to sit on.

"What a beautiful carpet!" Vaghinak said. "The mistress of this house must have woven it, I suppose?"

"I have no wife," Aran said. "She died ten years ago. My daughter Anait wove the carpet with her own hands."

"Even the tsar's palace boasts no carpet so beautiful. We

are pleased that your daughter is such a skilled weaver," the nobles said. "Her fame has reached the ears of the tsar. We come as matchmakers on his behalf. He wishes you to give your daughter in marriage to his only son, the heir to the throne."

The nobles expected Aran either to shake his head incredulously or leap from his seat for joy. But the shepherd did neither. He hung his head and his forefinger began to trace patterns on the carpet.

Said Vaghinak:

"What makes you so sad, Aran, my brother? We have brought you glad, not grievous tidings. We have no wish to take your daughter by force. Her marriage depends on your wish."

"My dear guests," Aran replied, "I will not force my daughter. If she agrees to marry the prince, then I will say nothing against it."

Just then Anait came in with a basket of ripe fruit. She bowed to the visitors, laid the fruit on a tray and served it to them, and then sat down at her rug-frame to weave. The nobles watched her, marvelling at the nimbleness of her fingers.

"Why do you work alone, Anait?" Vaghinak asked her. "I have heard that you have many pupils."

"So I have," Anait replied, "but I have let them all go to gather in the grape harvest."

"I have also heard that you teach your pupils to read and write."

"That I do," Anait replied again. "Now even our shepherds, while out with the herds, read and teach one another to read. All the tree-trunks in our forests are covered with writing. Fortress walls, rocks and cliffs bear inscriptions in charcoal. One man will write a word, then another, and so it goes on.

All our mountains and ravines are covered with writing."

"With us, learning is held in less esteem," said Vaghinak. "Townsfolk are lazy. But if you come to live with us, you will teach everyone to be diligent. Stop weaving for a moment, Anait, I have something to show you. See what fine gifts the tsar sends you!"

And Vaghinak took out many precious gems and silken gowns.

Anait cast a cursory glance at them.

"Why is the tsar so gracious to me?" she asked.

"Vachagan, the son of the tsar, met you by a spring and you gave him water to drink; he took a liking to you. We are now come by the tsar's orders to ask you to marry Vachagan. This ring, this necklace, these bracelets and everything else are for you."

"Then the hunter I saw was the tsar's son?"

"Yes."

"He is a fine young man. But does he know any trade?"

"He is the son of the tsar, Anait, and all of the tsar's subjects are his servants. What need has he of a trade?"

"That may be so, but fate plays tricks, and who is master today may be servant tomorrow. Everyone must have a trade, be he a tsar, a prince, or an ordinary man."

The nobles were surprised at Anait's words, but the shepherd Aran was pleased with his daughter.

"Then you refuse to marry the prince simply because he knows no trade?" the nobles asked.

"Yes. Take back all you have brought me. And tell the prince that I like him, but that I beg him to forgive me, for I have vowed not to marry a man who has no trade."

The tsar's envoys saw that Anait was firm in her decision and pressed her no more. Back at the palace they told the tsar all about it.

Learning of Anait's decision, the tsar and tsaritsa were overjoyed. Now Vachagan would surely think better of marrying her. But Vachagan said:

"Anait is right. I, too, must learn a trade, like all other people."

The tsar called a council of his nobles, and all unanimously agreed that the best and most suitable handicraft for a prince was the weaving of brocade.

A skilled craftsman was at once brought from Persia, and within one year Vachagan had learned the trade. Using fine gold thread, he wove a length of precious brocade and sent Vaghinak with it to Anait.

Said Anait when she received it:

"As the saying goes, the trials of fate he will meet unafraid, for poverty flees from a man with a trade. Tell the prince I agree to marry him, and give him this rug as a gift from me."

Preparations for the wedding were at once begun, and the celebrations lasted for seven days and seven nights.

IV

But soon after the wedding, Vaghinak, Vachagan's faithful friend and servant, disappeared. For a long time they searched for him until at last they lost all hope of finding him. Meanwhile, having lived to a ripe old age, the tsar and tsaritsa died, and Vachagan became tsar.

One day Anait said to her husband:

"I notice, my tsar, that you know your tsardom but poorly. People do not tell you the whole truth, they would have you believe that all is going well. But, perhaps, that is not altogether so? It would be a good thing if from time to time you undertook to wander through the land, now in the guise of a beggar, now in that of a tradesman or merchant."

"You are right, Anait," Vachagan replied. "I knew the people better when I used to hunt in the countryside. But how can I leave now? Who will rule in my absence?"

"I will," Anait said, adding: "And no one need know that you are away."

"Very well. Then I shall set out on my travels tomorrow. But if I do not come back in twenty days, know that either I am no longer alive or that I have come to some harm."

V

And so, dressed in the garb of a simple peasant, Tsar Vachagan began to roam through his tsardom. There was much that he saw and much that he heard, and after a time he came to the town of Perozh.

Now in the centre of the town was a large square and market-place with the shops of craftsmen and merchants all round it.

One day Vachagan was sitting in the square when he saw a crowd of people following a very old man. The old man moved very slowly. The way was cleared before him and bricks were placed under his feet for him to step on.

Vachagan asked of a passer-by who the old man was.

"Is it possible that you do not know!" the man exclaimed. "Why, he is the head priest and so pious that he will not even step on the ground for fear of crushing some insect."

Then a rug was spread on the square, and the head priest kneeled on it to rest himself. Vachagan pushed through the crowd to get nearer to the old man and hear what he had to say. The head priest had sharp eyes. Seeing Vachagan, he realised at once that he was a stranger.

"Who are you and what do you do for a living?" he asked.

"I am a workman from distant parts," Vachagan replied. "I have come to the town to seek work."

"Good. Come with me, I will give you work and will pay you well."

Vachagan nodded his agreement, and the head priest whispered something to his helpers, priests like himself, who at once went off in different directions.

After a time they returned with bearers laden with supplies of all kinds. Then the head priest rose and left the square, and Vachagan silently followed him.

In this way they came to the city gates.

Here the head priest blessed the people, who soon dispersed, leaving only the priests, the bearers and Vachagan.

With the town left behind them, they came to a high wall, in which was a gate. The head priest produced a huge key and opened the gate.

A large square lay within, and in the centre rose a temple with cells all round it. The bearers set down the bundles they were carrying, and the head priest led them and Vachagan to the other side of the temple, and opening an iron door, said:

"Go in, you will be given work there."

Stunned, they went in silently and found themselves in a dark underground dungeon. The head priest locked the door behind them, and knowing that the way back was cut off, they moved on.

VI

They walked a long time until suddenly a feeble light gleamed in the distance. They went towards it and soon arrived at a stone cave from which came groans and cries. Straining their ears to hear more, they looked round them in astonishment. At that moment a shadowy figure appeared in the darkness of the passage. As it came nearer it gradually took on shape and form. Vachagan moved toward it.

"Who are you—man or devil?" he called loudly. "If you are a man, tell us where we are."

The phantom moved closer and stopped, trembling, before them. It was a man, but a man in the saddest condition imaginable! He had the face of a corpse, sunken eyes and sharply protruding cheek-bones, and all the bones of his body were visible. Sobbing and stuttering, he said:

"Come with me. I will show you everything."

They followed him down a narrow corridor and came to a second cave. Many men, naked, writhed there in their death agony. In a third cave there stood huge cauldrons in which food seemed to be cooking. Vachagan bent over one of them and at once stepped back in horror, saying not a word to his comrades. They next found themselves in another corridor. Here, in the dim half-light there toiled several hundred men, all of them pale as death. Some were embroidering, some knitting, others sewing.

Said the man who resembled a corpse:

"The fiendish priest through whose wiles you find yourself in this dungeon, lured us here in the same way. I do not know how many years I have spent here, for there is no day and no night here, but only this endless, this eternal dusk. I know only that all who came here with me are dead. The priests lure men here who have a trade, as well as those who have none. The former they work to death, and the rest they take away to be slaughtered and then boiled in those horrible cauldrons you have seen. That devilish old head priest is not alone; he is aided by all the priests."

Vachagan, looking closely at the speaker, now saw him to be none other than his own faithful Vaghinak. But he said nothing lest the joy of their reunion snap the thin thread that bound Vaghinak to life.

VII

When Vaghinak had gone, Vachagan asked the men who were with him who they were and what work they could do. One said he was a tailor, another a weaver. The rest had no trade, but Vachagan decided to say they were his helpers.

Soon they heard steps, and a priest appeared before them accompanied by an armed crowd. Malice and cruelty were stamped on the priest's face.

"Are you the newcomers?" the priest asked.

"Yes, we are, and your servants, O merciful priest," Vachagan replied.

"Which of you knows a trade?"

"All of us!" Vachagan replied. "We know how to weave valuable brocade which is a hundred times more costly than gold."

174

"Can that be true?"

"That you can learn for yourself."

"Very well, I shall do that. Now tell me what tools and materials you need and then set to work in the common workshop."

"We shall not be able to do our work there; it is better for us to work here. And as for food, know that we do not eat meat and may die if we are forced to."

"Very well," said the priest. "You shall have bread and fruit, but should your work prove to be less valuable than you would have me believe, I will send you to the slaughter-house and have you tortured before you die."

The priest sent them some fruit and bread which they shared with Vaghinak and a number of others, and Vachagan set to work. He quickly weavéd a length of the most magnificent brocade and covered it with patterns which depicted all the horrors of the fearful dungeon he found himself in and which could only be read by the few initiated.

The priest was delighted with Vachagan's workmanship.
Said Vachagan:

"I told you that the brocade we worked was a hundred times more valuable than gold. Know that it is really worth twice as much as that, for certain talismans have been woven into the pattern. It is a pity that ordinary people cannot know their value. Only the all-wise Tsaritsa Anait will understand their meaning."

The greedy priest was amazed and decided to sell the brocade, but so that none should share in his profits. So, without saying a word of it to the head priest or even showing him the brocade, he set out with it for Vachagan's palace.

VIII

Anait ruled the country well, and all were satisfied. No one so much as suspected that the tsar was away. But the tsaritsa herself was filled with anxiety. Ten days had passed since the appointed time, but Vachagan had not returned. At night Anait had fearful dreams. By day she was visited by strange apparitions. Vachagan's dog Zangi continuously yelped or whined; his horse would not eat and whinnied pitifully like a foal that has lost its mother. The chickens crowed like cocks, and the cocks screeched like pheasants. The river waters rolled with a dull, hushed sound, without gurgling or splashing. The usually fearless Anait was terrified. Even her own shadow frightened her.

One morning she was told of the arrival of a merchant bringing rich wares.

Anait ordered the stranger to be brought in.

The man who entered had a terrible face. He bowed to the tsaritsa and held out a silver tray on which lay a length of gold brocade. Anait looked at it without noticing the pattern.

"What is the price of this brocade?" she asked.

"It is three hundred times dearer than gold, Your Majesty, if the workmanship and material alone are considered. And as for my industry and zeal in bringing it here, I leave it to Your Majesty to judge of their value."

"But why is it so very costly?"

"Most gracious Tsaritsa, it is endowed with a power which is beyond price. Just notice the pattern. Those are no simple figures, but talismans. He who wears a garment of this brocade will never know grief or sorrow."

"Can it be so?" Anait asked, and she unfolded the brocade. On it she saw inscribed no talismans, but letters worked into an intricate pattern. Anait read the message silently:

"My own incomparable Anait, I am held prisoner in a veritable inferno. The deliverer of this length of brocade is one of its fiendish keepers. Vaghinak is with me. Search for us east of Perozh in the dungeons of a temple enclosed by high walls. Without your help we shall perish. Vachagan."

Shaken to the depths of her being, Anait ran over the message a second and a third time, feigning to admire the pattern.

"You are right," she said, "these figures possess the power to cheer. Only this morning I was sad, and now I feel light at heart and gay. Your brocade is truly without price. I should not be sorry to give up half my tsardom for it. However, you must know yourself that no work of art can be greater than its creator."

"May God grant you a long life, Tsaritsa, you speak truly!"

"Then you must bring me the man who weaved this brocade. I wish to reward him as well as yourself."

"Most gracious Tsaritsa," replied the greedy priest, "I do not know who he is. I purchased the brocade from a Jew in India, who, in turn, bought it from an Arab, and as for the Arab, who can tell where he got it!"

"But you just told me yourself how much the work and material cost you, which means that you did not buy the brocade, but had it made."

"Most gracious Tsaritsa, that is what I was told in India. I. . . ."

"Be silent!" Anait cried, wrathfully. "I know who you are. Servants! Seize this man and throw him into a dungeon!"

IX

When her command had been carried out, Anait ordered her trumpeters to sound an alarm. The townsfolk gathered outside the palace, whispering anxiously among themselves. No one knew what had happened.

Armed from head to foot, Anait stepped out to the balcony.

"Hear me, townsfolk!" said she. "The life of your tsar is in danger. Let all who loved him and hold his life dear, follow me! By midday we must reach the town of Perozh."

In an hour's time all were armed. Anait mounted a goodly steed, and shouting "Forward! After me!" galloped off to Perozh. She did not stop on the way and only reined in her steaming horse on the central square in Perozh. The people of Perozh took her for a goddess descended from the skies and prostrated themselves before her.

"Where is the governor of this town?" Anait asked imperiously.

"I am the governor, and your servant, Your Majesty," said the governor, coming forward.

"You are too careless, you do not know what is occurring in the temple of your gods!"

"Indeed I do not, Your Majesty." And the man bowed.

"Do you know, at least, where the temple is?"

"You jest, Your Majesty. Of course I do."

"Then take me there."

The governor of the town led Anait to the temple, and the crowd of townsfolk followed them.

The priests, thinking that pilgrims had arrived, unlocked the first of the iron doors. Anait at once rode out on to the temple square and ordered the doors of the temple to be opened. Only then did the priests realise what had happened. The head priest rushed at the mounted Tsaritsa, but Anait's clever steed trampled him to death with its hoofs.

Meanwhile Anait's warriors had arrived, and the remaining priests were quickly dispatched. The people looked on in fear and bewilderment.

"Come near!" Anait cried. "See what is concealed in the sanctuary of your gods!"

The doors of the temple were quickly broken open. A fearful sight met the people's eyes.

Men looking like ghosts began crawling out from the dungeons. Some were close to death and too weak to stand. Others, blinded by the light of day, staggered and moved like crippled ants. The last to come out were Vachagan and Vaghinak. They walked with closed eyes, lest the bright light blind them.

The warriors burst into the dungeons and carried out the dead bodies and the instruments of torture. The townsfolk, shamefaced, helped them.

Then Anait joined Vachagan and Vaghinak in the tent where they were waiting. It had been hastily put up for them. Husband and wife sat down side by side and gazed long at each other. Vaghinak, weeping, pressed his lips to Anait's hand.

"Incomparable Tsaritsa," cried he, "today you have saved our lives!"

"Not so, Vaghinak," Vachagan told him. "Anait saved us long ago, the day she asked you if the son of your tsar had a trade. You remember how you laughed in answer?"

X

Throughout the towns and villages the tidings spread of Tsar Vachagan's fearful adventure. News of it was even carried to other lands, and all gave praise to Vachagan and Anait. The *ashugs*, or minstrels, made up songs about them. The songs, alas, have not come down to us, but the tale about Vachagan and Anait has happily survived.

THE TSAR AND THE WEAVER

An Armenian Fairy-Tale

Once upon a time there lived a tsar.

One day he was sitting on his throne, when the envoy of another tsar came to him from a distant land. Without saying a word, he chalked a circle round the tsar's throne and silently moved aside.

The tsar was puzzled.

"What does it mean?" he asked.

But the envoy said not a word.

This made the tsar anxious. He called his viziers and councillors and ordered them to explain what the line round his throne could mean.

The viziers and councillors examined the line carefully, but found nothing to say.

The tsar was very angry.

"Shame on you!" he cried. "Shame on you! Is there no one in the whole of my land who can guess the meaning of the line round my throne?..."

And the tsar gave strict orders for all the wise men of his tsardom to be called together that they might tell him the meaning of the chalk line. The tsar's orders further stated that if the wise men could not explain it, their heads would be cut off.

The viziers rushed to seek out the wise men. They scoured the city and all the villages, they knocked at every door. At last they came to a small house, which they entered and found quiet and empty, except for a cradle hanging there and rocking all by itself.

"What can it mean?" the viziers asked, wondering. "Why is the cradle rocking? There is no one here."

They stood there marvelling and then passed into the second room. Here also was a cradle and it, too, was rocking, although no one was about.

The viziers were very much surprised, and they climbed out on to the roof of the house. Wheat had been laid out on it to dry, and birds were wheeling over it. They wanted to peck at the wheat, but dared not, for a fan of reeds, fixed to the roof, swayed from side to side and scared them off.

The tsar's envoys were more surprised than ever.

"Why is the fan swaying?" they asked of one another. "There is no wind, and on the near-by trees not a bough, nor a leaf is stirring."

Climbing down from the roof, they again entered the house and went into the third and last room. There a weaver sat working at his loom.

"What miracle is this taking place in your house?" the tsar's envoys asked him. "Why do cradles rock of themselves in empty rooms? And why does the fan of reeds sway on the roof, though there is no wind?"

"It is no miracle," the weaver replied. "I am doing it all myself."

"You dare to laugh at us!" the tsar's viziers exclaimed. "How can you be doing it when you are sitting here, weaving?"

"Nothing could be simpler," the weaver replied. "I have three strings attached to my loom. One I have tied to the first cradle, the second to the second cradle, and the third to the fan of reeds. As I weave, the strings move, and they set in motion the cradles and the reeds on the roof."

The tsar's envoys looked closer and saw that, in truth, three strings were attached to the loom: two of them ran to the cradles and one to the fan of reeds.

"This is truly wonderful!" cried they. "The weaver is indeed wise. He is just the man we need! Come with us to the tsar, weaver, perhaps you will be able to solve the riddle."

"First tell me what it is," the weaver replied.

Said the viziers:

"The envoy of a tsar from a strange land recently came to our tsar. He took out a piece of chalk and drew a line round the throne. And no one, neither the tsar nor any of his attendants and councillors, can guess what this means. So, at the tsar's orders, we are seeking a wise man who can explain the meaning of the chalk line. If you are able to do it, the tsar will reward you richly."

The weaver listened to the tsar's envoys and fell into a deep reverie. Then he picked up two knucklebones, the kind children play with, dropped them into his pocket and went out into the yard to catch a chicken.

The viziers were perplexed, and exchanged glances.

"What do you want with a chicken?" asked they.

"I shall need it," the weaver replied, and put the chicken he had caught in a basket.

After this, they set off for the tsar's palace.

The weaver entered the palace, greeted the tsar, glanced at the white chalk line round the throne, and at the man who had drawn it, and threw the two knucklebones before him.

The other, without a word, took a handful of millet from his pocket and cast it on the floor.

The weaver laughed, took the chicken from the basket and set it down before the scattered grains. The chicken pecked at them hungrily, and soon not a grain of millet was left on the floor.

The stranger left in haste without uttering a word.

The tsar and his attendants had been watching the stranger and the weaver with growing astonishment. No one could guess what the two were about.

"What was the meaning of the stranger's actions?" the tsar asked.

"He wanted to show you," the weaver replied, "that the tsar of his land declares war on our land and means to besiege us from all sides. He also wanted to know whether you would fight or surrender. That is the meaning of the line round your throne."

"Yes, that's it," the tsar said. "Now I understand. But I still cannot understand why you threw two knucklebones at his feet."

Said the weaver:

"I threw the knucklebones to let him know that we are far stronger than they, and that they cannot vanquish us. In plain words the meaning of my action was: 'You are mere children compared with us, you would do well to stay at home and play knucklebones instead of waging war on us.'"

"I see!" said the tsar. "What you say makes it all clear. But I still don't know why the stranger threw a handful of millet on the floor and why you let the chicken out of the basket."

"That is not hard to explain, either," said the weaver. "By throwing the handful of millet on the floor the stranger wanted to show that his tsar's hordes are innumerable. And I set down the chicken to peck it all up to indicate that if they go to war against us, not one of their warriors will remain alive."

"Did he understand you?"

"He must have, for he retired in haste."

The tsar rewarded the weaver with costly gifts and said:

"Stay with me in my palace, weaver, and you shall be my grand vizier."

"No," the weaver replied. "I do not wish to be your vizier. I have my own affairs to attend to."

And with that he went away.

DEER-CHILD AND YELENA THE BEAUTIFUL

A Georgian Fairy-Tale

It may be true or it may be false, but it is said that there once lived a very rich tsar. One day he said to his hunters:

"Go out and kill the first animal you meet."

The hunters went forth and the first animal they met was a doe in a glade. They took aim and were about to shoot her, as the tsar had ordered, when they saw that a little boy was feeding at her udder. When the child saw them, he stopped sucking, threw his arms about the doe's neck, and fell to kissing and fondling her.

The hunters were astonished.

They carried the boy off with them and took him to the tsar, telling him what they had seen.

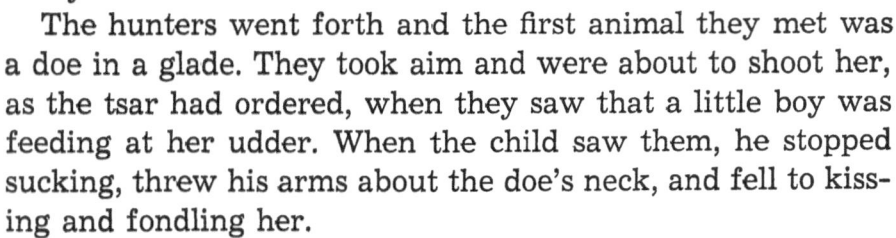

186

Now the tsar had a baby son who was the same age as the little boy the hunters had found, so he had them both christened together, and the foundling was named Deer-Child.

Deer-Child was brought up together with the prince, they slept in the same room and were suckled by the same nurse.

Some there are who grow by the year, but these two grew by the day and were twelve years old before they knew it. The tsar was happy with his two sons growing up in his palace.

One day the two boys went out to the fields with their bows and arrows. The prince shot an arrow, and the arrow hit the jug of an old woman passing by carrying water, and knocked off its handle.

The old woman turned and said:

"Curse you I will not, for you are an only son, but may your heart be rent for love of Yelena the Beautiful."

Deer-Child wondered to hear her.

"What does she mean?" he said.

But from that moment the prince could think of nothing and no one but Yelena the Beautiful. For the seeds of love had taken root in his heart and gave him no peace.

What was to be done? Three weeks passed by. The prince went about only half-alive. Love for a maiden he had never seen was draining his health and strength.

One day Deer-Child said to him:

"May your foster-brother die if he does not win Yelena the Beautiful for you!"

Then he went to the tsar and said:

"Father, order the blacksmith to make for me iron greaves

and an iron bow and arrows for I must go to seek Yelena the Beautiful."

The tsar agreed. An iron bow and arrows weighing fully five poods and a pair of iron greaves were fashioned for Deer-Child, and he and the prince set out together.

Said Deer-Child to his foster-father as he bade him good-bye:

"Have no fear, Father. You can depend on Deer-Child. Wait two years for us and remember this: we return with glory, or not at all."

So the two brothers went off together. They walked and they walked till they came to a dense, impenetrable forest. They made their way into it and saw a high cliff with a huge house at the top and a lovely garden in front of it. Now in this house lived five-headed and nine-headed man-eating giants.

Said the prince to Deer-Child:

"I am tired, my brother. Let us rest here a while."

"Very well," agreed Deer-Child.

And the prince lay down and closed his eyes.

"Lie here and sleep," said Deer-Child, "and I will go to the garden yonder and bring you some of its luscious fruits."

Not as one brother for another, but as a father for his son did Deer-Child care for the prince.

He reached the garden, and seeking out the finest apple-tree, began to pick some fruit.

Suddenly a nine-headed giant rushed out.

"Who dares to enter this garden?" he cried. "Here no birds fly in the sky, nor ants crawl over the ground for fear of me!"

"I am Deer-Child!" replied the youth in a loud voice.

At this the giant drew back, muttering to himself in fear and anger. For he, like all the giants, knew that Deer-Child's coming meant they were doomed. Indeed, so terrified were the giants that they rushed in all directions, trying to hide themselves. But Deer-Child found and killed them all, except for a single five-headed giant who was hiding in the attic.

Meanwhile the prince slept quietly in the shade.

Only when Deer-Child had cleared the house of the giants did he return and waken his brother. Now the giants' house and all their riches were theirs.

The brothers strolled in the garden and amused themselves in various ways, while Babahanjomi, the five-headed giant, sat on in the attic quivering with fear.

At last, overcoming his fear, he crawled out of the corner where he had been crouching, climbed down from the attic and made his appeal to Deer-Child:

"Do not kill me," said he, "and I will be a brother to you. All our riches will be yours."

Deer-Child smiled while the five-headed giant went on:

"What necessity urges you to leave your home and wander through the world from village to village and from town to town?"

Said Deer-Child:

"We have a task to perform. If, because you do not help us, we fail in our task, I will kill you as I killed the other giants. We are searching for Yelena the Beautiful, and you must search for her with us."

Now Babahanjomi had a little portable house which he could carry on his back wherever he went.

Said the giant:

"Get into this little house of mine, and we shall go to seek Yelena the Beautiful. But it will not be easy to win her. Many there are who would have her for themselves."

And the two brothers stepped into the giant's house and rode off on his back.

They travelled in this way for three months or more, and at last they reached a river.

"I am tired," said the prince to Deer-Child, "let us rest."

And, of course, Babahanjomi was even more tired, so the brothers got out of his little house and sat down by the river to rest. They were very thirsty, and tried drinking from the river, but found the water was salty.

"Why is the water salty?" asked Deer-Child, surprised.

"It is not water, but tears," Babahanjomi replied. "There is a five-headed giant living higher up the river. He, too, loves Yelena the Beautiful, but she refuses him. Love for her burns him up like fire, and he is weeping rivers of tears."

Deer-Child listened in great wonder.

"My name is not Deer-Child," said he, "if I do not win Yelena the Beautiful for my brother."

They went to the giant who lived higher up the river, and Deer-Child said to him:

"Tell us, giant, is your love for Yelena the Beautiful so great?"

The giant wept on, and his tears flowed and formed a river.

"I don't care if I die if I can only see her once," he replied.

"Well," said Deer-Child, "you shall see her, I promise, when we carry her home with us."

With that they continued on their way.

Some months passed by, and they still pressed on. Though they shot and ate every wild animal they chanced to meet, their food was running out. On and on they walked till at last they reached a small grove. They had not yet had any sign of Yelena the Beautiful.

Said Deer-Child:

"Yonder lies a village. I shall go and ask, perhaps someone in the village knows where to look for Yelena the Beautiful."

And leaving Babahanjomi with his little house and the prince inside it, Deer-Child set out for the village. He saw an old woman by her hut and said to her:

"Tell me, mother, in the name of the love of all mothers for their children, do you know where I can find Yelena the Beautiful?"

The old woman was much surprised. She knew how difficult it was to approach Yelena the Beautiful and wondered at the simple speech of the youth.

"To find her is a very, very hard thing to do, my son," said she. "You know little about her, it seems. She is loved by the great Tsar Wind who is ever seeking ways of carrying her off from her home. That is why she is kept behind nine locks and never sees a ray of sunlight: her family fear she will be spirited away."

And the old woman went on to tell Deer-Child the whereabouts of Yelena the Beautiful.

"Her castle," said she, "stands in the back of a large garden and is surrounded by a high wall, and Yelena the Beautiful lives there with her mother and brothers."

"But how are we to get to her?" Deer-Child asked. "My brother wants to marry her."

"That is not easy," said the old woman. "Yelena the Beautiful has many wooers, and her family will not want her to marry your brother. She sets her wooers three tasks to do and promises to marry the man who carries them out. But those who fail, her brothers kill."

Deer-Child smiled. What could Yelena the Beautiful conceive that he and his brother could not perform?... And he returned to where he had left his brother and Babahanjomi.

The giant hoisted to his back the little house with Deer-Child and the prince inside and on they moved again.

They reached the castle of Yelena the Beautiful, and Deer-Child was the first to venture inside.

Now the mother of Yelena the Beautiful was a sorceress, and she could both kill a man and bring him back to life.

She looked at Deer-Child, and found him so tall and strong and handsome that she could hardly keep her eyes off him.

"Who are you and what brings you here?" she asked.

Said Deer-Child:

"I come as a friend, not a foe."

"But what do you want?"

"I want your Yelena the Beautiful for my sister-in-law."

Now Yelena had three brothers, but all three were out hunting in the forest at the time.

"Stay here," said the mother of Yelena the Beautiful, "and wait for my sons to return. You will talk to them, and it will all be arranged."

So Deer-Child sat down in the garden to·wait for the brothers of Yelena the Beautiful.

Meanwhile, the prince and Babahanjomi, who were waiting for Deer-Child, feared lest the great Tsar Wind clash with him and kill him, so they decided to see for themselves how he was faring.

As for the brothers of Yelena the Beautiful, they made their appearance as darkness fell, one carrying a whole deer over his shoulder, the second—a roe, and the third—a tree-trunk for lighting a fire.

They smelt a stranger, and they asked of their mother:

"Who is here, Mother?"

"One who has come as a friend, my children. You must not harm him," the mother replied.

Meanwhile, Babahanjomi had brought the prince to the castle, and the prince stood there and waited to see what would happen.

The brothers of Yelena the Beautiful set about skinning the deer, and Deer-Child came up and joined them, and in the time they spent over one leg, Deer-Child, quick as lightning, had skinned the whole carcase. The three brothers looked at him, wondering.

They sat down to eat, and Deer-Child snatched up and swallowed great hunks of meat. And again the three brothers looked at him in wonder.

They finished supper and then went to bed. Next morning Yelena the Beautiful said:

"If the prince carries out the three tasks I set him, then I will marry him; if he fails, then I will not."

The prince was brought before her, and Yelena the Beautiful spoke to him; but the poor youth stood petrified, not uttering a sound, too dazed to understand what was happening. For the truth of the matter was that the mother of Yelena the Beautiful had cast a spell over him.

"Leave me!" cried Yelena the Beautiful, and expelled the prince from the chamber.

The prince stumbled out like a drunken man, and Deer-Child hurried to him and asked:

"Well, what did she say to you?"

"I do not know, my brother, I was too dazed," replied the prince.

Deer-Child was very angry, and he went off to ask Yelena the Beautiful to receive his brother a second time.

But the second time, too, the prince remained silent while in her presence, and he left Yelena the Beautiful as in a dream.

Deer-Child told Babahanjomi all about it, and they put their heads together and agreed on what they should do. Then Deer-Child again approached Yelena the Beautiful and asked her to receive the prince a third time.

The prince stood like a graven image before Yelena the Beautiful, for her mother had again bewitched him. But Babahanjomi came up, and taking out some writings, of the kind used to break spells, threw them into the chamber where Yelena the Beautiful sat talking to the prince.

The walls swayed suddenly, and the prince came to his senses. Now that the spell was broken and his eyes fell on Yelena the Beautiful, he ran to her and seized her by the hand.

"You are mine! You are mine!" he cried.

Deer-Child was overjoyed, and so, too, was Yelena the Beautiful, for she knew that her mother bewitched her wooers to prevent her marrying. So she and the prince came out together, smiling and happy.

The following morning the bride and groom went strolling in the garden, and Deer-Child stood watching near by and rejoicing in the sight of them. Suddenly the great Tsar Wind saw Yelena the Beautiful and pounced upon the prince. Lifting him up, he whirled and spun him round and round and then dashed him to the ground. Then he caught up Yelena the Beautiful and carried her high up into the sky.

When Deer-Child saw his brother lying lifeless on the ground, he was prostrated with grief and forgot Yelena the Beautiful. He now recalled that the old woman he had met had warned him about the great Tsar Wind; but, alas, it was too late.

Deer-Child sat down and wept bitterly, and the mother of Yelena the Beautiful came up to him and said:

"Do not weep, I will bring your brother back to life. But the great Tsar Wind has stolen Yelena the Beautiful, and how we are to get her back I do not know."

She brought out a kerchief and passed it over the face of the prince, who at once came back to life. He rose, rubbed his eyes and said:

"I have slept a long time."

But when he looked round him and saw that Yelena the Beautiful was gone, he began weeping and sobbing, for he did not know what to do.

Then Deer-Child went to Babahanjomi and said:

"The great Tsar Wind has carried off the bride. We must get her back at whatever cost."

Said the giant:

"May Babahanjomi drop dead on the spot if he does not help you! Look in my right ear, and you'll find a saddle there, look in my left ear, and you'll find a bridle and a lash. Take them out and bridle me, and we shall set off at once."

Leaving the prince in the house of Yelena the Beautiful, Deer-Child bridled Babahanjomi, lashed the saddle to his back with nine bands and passed nine bits through his five mouths.

"Now jump on my back," Babahanjomi said, "and give me three hard cracks with your whip that will flay nine strips of skin from my back. After that hold on and do not be afraid, I will fly fast as the wind!"

Before doing as Babahanjomi told him, Deer-Child went to say good-bye to the prince, his brother.

"Stay here and wait for us," said he, "we are going to seek for Yelena the Beautiful."

Then he jumped on the giant's back and cracked his whip three times across his back, flaying nine strips of skin from it. The giant moaned and whistled, he struck the ground with his body, and sweeping upwards, broke through the clouds. Away they flew across the sky, and only when they spied a field did they come down again. There was an old woman in the field, and Deer-Child asked her if she knew where the great Tsar Wind lived.

The old woman began to sob and to wail.

"My son, my son," cried she, "what brings you here? How can you dare to show yourself? The great Tsar Wind will smell a stranger, he will know you are here, and he will kill us all! A while ago he brought here a maiden so lovely that nothing under the sun can vie with her beauty. The Tsar Wind blew so hard that all that could be heard was his moaning and whistling, and everything around him crashed to the ground."

"It is this very maiden that I am seeking," Deer-Child said. "You must show me where the great Tsar Wind dwells."

"Very well," agreed the old woman, but she trembled with fear and could hardly breathe.

Deer-Child alighted, hid the saddle, bridle and whip in the giant's ears and followed the old woman.

Babahanjomi remained behind. He walked about, examined everything, did whatever came into his head, and even ate up all the Tsar Wind's chickens.

The old woman brought Deer-Child to the great Tsar Wind's castle and went away.

Now that very morning the Tsar had gone out hunting, so Yelena the Beautiful was left alone in the castle, weeping.

Deer-Child came to the door of her chamber, kicked it open and entered.

"How did you get here?" asked Yelena the Beautiful. "And what has happened to my poor bridegroom?"

And she embraced and kissed Deer-Child who told her of all that had taken place.

"I have come to take you away from here," said he.

"You will never be able to do it!" cried Yelena the Beautiful. "The great Tsar Wind, may he be cursed, will kill us both!"

Then Deer-Child went to the old woman who had shown him the way to the great Tsar Wind's castle, and asked for advice how to carry off Yelena the Beautiful and rid them of the great Tsar Wind.

Said the old woman:

"First go and tell Yelena the Beautiful that the next time the great Tsar Wind leaves for the hunt, she must quickly decorate one corner of the house with flowers and then, on his return, meet him with a sad countenance, to make it appear that she had sorely missed him."

Next morning, the moment the great Tsar Wind left the castle, Yelena the Beautiful went to the garden, picked some flowers and busied herself like a child at play, decorating a corner of the house.

The tsar came home in the evening and he marvelled at the sight of her.

"Why are you fussing about with flowers like a child?" he asked.

"What else am I to do?" said she. "I have to find something to amuse me while you are away. If only you would show me where your soul lies hidden, I should not be so bored and lonely."

"What do you want with my soul, my beauty?"

"How strange you are! If I knew where it was, I could at least kiss and fondle it while waiting for your return. I am your wife, don't forget. Please tell me where it is."

"Very well," said the great Tsar Wind. "I will tell you where it is, since you wish it."

And taking her to the roof of his castle, he said:

"Do you see that deer in the glade yonder? Three men cut the grass for him, and he eats it up all by himself, so that they can hardly keep up with him. Well, in that deer's head there are three small boxes, and my soul is hidden in them."

"But might not someone kill the deer?" asked Yelena the Beautiful.

"No, for he can only be killed with my own bow and arrows," the Tsar replied. "In each of those boxes there is a bird. If one of the birds is killed, I shall turn to stone from my feet to my knees; if the second one is killed, I shall turn to stone up to my waist; and if the third one is killed, I shall die. Now do you understand where my soul is?"

Morning came, and the great Tsar Wind went off on business of his own, and Yelena the Beautiful took his bow and arrows and gave them to Deer-Child, instructing him as to how the great Tsar Wind could be killed.

Deer-Child was overjoyed. He took the bow and arrows and went to the glade where the deer was browsing. He shot an arrow, killed the deer, and running up to him, cut his head in two and took out the boxes.

Now as soon as the deer had dropped dead, the great Tsar Wind felt that something was wrong and hurried home.

But Deer-Child wrung the first little bird's neck, and the great Tsar Wind's legs turned to stone. He wrung the second little bird's neck, and a numbness came over the great Tsar Wind's body so that he could barely drag himself to the threshold.

Said the great Tsar Wind to Yelena the Beautiful:

"You have betrayed me, Yelena the Beautiful!" And he made to climb the stairs, but Deer-Child seized the third little bird in his hands.

"This is to pay you for the evil you have wrought!" he cried, and he wrung the third little bird's neck.

The great Tsar Wind fell dead to the ground, and Deer-Child went up to Yelena the Beautiful and told her it was time for them to begin their journey.

"Very well," replied Yelena the Beautiful. "But first you must pass through nine rooms in the castle and there, in the tenth, you will find tethered the great Tsar Wind's horse. It is as fast as the wind, and it will get us home in a trice."

Deer-Child found the great Tsar Wind's horse, and he called Babahanjomi. He took all the horse-trappings out of his ears, got on his back, put Yelena the Beautiful on the horse, and away they flew!

Thus was Yelena the Beautiful reunited with her prince. They were married with grand celebrations, and everyone thanked Deer-Child for bringing it to pass.

As for the old tsar, the prince's father and Deer-Child's foster-father, he had decided his sons were dead and had been so overcome with grief that he had ordered mourning throughout his tsardom and spent the days in weeping.

Meanwhile, after feasting with the bride's family, the prince, Deer-Child and Yelena the Beautiful were on their way home in the little house on Babahanjomi's back.

As they passed the giant who had wept a river of tears out of love for Yelena the Beautiful, Deer-Child said:

"Well, giant, would you like to see Yelena the Beautiful?"

"Ah, Deer-Child, who would let me look at her!" the giant replied.

"Well, she is here, so look if you wish," said Deer-Child.

The giant looked, was blinded by the beauty of Yelena the Beautiful, and wasted away and dropped dead before their eyes.

Deer-Child and the others continued on their way, and after spending the night in the empty house of the nine-headed giants, moved on again.

Five more months of travel lay ahead when they stopped by a forest for a rest.

In the night three pigeons suddenly flew up, perched on the bough of a tree, and one of them said:

"When the old tsar learns that his son is coming with Yelena the Beautiful, he will send him a gun for a gift; the gun will go off and kill the prince. But whoever overhears us and speaks of it, will turn to stone and die."

"So will it be!" echoed the other two pigeons.

Said the second pigeon:

"When the old tsar learns that his son is near, he will go out to meet him, leading a horse for him, and the horse will throw the prince and kill him."

"So will it be!" the other two pigeons repeated, adding: "But whoever overhears us and speaks of it, will turn to stone and die."

Said the third pigeon:

"And when the bride and groom arrive, the terrible monster *gveleshapi* will come in the night and choke them both to death. But whoever overhears us and speaks of it, will turn to stone and die."

And with these words they flew away.

Deer-Child heard it all, but said nothing.

Morning came, and they all climbed into the giant's little house and set off on their way.

The old tsar, learning that his son was alive and well and was coming home with Yelena the Beautiful, sent him a gun for a gift, but before the prince could so much as touch it, Deer-Child rushed ahead, snatched the gun and flung it far away.

"My father the tsar honoured me with the gift of a gun, but Deer-Child would not let me have it," said the prince to himself, bitterly disappointed.

They went on again, and the old tsar sent his son a horse, but Deer-Child would not let the prince touch it and sent it back. This grieved the prince still more.

They arrived home, and the old tsar welcomed them warmly and another feast was held to celebrate the wedding.

Then Deer-Child came out from the castle and he said to Babahanjomi:

"Thank you for your faithful service. You are free now to go and live where you will in peace."

The giant went away, but Deer-Child stole to the bridal chamber and stood at the door, waiting. The bride and groom slept, but Deer-Child stayed awake. He stood on guard, his sword ready, knowing that his foster-brother's life was in his hands.

On the stroke of midnight the *gveleshapi* appeared. He crept up stealthily to the bridal bed, and opening wide his jaws, was about to pounce on the bride and groom and choke them to death. But Deer-Child lifted his sword and with a flourish killed the monster. After that he cut up his body and threw the pieces under the bed.

Morning came, and the bride and groom rose, all unaware of what had occurred in the night.

But when the servants came to clean the bridal chamber they found pieces of carrion under the bed, and the tsar was enraged, for he thought that someone was mocking him.

They began to talk and to reason and to ask themselves who had done it, and they put all the blame on Deer-Child. For had he not shown lack of respect for the prince by throwing away the tsar's gun and sending away his horse! Who but Deer-Child could have left the carrion in the bridal chamber and thus made them all an object of ridicule!

Said Deer-Child:

"I wished you only well. Would you have me die, while you live in happiness?"

But they were sorely vexed with him and demanded that he tell them where the carrion had come from.

"Very well," said Deer-Child, "I will tell you what you wish to know, but may grief not weigh you down when you understand that you have caused the death of the one who has laboured hard to bring about your happiness. Now listen. When we camped in the field on the edge of the forest, three pigeons flew up in the night, and perching on a bough, began to speak. The first one said: 'When the bridal train comes near, the old tsar will send his son a gun and it will go off and kill him. But he who speaks of it will turn to stone.'"

And no sooner were the words out of his mouth than Deer-Child turned to stone from his feet to his knees.

Now they knew why it was he had not spoken before, and they began to plead with him to be silent, saying:

"O Deer-Child, say no more, say no more!"

But Deer-Child replied:

"No, now I have begun, I will go on. So listen.... The second pigeon said: 'The old tsar will send his son a horse, and the prince will fall from his back and be killed. But whoever speaks of it will turn to stone.'"

And Deer-Child turned to stone to his waist.

"Stop! Say no more!" they all begged him.

"No," said Deer-Child. "You would not believe me before —now it is too late. So listen. The third pigeon said: 'In the night, when the bride and groom go into their chamber, the *gveleshapi* will come and choke them to death—' "

And before he could say any more, Deer-Child turned completely to stone.

The old tsar and the prince cried bitter tears, but, of course, this availed them nothing.

Yelena the Beautiful was heavy with child, but not even this gave joy to the prince.

"I must bring to life my faithful friend and brother, at whatever cost to me!" thought the prince to himself.

He put on his iron greaves, took an iron staff and set out to roam the world. He wandered from place to place and he asked everyone he met if they knew how to bring his foster-brother back to life. One day, being very weary, he sat down by a forest to rest. Suddenly an old man came out of the forest, and of him, too, the prince asked what he had asked of all the others.

Said the old man:

"Go home, for that which will save your foster-brother is in your own home."

But because the prince did not understand what this meant, the old man said again:

"Do not you know that a son, a golden-haired child, has been born to you? If you want your foster-brother to live, you must sacrifice your son. Kill him in his cradle, boil him and pour the water over your foster-brother. That will bring him back to life."

The prince heeded the old man's words and set off homeward.

Said he to himself:

"Children I will have, but never more a friend and brother like Deer-Child."

He came home and found his son lying in the cradle. His golden curls gleamed and shone and he was as bright as the moon in the sky!

The prince told Yelena the Beautiful what he had been told to do, and she agreed it must be done.

"For," said she, "we must do everything to bring Deer-Child back to life. To friends one must be faithful no matter what the price."

They did everything the old man had told the prince to do, and Deer-Child stirred, opened his eyes and came back to life.

In the morning Yelena the Beautiful went to her son's cradle. She was a mother, and her heart bled for her son, even though she had sacrificed him for friendship's sake. Suddenly there was a movement in the cradle. She turned back the sheets, and lo! there was her son, alive and well.

Everyone was overjoyed.

They slaughtered a cow and fifteen sheep and they roasted them whole on spits. For fourteen days they feasted and drank, and never stopped to clear the tables.

THE LION AND THE HARE

A Georgian Fairy-Tale

In a certain forest many animals were wont to gather, but each time the Lion would put in an appearance and pounce upon one of them and devour him on the spot. So the unhappy animals were in constant fear.

One day they all came to the forest as usual and began discussing what to do to rid themselves of this perpetual fear. They put their heads together, they talked and reasoned a long time and at last decided to pay the Lion a lifelong tribute, to deliver it to him themselves and to ask him in return to release them from the daily terror for their lives. And this resolved on, they went and told the Lion about it.

The Lion agreed to the proposal on condition that the tribute be delivered to him at an appointed time and without a moment's delay.

"Otherwise I shall kill you all!" said he.

And so every day from that day on the animals began delivering one of their own number for the Lion's dinner.

By and by the Hare's turn came to be taken to the Lion.

"Oh, well, it's my turn and there's nothing for it," said the Hare. "Only please let me go to the Lion alone. I shall try to do away with him. Perhaps I shall be able to save myself from death and the rest of you from misery and distress."

The animals burst out laughing. What a braggart was this squint-eyed little coward of a hare!

Now the Lion lay in his den, and he was very hungry. He waited for his victim's arrival with eyes that flashed fire and gnashing teeth. He was about to go and make short work of all the animals when the Hare appeared, purposely late.

Said the Lion, looking fiercely at the Hare:

"How dared you come so late!"

"Sire," said the Hare meekly, "I was entrusted with the task of bringing a hare for your dinner, and I was leading him here, but another lion attacked us on the way; he seized the other hare and dragged him off to a deep ravine."

"Come, show me where he is!" the Lion roared.

The Hare led the Lion to a well.

"He is down there, Sire," said he, "only I am afraid to look down at him alone. Take me in your paws, and I will show him to you."

The Lion took the Hare in his paws, they looked down into the well and saw their own reflection at the bottom: a lion holding a hare in his paws and gazing up at them.

The Lion, enraged, threw the Hare aside and plunged into the well to punish his rival and take away his prey. But the well was deep, and the fierce Lion was drowned.

Hearing about it, the animals rejoiced that they were delivered from so cruel an enemy, and they thanked the Hare very warmly indeed.

A LESSON IN WISDOM

A Georgian Fairy-Tale

A Bear, a Wolf and a Fox once met and began complaining of how they were often obliged to go hungry for so long that they got cramps in their bellies. They bewailed their sad lot, they talked it all over and decided to live as brothers. From now on, said they, we shall share whatever food comes our way. Thus resolved, they embraced in true brotherly fashion, vowed to be faithful to one another and together set out to hunt for prey.

They walked along, looking out for something to pounce upon, and after a while came upon a young wounded deer. Killing it off on the spot, they seated themselves in the shade on the grass and began dividing their booty.

Said the Bear to the Wolf whose jaws were stiff from gnashing his teeth in hunger:

"Come, Wolf, you divide the deer among us."

"Very well," the Wolf agreed. "The head will go to you, Bear, you being our lord and master, the body to me, and the legs to the Fox, since she is so fleet of foot."

But the Wolf had not finished before the Bear struck him such a blow on the head with his paw that the mountains rang with the sound of it. The Wolf gave a howl of pain and fell in a heap. And the Bear turned to the Fox and said:

"And now, Mistress Fox, you divide the deer."

The Fox, who was very sly, rose and said in flattering tones:

"The deer's head is yours by right, Bear, for you are our lord and master; the deer's body is yours, for you have always cared for us like a father; and the deer's legs are yours too, for you have ever stepped forward to benefit us."

"You are clever indeed, Mistress Fox," said the Bear. "Whoever taught you this very wise and sensible way of dividing booty?"

"How could I help learning wisdom, my lord" the Fox replied. "I have watched you giving the Wolf a lesson!"

ALTYN-SAKA THE GOLDEN KNUCKLEBONE

A Bashkir Fairy-Tale

Once upon a time there lived an old man and an old woman. They had only one son, whom everyone called Altyn-saka the Golden Knucklebone, because he owned a golden knucklebone. Altyn-saka played knucklebones better than anyone: no one could beat him at the game.

One day the old man went to a lake to water his horses. He drove the herd close to the water, but the horses shook their manes and tails, pawed at the ground with their hoofs, neighed anxiously and insisted on backing away from the lake: someone was clearly snatching at their manes and pulling at their mouths and not letting them drink.

"What can it be?" the old man asked himself. "I had better go and see."

But no sooner had he bent over the water than all of a sudden someone clutched him by the beard! The old man tried to wrench himself free, but could not.

He looked, and he saw that his beard was held by no other than Ubyr, the old witch herself.

"Do not hold me, Ubyr, let me go!" the old man cried. "I will give you a flock of sheep if you do."

"I don't need your old sheep," Ubyr replied.

"A herd of horses, then."

"I don't need your old horses."

"What shall I give you then?"

"Give me that of which you have but one in your yurta."*

In his fright the old man did not stop to think what it was of which he had but one.

"Very well," said he, "you shall have it, only let me go."

And Ubyr released him, saying:

"Remember, I'll find you anywhere, no one can hide from me!"

The old man came home, and it was then that he realised what it was Ubyr had asked of him. It was his son she had meant, his dear Altyn-saka, for he had but one son.

The old man felt very sad and woebegone, but he said nothing about it to his wife and son.

"We had better move on to new camping grounds, the lands here are poor," was all he said.

So they moved on to a new camping site and set up their yurta there, but the very next day Altyn-saka missed his golden knucklebone.

"Where is my golden knucklebone?" asked he.

Said the old man:

* Yurta—tent of thick felt.—Tr.

"We must have left it at our old camp. Only you mustn't go there, for Ubyr will get you."

And he told Altyn-saka of all that had happened to him on the lake shore.

Altyn-saka listened carefully to his father, then said:

"I am not afraid of Ubyr! She will never catch me. I am going back, only tell me which horse I should ride."

The father tried to dissuade his son, but Altyn-saka stood firm: he was not afraid of Ubyr, go he would, and that was that! There was no way of keeping him from doing what he wanted.

Said the father:

"Very well, let it be as you wish. And now go out to where the herd is, swing your *korok** and rattle your bridle, and whichever horse runs up to you, that is the one you must ride."

Altyn-saka went to where the herd was grazing, he swung his *korok* and he rattled his bridle, and at once a scraggy, rough-coated colt ran up to him.

Altyn-saka chased him away, and going to his father, asked him:

"Tell me, Father, which horse should I ride?"

"Did I not tell you to swing your *korok* and rattle your bridle?" the father said.

And Altyn-saka went out again to where the herd was grazing, he swung his *korok* and he rattled his bridle and the very same colt ran up to him.

"I shall have to ride this colt, it seems," said Altyn-saka.

* *Korok*—a kind of lasso, a light pole with a loop of rope at the end.–*Tr.*

213

He touched the colt's neck, and lo! its dirty, tangled coat fell away; he put the bridle on him, and the colt became strong and sleek; he led him out of the enclosure, and the colt turned into a tall and stately horse; he saddled him, and he became the best and most handsome steed in the herd.

Said the horse to Altyn-saka:

"Where are you going, Altyn-saka?"

"I am going to our old camp to get my golden knucklebone," Altyn-saka replied.

"Ubyr is waiting for you there," said the horse. "She will tell you to get off my back and pick up your knucklebone, but you must not listen to her. For if you get off my back, she will eat you up. Be swifter than a falcon, bend down quickly and seize your golden knucklebone."

Altyn-saka jumped on his horse and rode back to the old camping site. He looked, and he saw Ubyr sitting by a camp-fire, warming her hands.

Said Altyn-saka:

"Give me back my golden knucklebone, grandma."

"Your knucklebone is lying on the ground, my son," Ubyr replied. "Get off your horse and pick it up. My back aches so that I cannot get up."

Altyn-saka's horse bent down low to the ground, and Altyn-saka snatched up his golden knucklebone and galloped away. Ubyr jumped up with a howl of rage. She spat once, and a great black horse stood beside her, she spat a second time, and some reins appeared. Ubyr jumped on her horse and galloped after Altyn-saka.

Fast as the wind they went, Altyn-saka on his bay horse and Ubyr on her great black steed. Very, very close she got to him and was about to seize him when her horse stumbled, snorted loudly, and limping badly, dropped behind.

Ubyr pulled at the reins and dug her heels into the horse's sides, but the horse's speed became slower and slower, and Ubyr flew into a passion. She was so angry that she ate up her horse and had to run on foot after Altyn-saka.

On and on Ubyr ran, spurring her own self by punching herself on the sides and back with her fists. She caught up with the bay horse and bit through his right leg, but he galloped on on three legs. Ubyr did not drop behind. She caught up with the bay horse again and bit through his left leg, and the horse mustered his last remaining strength and plunged ahead, bearing Altyn-saka away from Ubyr. But he had not much strength left, and galloping up to the side of a lake said:

"I cannot run any more. I will hide from Ubyr in the lake, and you must hurry and climb that oak-tree yonder. When my legs heal, I will carry you further."

And with these words the horse dived into the lake. Altyn-saka quickly climbed the oak-tree by the lake and hid himself in its topmost branches.

Ubyr ran up, she saw Altyn-saka in the oak-tree and cried:
"I've got you now! I will drag you down and eat you up!"

She spat once, and an axe appeared. Then she pulled out a tooth, and whetting her axe on it till it became quite sharp, began hacking down the oak-tree, the chips flying to all sides as she worked.

A Fox ran up at the sound.

"Why are you chopping down the oak-tree, grandma?" asked the Fox.

"Cannot you see who is sitting in it!" Ubyr returned. "I will chop down the oak-tree, seize Altyn-saka the Golden Knucklebone and eat him up."

The Fox looked up and saw a handsome lad sitting in the top of the oak-tree. She took pity on him and said:

"You are old, Ubyr! You must not wear yourself out. Let me chop down the oak-tree for you."

"No, no!" Ubyr said. "I will chop it down myself and eat up Altyn-saka."

But the Fox would not be put off so easily and said:

"I will chop down the oak-tree, and you will eat him up."

Ubyr gave the Fox her axe, lay down under the oak-tree and at once fell asleep. She snored as she slept, and sparks and smoke poured from her mouth and nose.

While Ubyr slept, the Fox threw the axe and the tooth Ubyr had used as a whetstone in the lake, and gathering up all the chips, fitted them into the cuts in the tree made by Ubyr's axe. Then she spat on the cuts and licked them, and at once the chips grew fast to the tree, and it became whole again.

Then the Fox said good-bye to Altyn-saka and ran away.

Ubyr woke up, took one glance at the oak-tree and said:

"What do I see! The oak is whole again as though I had never touched it."

And she began cursing the Fox and calling her all the bad names she could think of.

Then she spat once, and an axe appeared. She pulled another tooth out of her mouth and began whetting the axe. She kept looking up at Altyn-saka as she worked and saying:

"I will chop down the oak-tree and eat you up."

When her axe was sharp, Ubyr again began hacking down the oak-tree. The chips flew to all sides, and the tree shook and trembled. Another stroke of the axe, and down it would fall!

All of a sudden a second Fox ran up.

"What are you doing, grandma?" asked she of Ubyr.

"Chopping down the oak-tree."

"Whatever for?"

"I want to get at Altyn-saka the Golden Knucklebone up there and eat him up."

Said the Fox:

"You must not strain yourself. Let me chop down the oak-tree for you."

"No, no," Ubyr grumbled, "I can manage. I want to eat up Altyn-saka myself."

"And so you shall," the Fox replied. "I will only chop down the oak-tree."

"No!" Ubyr cried. "I will not give you my axe. There was another Fox here who promised to help me, but she fooled me."

"What colour was this Fox?" the Fox asked.

"Red."

"You must never trust red foxes, grandma," said the Fox. "Red foxes are liars, all of them. Only we black foxes can be trusted."

Ubyr looked and saw, indeed, that the Fox was black. So she gave her the axe and lay down and at once began to snore, and sparks and smoke poured from her mouth and nose.

The black Fox threw Ubyr's axe and tooth into the lake, fitted the chips into the cut in the tree, spat on them and licked them, and lo and behold! they grew fast to the tree which became whole again.

Then the Fox said good-bye to Altyn-saka and ran away.

Soon after, Ubyr awoke. She looked at the oak-tree and cried:

"Why, what is this?... The oak is whole again!"

Ubyr spat, and an axe appeared. She pulled a third tooth out of her mouth and began whetting the axe, and when it was quite sharp started chopping down the oak-tree again. And she cursed Altyn-saka and the Fox as she worked, calling them the ugliest names she could think of.

At last the oak-tree was cut halfway through, and Altyn-saka looked down and thought to himself:

"Ubyr will get me now."

All of a sudden a white Fox came running up to the oak-tree and said to Ubyr:

"Let me help you chop down the oak-tree, grandma."

"Be off with you while you have the chance!" Ubyr cried. "Twice already have foxes fooled me and run away."

"What colour were they, grandma?" asked the Fox.

"One was red, and the other black," Ubyr replied.

"You must never trust red or black foxes, grandma," said the Fox. "They are terrible liars. Only we white field foxes can be trusted. I won't fool you, I will help you."

Ubyr believed the Fox, and handing over her axe, went to sleep. And the Fox threw into the lake the axe and the tooth Ubyr had used for a whetstone, and quickly gathering up the chips, fitted them into the cut in the tree. She spat on them and she licked them, and they grew fast to the tree.

Said the Fox to Altyn-saka:

"Thrice have I helped you, Altyn-saka the Golden Knuckle-bone, I smeared my fur with black, and then with white clay so that Ubyr might not know me. I can do nothing more for you."

And bidding him good-bye, she ran away.

Soon after that Ubyr woke up.

"What is this that I see!" cried she. "It is as if I had not touched the tree at all."

She spat, and an axe appeared. She pulled out her last tooth and began whetting the axe, and when it was sharp, started chopping down the oak-tree, muttering as she worked:

"I will take no more helpers! I will manage alone now."

The chips flew to all sides, and the oak swayed and creaked and seemed about to crash down.

Altyn-saka sat there, and he saw that now Ubyr would surely get him.

"What shall I do?" he asked himself.

All of a sudden a Raven flew up and perched on the top of the oak-tree.

"Hear me, Raven, hear me, my good friend!" pleaded Altyn-saka. "You fly everywhere and you go everywhere. Fly to our new camp, find my two dogs Akkulak and Aktyrnak, and tell them to come quickly, for I need their help."

"I will not!" the Raven replied. "I hope Ubyr gets you, for I shall then have a share of the booty."

And perching comfortably on a bough, he settled down to wait.

Altyn-saka looked to all sides to see if help could be expected from anywhere. Just then a Magpie flew up.

Said Altyn-saka:

"Hear me, Magpie, hear me, my good friend! You fly everywhere and you go everywhere. Fly to our new camp and tell my dogs Akkulak and Aktyrnak to come quickly, for I need their help."

"I will not!" the Magpie replied. "I want Ubyr to get you, for then a bit of the booty will surely fall to me."

Altyn-saka became very sad and crestfallen.

"My end is near," thought he.

All of a sudden a flock of sparrows appeared, flying just over his head.

Said Altyn-saka:

"Hear me, grey sparrows, hear me, my good friends! Fly to our new camp, find my dogs Akkulak and Aktyrnak and tell them that the old witch Ubyr wants to eat up their master."

"We shall find them! We shall find them! We shall tell them! We shall tell them!" chirped the sparrows, and away they flew very fast to Altyn-saka's camp.

They came to the camp and they found Altyn-saka's two dogs fast asleep. They had been running about in search of their master and this had worn them out so that they had dropped down like logs. The sparrows began to peck at the dogs' ears, trying to waken them; then they set up a great chirruping and fluttering.

"Come, Akkulak, come, Aktyrnak," they chirruped. "Hurry and run to the big oak-tree that grows by the lake and save your master. Ubyr wants to eat him up."

Akkulak and Aktyrnak started up and rushed for the lake.

The sparrows flew over the road, and the dogs followed, raising clouds of dust as they ran.

Ubyr saw the dust, and she said to Altyn-saka:

"Look, Altyn-saka the Golden Knucklebone, look! What are those clouds of dust on the road?"

"They bring joy to me and grief to you!" Altyn-saka replied.

Ubyr heard the patter of the dogs' feet, and she asked:

"Do you hear that, Altyn-saka the Golden Knucklebone, what are those peals of thunder?"

"They bring joy to me and grief to you!" Altyn-saka replied.

Just then Akkulak and Aktyrnak ran up. They rushed at Ubyr and began to bite and to worry her.

Ubyr was frightened, she threw her axe in the lake and plunged in after it.

Said the dogs to Altyn-saka:

"We are going to dive in after Ubyr, and you stay here and watch the water. If we kill Ubyr, the water in the lake will turn black; if Ubyr kills us, it will turn red."

And with these words they plunged in.

The water in the lake began seething and boiling.

Altyn-saka looked, and he saw that it was turning red.

"Ubyr has killed my dogs!" said he to himself.

He looked again, and lo! the water was now black.

Altyn-saka was overjoyed. He laughed in glee and climbed down from the oak-tree, and Akkulak and Aktyrnak came out of the water and began shaking themselves.

"Why did the water in the lake first turn red?" Altyn-saka asked.

Said Aktyrnak:

"Because Ubyr was beginning to get the better of us and even bit off one of my ears. But we soon made short work of her."

The bay horse followed the dogs out of the lake.

"Come, Altyn-saka the Golden Knucklebone," said he, "jump on my back, and I will take you home."

And so Altyn-saka returned to his camp safe and sound. His mother and father were very happy, and they held a great feast to which they invited all their kith and kin, and all their friends and acquaintances. For nine days they ate and for nine days they drank and for nine whole days they made merry!

TSARKIN KHAN
AND THE ARCHER

A Kalmyk Fairy-Tale

In olden times, in the realm of Tsarkin Khan there lived an Archer who was brave and handsome and strong. One day he went to the shore of a lake to hunt wild fowl, and he saw three golden-crowned swans. The Archer at once fell flat on the ground, hid himself in the rushes and lay in wait.

The three golden-crowned swans flew down to the shore, cast off their feathers and turned into three beautiful maidens who entered the water to bathe.

The Archer crept near, seized the cast-off plumage of one of the swans and again hid himself in the rushes.

The swan-maidens bathed, they came out of the water and two of them at once donned their feathers, but the third could not find hers. The two swans flew up into the air and began looking out for their sister's feathers, but they could not see them anywhere.

"It is the will of fate, sister!" cried they and flew away.

The swan-maiden was left alone. She ran up and down the shore, looking for her feathers and weeping bitterly.

"If he who finds my feathers and returns them to me is poor," said she, "I will make him rich. If he is ugly, I will make him handsome. I will give him anything he asks for... Aye, I will grant his every wish!"

So did she speak, the while she continued to run up and down the shore, sobbing piteously.

Then the Archer came out from behind the clump of rushes and said:

"Do not grieve, swan-maiden, but come to me. I have your feathers."

Seeing her feathers in the hands of the handsome Archer, the swan-maiden was well pleased and came up to him shyly.

"O my brother," said she, "you have done one kind deed in finding my feathers. Now do another and let me have them back. In return, you shall have anything you desire, I will grant your every wish."

"There is nothing I want but your own dear self," replied the Archer. "Will you be my wife?"

The swan-maiden looked at the Archer, and seeing him so young and tall and handsome, said softly:

"Yes."

Then the Archer took her by the hand, led her to the nomad camp where he lived, and married her. They had only the Archer's *kibitka*, his poor tent, for a home, but they loved one another dearly, could not bear to be out of each other's sight or to separate for even a moment.

Some little time passed by, and Tsarkin Khan heard that his Archer was married to a woman of rare and dazzling beauty. The Khan, being curious to learn if this were true, went himself to the Archer's tent and was astonished to see that those who had spoken of the Archer's wife had not exaggerated: never had there been anyone so beautiful! She was as lovely as a daughter of the Sun. One could never tire of gazing at her, nor could any woman in his realm be compared with her.

Having feasted his eyes on the swan-maiden's beauty, Tsarkin Khan returned to his palace and at once called together his *darkhans*, his viziers and councillors, regaled them with the best of foods and drinks, and then said:

"O my *darkhans*, you whom I hold as dear as life itself, I ask for your counsel."

"You shall have it, O Khan!" the *darkhans* replied in unison.

Said Tsarkin Khan:

"One of my archers has a wife whose beauty is such as has never been seen on earth. Her equal cannot be found; it is not possible to meet another like her: she outshines all!"

And Tsarkin Khan went on to speak of the proud bearing and lovely features of the Archer's young wife, of her sweet voice and of the graceful way she walked, of her eyes and of her long, plaited hair.

"And this woman of beauty so rare that it is as the rays of the sun is the wife of a simple archer," said he in conclusion. "Advise me. Tell me how I can have her for my own."

Some of the *darkhans* pondered and said:

"Steal her from her home and keep her secretly in the palace."

Others thought hard and said:

"Kill the Archer and marry her."

Others still said:

"Do not kill the Archer, but banish him from your domains; then you can take away his wife without any trouble."

When all of them had spoken, the chief *darkhan*, he who sat on the right-hand side of the Khan, rose to his feet.

"There is no wisdom in any of these counsels," said he. "To steal a woman from her home and keep her secretly in the Khan's palace is imprudent, for sooner or later the people will learn about it. To kill the Archer and marry his widow is dangerous, for the people may rebel, and then there will never be an end to trouble. To banish the Archer is foolish, for he will return in secret and take his wife away. Nay, what we must use here is cunning."

"What is it you advise then?" Tsarkin Khan asked.

Said the chief *darkhan*:

"I have heard tell that in the land of the setting sun, on the steep and precipitous bank of a wide river, there dwells a tigress and her cubs. They say that this tigress is more savage and ferocious than any beast to be found on the earth. You, my Khan, must order the Archer to bring you some of the milk of the tigress. He will not come back, for the tigress is sure to tear him to pieces. You will then find it easy to get his beautiful wife for yourself. It should not be hard to send the Archer on this errand, for he will not dare to disobey his Khan's command."

This crafty plan of the chief *darkhan* found favour with both Tsarkin Khan himself and all his councillors.

"That is a wise plan," said they.

Tsarkin Khan did as his *darkhan* advised. He pretended to be gravely ill and sent for the Archer.

The Archer came, and the Khan, moaning and sighing loudly, said to him:

"You can see for yourself that I am stricken by a grave and mortal disease. The remedy to cure my ailment is to be found in the land of the setting sun. There, on the steep, precipitous bank of a wide river, dwells a huge tigress with her cubs. Only the milk of this tigress can restore me to health and strength. Go at once and bring me some."

And Tsarkin Khan moaned the louder and writhed as if in pain.

The Archer returned to his tent and prepared himself for a distant journey. He put on his best clothing and he armed himself with his best weapons.

"Where are you going?" his wife asked.

"The Khan is dangerously ill. He can only be cured if he drinks of the milk of the tigress that lives on the steep bank of a wide river in the land of the setting sun. He has ordered me to go there without delay. I go against my will, but I cannot disobey."

The Archer's wife understood that it was not without some hidden motive that Tsarkin Khan was sending her husband for the milk of the tigress, that he had some evil purpose in mind. She took her yellow-flowered kerchief, gave it to her husband and said to him:

"Always have this kerchief with you, for it will save you

from death. When the tigress is about to pounce upon you, pull it out and flourish it, and she will at once become meek and gentle and allow you to milk her. She knows me, for she has lived at my house."

The Archer took the yellow-flowered kerchief, saddled his horse, and taking leave of his young wife, set off at a gallop for the land of the setting sun.

Lower than the clouds, but higher than the tops of the nomad tents he sped, leaving behind him hills and gorges, salt-water lakes and quicksands. In such haste was he to carry out the Khan's command and return to his wife that he did not stop to eat during the day or to sleep at night and forgot to count the days and nights.

In this way he travelled a long time until at last he reached a precipice overhanging a river as broad as the sea. Here dwelt the huge tigress and her cubs.

The tigress saw the Archer when he was a whole day's ride away; she let out a deafening roar and leapt forward, wishing to pounce upon him and tear him to bits. But the Archer, quick as lightning, pulled out the yellow-flowered kerchief his wife had given him and flourished it. The tigress stood stock-still and at once stopped roaring.

"Tell me, brave Archer, where did you get the kerchief?" she asked him.

"My wife gave it to me," the Archer replied.

"And now tell me why you have come here," the tigress went on.

"My Khan has fallen dangerously ill," the Archer told her, "and he has ordered me to bring some of your milk to him."

"In that case," the tigress said, "dismount quickly and I will let you milk me. You can fill your whole *bortago** full of milk."

The Archer alighted and milked the tigress. When his *bortago* was full, he strapped it tightly to his saddle, thanked the tigress and wished her good health.

"I wish you the same," the tigress said. "Go home to your wife, make your Khan well again, and may fortune smile upon you always."

And saying this, the tigress went back to her cubs, and the Archer jumped on his horse and set off homeward.

As soon as he arrived, he carried his *bortago* to the Khan.

All Tsarkin Khan could do was to take a sip of the milk and say:

"Ah, I am well again."

After that he told the Archer to leave him and at once called together his *darkhans*.

"It was a wise counsel my chief *darkhan* gave me, but it has been of no avail," said he. "The tigress should have torn the Archer to pieces; instead, he has returned home safe and sound. What errand shall I send him on, so that he may never come back here again?"

The *darkhans* began to think and to ponder, but rack their brains as they would, there was nothing they could think of, nor did they utter a single wise word.

Then the chief *darkhan*, he who sat on the left-hand side of the Khan, rose and said:

* *Bortago*—a flat vessel of leather.—*Ed.*

"We sent the Archer to a place where we thought he would perish. That it did not happen only means that we know of no way of ridding ourselves of him. It is my belief that there remains for us but one thing to do: to get together the worst, most confirmed rascals and scoundrels, fill them up with drink and rich food, and try to discover whether they know of a way of putting the Archer to death and ridding the Khan of him for ever."

"The chief *darkhan* has spoken truly, that is what we must do," they all agreed.

On the appointed day Tsarkin Khan and his *darkhans* secretly invited to the palace a company of rogues, thieves, swindlers and cutthroats of every kind on earth; they filled them with drink and rich food and began trying to discover whether anyone among them could rid the Khan of his Archer.

"If there is no one among you who can help the Khan," said they, "perhaps you know of someone who would stealthily get rid of the Archer?"

And so saying, Tsarkin Khan and his *darkhans* began to stroll among the ill-assorted company, waiting to hear what the knaves and rogues had to say in reply. But no reply came. The knaves and rogues kept as mum as if their mouths were full of the meat they had been eating. Then the *darkhans* put the same question again, and again the knaves and rogues were silent. Suddenly one among them, a man blind on one eye and a cunning devil if there ever was one, jumped up from his seat, threw open his robe, and smiting his chest with his fist, cried:

"I know what to do!"

Tsarkin Khan was well pleased and said loudly:

"Speak out then and tell us what to do!"

Said the one-eyed man:

"You must send the Archer No-One-Knows-Where and command him to bring you No-One-Knows-What. He will go to seek something that has no shape, no form and no place, and not being able to find it, will never dare to appear in these parts again."

Tsarkin Khan and his *darkhans* were delighted with the one-eyed man's suggestion, and rewarding him richly, sent him away.

In order to find some pretext for his new orders to the Archer, Tsarkin Khan again pretended to be gravely ill, and summoning the Archer, said to him with many moans and sighs:

"I am gravely sick again, and I can only be cured if you go No-One-Knows-Where and bring me No-One-Knows-What. No one but you can do it. Go at once and bring me that which has no shape, no form and no place."

"But where am I to go and what am I to bring?" the Archer asked.

"I don't know, I don't know," said Tsarkin Khan. "All I know is that you are the only one who can do it. If you fail, I shall die."

And he began moaning louder than ever and writhing as if in pain.

The Archer went back to his *kibitka* and began to think what he should do. For three days and three nights he pondered. During the day he would climb to the top of a hill, and at night he could not sleep but turned and twisted on his thick mat of felt. He thought long and he thought hard, but nothing could he devise. Yet he would not breathe a word of it to his wife for fear of worrying her.

Three days passed by, and then the Archer saddled his horse.

"Perhaps if I follow my nose I shall get wherever it is the Khan is sending me," said he to himself, and springing up on to the horse's back, he called his wife to bid her good-bye.

"Where are you going?" she asked him.

"The Khan is ill again," the Archer replied. "He has commanded me to go No-One-Knows-Where to seek No-One-Knows-What."

Said the Archer's wife on hearing this:

"You won't get there on horseback, you had better go on foot. Here is a ball of thread for you. Take three steps, and then throw it down. Whichever way it rolls, there you must go. Here, too, is a golden comb. You must take it with you and comb your hair with it every morning."

The Archer said good-bye to his young wife, took three steps and threw down the ball of thread. The ball of thread started rolling very, very fast, and the Archer walked after it.

He followed it over salt-marshes and quicksands, up high hills and down deep gullies, past lakes and camping grounds and through dense growths of rushes. During the day he would not stop to eat, at night he would not sleep, and he lost count of the days, weeks and months that passed. At last the ball of thread rolled into a great, dark forest, and the Archer entered the forest and walked on in its wake. Day in and day out he walked, without rest or sleep, and the ball of thread kept rolling on and on. Finally it rolled up to a little *kibitka* of felt and vanished, for all the world just as if it had melted away.

"What am I to do now?" the Archer asked himself. "I suppose I must go inside."

And lifting up the hanging of thick felt, he entered the *kibitka* and was met by a little woman who was very, very beautiful.

"Who are you, whence do you hail and whither are you bound?" she asked him.

"I am the Khan's Archer," the Archer replied, "and I am going No-One-Knows-Where to seek No-One-Knows-What."

The little woman asked the Archer no more, but put food before him and then sent him to bed; and the Archer fell asleep the moment he lay down.

In the morning he rose, washed and began combing his hair with the golden comb, and the little woman, mistress of the little *kibitka*, saw him and asked:

"Where did you get that golden comb?"

"My wife gave it me," the Archer replied.

The little woman was overjoyed.

"In that case," said she, "you are my kinsman, for your wife is my younger sister. Why did not you tell me about it yesterday?"

And placing all kinds of delicious foods and drinks before him, she said:

"Give your weary feet a rest after so long and hard a journey, and stay with me three more days."

The Archer gladly agreed and stayed another three days in the little woman's *kibitka*.

On the third day, when the Archer had rested, the little woman said to him:

"Now tell me where you are going and why."

Said the Archer:

"My Khan is gravely sick and has ordered me to go No-One-Knows-Where and bring him No-One-Knows-What. What that is I do not know. My wife, your younger sister, gave me a ball of thread and told me to follow it, and it led me to you. But where I am to go now I do not know, for the ball of thread has vanished."

At this, the little woman, mistress of the little *kibitka*, gave the Archer a ball of silken thread and said:

"Follow this ball of thread. It will take you to my elder sister. Perhaps she can tell you where you must go to find that which has no shape, no form and no place."

So the Archer set off again after the ball of silken thread. Day after day he walked, and night after night, and never stopped for rest. He left the great, dark forest behind him and walked across a steppe for thirty days and thirty nights until he reached another forest, as large and dark as the first.

The ball of thread wound in and out among the trees and bushes, and the branches scratched the Archer's hands and body and struck him in the face, but he went on and on, without stopping.

At last the ball of thread rolled up to the entrance of a tiny little *kibitka* of felt which stood in the middle of the forest, and vanished.

A tiny little woman who was very, very beautiful came out of the *kibitka*.

"Who are you, whence do you hail and whither are you bound?" she asked of the Archer.

"I am a wayfarer," the Archer replied. "I come from afar and I am going far away."

The tiny little woman, mistress of the tiny little *kibitka*, asked the Archer nothing more, but invited him to come in, gave him food and drink and sent him to bed.

In the morning the Archer rose, washed, and began combing his hair with the golden comb. The tiny little woman, mistress of the tiny little *kibitka*, saw him and asked:

"Where did you get that golden comb?"

"My wife gave it me," the Archer replied.

The tiny little woman's face brightened with pleasure, and she said:

"In that case, you are my kinsman, for your wife is my youngest sister. Why did you not tell me about it before?"

And she brought out all she had in the house, the best foods and the best drinks, and began to regale the Archer.

Said she when he had had his fill:

"You must give your weary feet a good, long rest. Stay with me for a time."

So the Archer spent three days and three nights in the tiny little woman's *kibitka*, and on the fourth day she asked him to tell her where he was going and why.

"Do not hide anything from me," she said.

The Archer told the tiny little woman all about everything, about where he was going and why, and the tiny little woman listened to his story, shook her head and said:

"I do not know the whereabouts of the place you are bound for. I shall ask my helpers."

And she took her golden horn, went out of her *kibitka* and blew a loud blast.

There sounded one hundred and eight sad notes and sixty-two gay notes, and at once there ran up, flew up, crawled up and hopped up the wild beasts of the steppe and the forest, the birds of the sky, the worms from under the ground, and every living thing there is. They came and they gathered in a circle round the tiny little woman, mistress of the tiny little *kibitka*.

Said the tiny little woman:

"Beasts and birds, you who go everywhere, who run far and fly far, who know all and hear all, is there one among you who knows where that is found which has no shape, no form and no place? Let him who knows come forward and say: 'I know,' and let them who do not know say: 'We do not know,' and then all of you can go back to where you came from."

Said the birds:

"We do not know!" and at once flew away.

Said the beasts:

"We do not know!" and at once ran away to the steppes and forests.

Said the worms and insects:

"We do not know!" and at once crawled away.

Then the tiny little woman picked up her horn and blew another blast, and there sounded one hundred and eight sad notes and sixty-two gay notes, and all the creatures living in the water gathered round her: fishes and turtles and frogs and snakes and crayfish.

Said the tiny little woman, mistress of the tiny little *kibitka*:

"Snakes and fishes, you who go everywhere, you who swim in far-off waters, you who know all and hear all, answer me: is there one among you who knows where that is found which has no shape, no form and no place? Let him who knows come forward and say: 'I know,' and let them who do not know, say: 'We do not know,' and then all of you can go back to where you came from."

"We do not know! We do not know! We do not know!" cried the fishes, the turtles, the snakes, the frogs and the crayfish, and they went back to their lakes, rivers and swamps.

Only one large crayfish did not leave. He first crawled to the water, then back to the *kibitka* and again returned to the water.

The tiny little woman, mistress of the tiny little *kibitka*, seeing that the crayfish was undecided as to what he should do, said:

"You are the Khan of all the crayfish, are you not?"

"I am," replied the crayfish.

"What do you know? What have you heard? What do you wish to say? Be it true, or be it false, speak out just the same."

Said the crayfish:

"I do not know if what I know is true."

"That is as it may be, but you must say whatever you have to say," insisted the tiny little woman, mistress of the tiny little *kibitka*.

"Well," the crayfish began, "let him who seeks that which has no shape, form or place, travel southwards; after a month's travels he will reach a large sea. If he is unable to cross the sea, let him turn westwards, and after another month's travels he will get to a ford. When he has crossed the sea and reached the opposite shore, he will come upon a wide road. This road leads southwards. If he follows it for a month he will see a great, dense forest to the east of him. A two-wheel track leads from the road to the forest. There the way ends. What lies beyond, I do not know."

And saying this, the crayfish crawled away to his lake.

"Well, brave Archer, did you hear the words of the Khan of the crayfish?" the tiny little woman asked.

"I did," replied the Archer.

"In that case, you may start on your way. Perhaps you will find what you are looking for. No one else knows anything about it. From now on you will have to fend for yourself!"

She gave the Archer food and helped him get ready, and after taking leave of her, he set off on his journey.

On and on he walked, day after day, never stopping for so much as a moment; it was a whole month before he finally reached the sea. He looked out across it and realising he would never be able to cross it, turned westwards and walked along the shore. After a month of journeying he came to the ford, crossed the sea, found the wide road on the opposite shore and followed it for another month. At last to the east of him lay a great, dense forest and he proceeded in that direction, not stopping for a moment, until he came upon a wide, two-wheel track. He turned off the road and followed the track, and it was three days and three nights before he finally reached the forest.

He entered the forest and saw the two-wheel track winding in and out among the trees. He followed it till it brought him to an impenetrable thicket where it abruptly vanished. The Archer then began working his way through the thicket.

The trees there were tall and dark, they covered the sky with their branches, so that not a ray of sun or a gleam of light came through. There was no path to be seen anywhere: not ahead, nor to the right, nor to the left. The Archer stopped and said to himself:

"What am I going to do? I have come too far to go back now."

He looked round him and all of a sudden noticed a hole in the ground. He climbed down the hole, and finding himself in an underground passage, began groping his way along it. On and on he went until he came to a hut dug out in the ground. He entered and looked all round him, but there was no one there. He listened, but not a sound did he hear. And yet he could see that someone was in the habit of visiting the place.

"I do not know who lives here," said the Archer to himself, "but I must take care lest I come to harm."

And seeing a deep niche in the wall, he crawled into it and at once fell fast asleep.

Through his sleep he heard the clatter of cart-wheels, and so loud was the sound that he knew this was no ordinary cart.

He hid himself as best he could and lay there quiet as a mouse, thinking:

"I wonder what will happen now."

At first he heard the cart come to a halt at the door of the hut, and then a young giant of the most formidable appearance entered. He was clad in rich garments, and costly weapons hung at his belt. The giant took off his weapons and hung them on the wall, and then he took off his garments and hung them on the opposite wall. After that he sat down cross-legged and said:

"Come, Murza, I am hungry!"

No sooner were the words out of his mouth than a yellow-flowered cloth unfolded before him, and on it appeared the finest and most delicious dishes and drinks and the choicest fruits, everything to please the palate and cheer the heart.

The giant had his fill of the food and the drink, and then he said:

"Come, Murza, take it away!"

And at once the yellow-flowered cloth, with all its platters, jugs and cups, vanished for all the world just as if it had melted away.

The giant donned his garments, took his weapons and left the underground hut. At once there came the rumble and clatter of cart-wheels dying away in the distance: the giant had gone.

The Archer crawled out of his hiding-place and looked around him, but he saw nothing and no one. He stood there wondering and he said to himself:

"Who was the giant that came here in his cart? And who was it that served him all those fine dishes? And where has the food disappeared that he left untouched? I think I shall try and do all that he did."

The Archer then removed his weapons and hung them on the hook the giant had used; he took off his garments and hung them on the second hook the giant had used. After that he sat down cross-legged on the felt mat and said:

"Come, Murza, I am hungry!"

At once a yellow-flowered cloth unfolded before him, laden

with the choicest foods and the finest drinks, everything to please the palate and cheer the heart.

The Archer ate and drank and then said:

"Where are you, Murza? Come, sit down and eat and drink your fill."

At this Murza appeared and at once sat down and began to eat, and when he had finished, he said:

"For thirty whole years have I served food and drink to the giant who was here a while ago, and not once did he invite me to eat or drink with him. Not so you. I served you only once, and you thought of me and invited me to partake of your repast. I shall be better off with you. Take me with you."

"Gladly," the Archer replied. "I realise now that, without knowing it, it was you I came for and searched for and finally found so unexpectedly."

"Well, from this day on I shall be yours and will follow you everywhere," Murza declared.

"Very well," agreed the Archer, "let it be so."

They came out of the underground hut and went along together, Murza keeping always at the Archer's side, but remaining invisible to all eyes.

Whether they were long on the way or not no one knows, but suddenly there was a loud clatter of wheels.

Said Murza to the Archer:

"That is my former master coming on his eight black horses with white stars on their heads. He must be hungry, and he will call on me to serve him, but there will be nobody to answer his call."

They went on, and late in the evening reached a spot that

looked lonely and desolate. A dark, smoky *kibitka* stood there, its covering of felt worn and full of holes.

The Archer went into the *kibitka*, and there he found a *dayanchi*, a hermit, making bows of obeisance and so absorbed in prayer that he paid not the slightest attention to the Archer's appearance.

"O most venerable *dayanchi*," the Archer said, "there is something I wish to ask of you. Allow me to spend the night in your *kibitka*."

The *dayanchi* interrupted his prayers and said:

"No man has appeared in these parts before. Whence do you hail and whither are you bound?"

"I have travelled to distant lands on my Khan's orders, and now I am on my way home again," the Archer replied.

Said the *dayanchi*:

"You are welcome to spend the night here, but I have no food to offer you, no *shulun*, no mutton stew, and no tea, nothing at all. I have not so much as a pot or a tripod in my *kibitka*."

"I do not want anything," the Archer replied. "All I need is a place to spend the night."

"Well, then, you may stay!" said the *dayanchi*, and prostrating himself on the floor, began to pray again. But just before going to bed he took out his supplies and sat down to eat: his meal consisted of wild raspberries gathered in the clefts of the rocks and of dried sloes and hawthorn fruits from the forest.

The *dayanchi* sat there, eating, and he said to the Archer:

"Do you see what I am eating? I dare not offer you such poor fare. Besides, there is not enough of it. I have little time to gather fruit, for I must devote myself to prayer."

But this left the Archer unmoved.

"You eat your food," he said, "and I will eat mine." And he added loudly:

"Come, Murza, I am hungry!"

No sooner were the words out of his mouth than a yellow-flowered cloth unfolded before him, set with platters of food and jugs of *koumiss*,* with everything, in short, to please the palate and cheer the heart.

The Archer sat down to the feast and he said to the *dayanchi*:

"Well, now, most venerable *dayanchi*, why do you not join me and try some of my food?"

The *dayanchi* sat down, wondering, beside the Archer and began to eat and to praise what he ate. And the Archer called Murza and invited him. too, to partake of the feast.

When they had all had their fill, they rose, and the Archer said:

"Take it away, Murza."

And at once all that had been on the yellow-flowered cloth, as well as the cloth itself, vanished.

The *dayanchi*, who was well pleased with the dainty foods he had eaten, began pleading with the Archer to trade with him.

"Do please give me this Murza of yours with his magic cloth, my brave Archer," he begged. "You shall have something very fine in return."

"Oh, no," the Archer replied. "I would not trade Murza for anything. I need him myself."

---

* *Koumiss*–a drink of fermented mare's milk.–*Tr.*

But the *dayanchi* would not be put off and continued to plead all the night long with the Archer.

"Come, brave Archer," said he, "I will give you something even more wonderful than your Murza in exchange for him."

"What can you give me?" the Archer asked.

"I will show you," said the *dayanchi*, and he took out a *khadak*, a long silken kerchief, and told the Archer to come outside with him. The Archer did so, and the *dayanchi* waved the *khadak* and said:

"Appear, palace!"

In the same instant a magnificent palace, its roof nearly touching the sky, appeared before them. Its beauty was such as had never been seen; on the outside it was ornamented with silver and gold and studded with coral, pearls and precious stones, and inside, its appointments and wall decorations were quite dazzling—such richness and splendour was not to be found in the palaces of the mightiest khans.

Said the *dayanchi* to the Archer:

"You are young, brave Archer, and you will have need of the palace. As for me, all I want is something to please the palate. So take my *khadak*, my magic kerchief, and let me have Murza with his yellow-flowered cloth."

But plead as the *dayanchi* might, the Archer would not agree.

"No, no," said he, "I cannot give up my Murza."

But Murza whispered in his ear:

"Trade with him. The palace will be yours, and I will be yours, too, you will see."

And the Archer heeded Murza's words and agreed to trade with the *dayanchi*.

The *dayanchi* then waved his magic kerchief and said: "Vanish!" and at once the palace disappeared.

And the Archer took the kerchief from him and said: "Now Murza is yours."

And saying good-bye to the *dayanchi*, he went on his way.

He reached a mountain pass, skirted it and said to himself: "I acted rashly. I should not have made the exchange. Now I have this magnificent palace, but no Murza. Where is he and what is he doing now, I wonder?"

All of a sudden what did he hear but Murza's own voice, saying:

"Do not grieve, brave Archer, I am at your side. Never will I part with you!"

"What about the *dayanchi*?" the Archer asked.

"Let him pray," Murza replied. "I will not be a servant to him."

The Archer was overjoyed and went on. At times he would walk and at others he would run, so eager was he to get back home to his young and beautiful wife. On and on he went without stopping, never counting the passing days and nights, till at last he reached the sea.

"If I am to go all the way round the sea," said he to himself, "I shall have to travel for another month. But, perhaps, I shall meet some boatmen here."

He went along the seashore and what did he see but a large ship at anchor. There were many warriors on board, and they were all waiting to sail across. The Archer came close and said:

"I come from far, far away, brave warriors. Do me a kindness, take me with you to the opposite shore."

Said the commander of the warriors:

"That we will, come on board."

The Archer boarded the ship and set sail together with the warriors.

After a time the warriors grew hungry and sat down to eat. Said the Archer:

"Won't you give me something to eat too?"

"A fine way to behave!" the warriors cried. "We let you board our ship, and now you want us to feed you into the bargain! And what have we to gain from you? We are only allowed so much food to a man, we cannot share it with anyone."

Said the Archer:

"Your food is meted out to you, but mine is not. If I so desire, I can feed you all, and there will still be enough left for as many more."

The warriors were stung to the quick.

"Braggart! Liar!" they cried in angry tones. And they went and told their commander all about it.

The commander at once called the Archer and said to him:

"I hear you have been bragging that you can feed all my warriors at once?"

"I was only telling the truth," the Archer replied.

"If that is so, then do it, and we shall believe that you are honest and truthful. But should your words prove false, do not expect mercy. We shall tie a stone as big as an ox round your neck and throw you overboard."

"Very well," said the Archer, "I will prove to you that I spoke truly! Sit down, all of you, in two rows, but mind you leave a wide passage between."

The warriors did as the Archer asked; they seated themselves in two rows, one facing the other, and so many were they that the rows stetched from one end of the ship to the other.

"Come, Murza," the Archer said, "these warriors are hungry, feed them well!"

In the same instant, from one end of the ship to the other, in the passage between the rows, a yellow-flowered cloth unfolded, set with all kinds of foods and drinks and berries and fruits, everything, in short, to please the palate and cheer the heart.

The warriors ate and drank their fill, but the food and the drink did not diminish, and there still remained enough to feed as many more.

"Have you had enough?" the Archer asked.

"Yes!" the warriors cried.

"Good!" said the Archer. "Come, Murza, take it away!"

In the same instant everything vanished: the cloth and the platters, the jugs and the cups.

The warriors opened their mouths in astonishment.

"Never have we seen anything so wonderful," said they.

And they began to talk among themselves, trying to think how to get Murza and his magic cloth for themselves.

"Sell him to us," said they to the Archer.

"Oh, no," replied the Archer. "He is not for sale."

And no matter how hard they pleaded and how much gold they offered, they could not persuade the Archer to do as they asked.

"If you do not want to sell him," said they, "then let us trade. We will give you something no less wonderful in return."

"What can you give me?" the Archer asked. "Nothing can be more precious to me than my Murza. I need him more than anything."

The warriors brought out a gold stick, with one end thin and the other thick, showed it to the Archer and said:

"We will give you this stick. It is a magic stick. If you strike at the ground with the thick end, mounted warriors will appear without count or number, every man of them clad in shining armour and bearing a sword of steel; and if you strike at the ground with the thin end, archers will appear without count or number, each one armed with a bow and arrows."

Seeing the magic stick, Murza whispered in the Archer's ear:

"Trade with them, do, brave Archer. The stick will be yours, and I will be yours too."

And the Archer heeded his words and took the golden stick in exchange for Murza.

Soon afterwards they reached the opposite shore and left the ship, the warriors going off in one direction and the Archer in another.

He walked along and he said to himself:

"Where can my Murza be now?"

But Murza did not reply and did not appear.

The Archer walked on for another day and another night and then he said again:

"Where are you, Murza, my dear friend?"

But Murza did not reply and did not appear.

The Archer went on, but when another two days and two nights and passed, he again called to his friend, saying:

"Where are you, Murza? Answer me!"

But Murza did not reply and did not appear.

The Archer was quite overcome with grief.

"He has fooled me, after all," said he to himself. "I should never have traded with those warriors!"

The evening of the fifth day came, and the Archer said to himself:

"I think I shall call him one last time!" and he cried loudly:

"Answer me, Murza! Where are you?"

And all of a sudden what did he hear but Murza's own voice, saying:

"Do not grieve, brave Archer! Your Murza is here at your side. I came at midday."

The Archer was overjoyed. He sat down on the ground and said:

"I am half-dead with hunger. Let us eat quickly!"

At once the yellow-flowered cloth unfolded, set with foods of all kind. The Archer and Murza ate their fill and then went on. They walked a long time, and the days and the nights were as one to them, but at last, on the stroke of midnight, they arrived in the realm of Tsarkin Khan.

The Archer walked into his *kibitka* and roused his wife.

"Wake up!" said he. "I have come."

The wife was overjoyed and rose quickly and made up the fire.

"Are you in good health?" asked she.

And they fell to telling each other about how they had lived all the long days and about what had passed.

"How is the Khan faring?" asked the Archer. "Is he sick still?"

"From the very first day you left," the wife replied, "the Khan has been well. Three times already has he visited me to try and persuade me to become his wife. But each time he came I said to him: 'It is not fit for me to think of remarrying. My husband went to seek the remedy you asked for, and, for all I know, he may be alive. How can I marry you?' But the Khan kept repeating: 'No, your husband is dead. He died long ago.' So I said to him: 'Show me his bones if you want me to believe you. When I see them I shall know what answer to make.' At these words the Khan became very angry, and he ordered all my herds and all my belongings to be taken from me. Now there is nothing left to us but our empty *kibitka*."

When the Archer heard what his wife had to say he fell into a great passion.

"Let us go to the Khan!" cried he. "I will punish him for his treachery and lawless ways."

They came to the Khan's palace, and a little distance away from it the Archer halted, waved his magic kerchief and said:

"Let a palace appear on this spot!"

At once a great palace rose up, so tall that it reached to the clouds, and so rich and beautiful that the Khans's palace was as a poor hovel beside it.

The Archer and his wife entered the palace, and the Archer said:

"Come, Murza, we are hungry, feed us!"

They ate their fill, and then the Archer came out of the palace and struck the ground with the thin end of his golden stick. In the same instant men appeared without count or number, armed with bows and arrows. They took their stand at the palace doors and awaited the Archer's command.

Said the Archer:

"Let no one in until I awake and rise from bed."

In the morning, the servants of the Khan saw a huge and magnificent palace towering beside that of the Khan, and they did not know what to make of it.

"What miracle is this?" asked they. "Has the great God Burkhan set up this palace in the night or has it been built by the devil?"

And they ran to Tsarkin Khan to tell him about it.

Tsarkin Khan came out and looked at the palace and was so overcome with astonishment that he nearly lost his wits.

"What is this?" he asked. "Never in all my life, as far back as I can remember, have I seen or even heard of such a palace.

Who has built it and who lives in it? Go and bring him to me!"

Away went the Khan's envoys to fulfil his command.

They came to the Archer's palace and they asked of the two guards at the door, tall men both and stern-looking:

"Whose palace is this? Who lives in it? And who are you that guard it? Have you dropped from the sky or sprung up from the ground? Answer us at once!"

But the two guards in their turn asked in menacing tones:

"And who are you that ask us so many questions?"

"We are the envoys of the mighty Tsarkin Khan. He has commanded us to report to him all that we learn from you."

"Who is this Tsarkin Khan?" the guards asked. "We have never heard of him, nor do we desire to hear of him. We have our own Khan, and he is in his palace, sleeping. Be

251

off with you now, while you still have your heads on your shoulders!"

The envoys were frightened. They rushed to Tsarkin Khan and told him of all that they had seen and heard. But Tsarkin Khan flew into a rage and upbraided them in loud and angry tones.

"I did not send you there to talk with the guards," said he. "I sent you to bring me their lord and master."

And ordering the two envoys to be severely punished, he summoned two of his best warriors, great, tall men both, and said:

"Seize the owner of yonder palace and drag him here to me!"

The Khan's two warriors came to the palace and tried to open the doors, but the guards thrust them aside.

"Who are you? Stand back if you value your lives!" they cried.

Said Tsarkin Khan's two warriors:

"We were not sent to speak with you. We were sent to seize the owner of this palace and to deliver him to our Khan."

And they began trying to break their way into the palace again.

But the guards seized them and began thrashing and beating them.

"That Khan of yours is nothing to us!" they cried. "We neither know, nor wish to know him."

And having flogged the Khan's warriors, they drove them away.

Limping and groaning, the warriors dragged themselves into Tsarkin Khan's presence.

"The guards did not let us into the palace," they cried.

"We could not hold out against them. We have less than half their strength."

Hearing them, Tsarkin Khan called his *darkhans* to take counsel of them.

"Speak up and tell me what we should do," he said. "A powerful enemy has entrenched himself in yonder palace."

Said the *darkhans*:

"Send your host against him."

And Tsarkin Khan at once ordered his host to be mustered and brought before him.

"Let every man come who can so much as hold himself up on horseback!" said he. "And the sooner the better."

Tsarkin Khan's captains mustered his host and brought it before him. Thirty-three regiments surrounded the Archer's palace, in thirty-three rows they stood, and on Tsarkin Khan's command, his heralds called:

"Come ye out while the sun shines overhead and measure your strength with ours!"

The Archer heard the challenge, and opening his window, leaned out as far as his waist.

"Who are you and why have you gathered here?" he called.

And the warriors replied:

"We are the host of the mighty Tsarkin Khan."

Said the Archer:

"I am no enemy to Tsarkin Khan, nor am I his friend. I live in my own palace and do not war with him. But if Tsarkin Khan wishes to do battle, then let him say so openly, and fight him I will!"

"I wish to do battle!" cried Tsarkin Khan.

At this the Archer came out of his palace and struck the ground with the thick end of his golden stick. In the same instant there appeared so many mounted warriors that they could neither be counted nor taken in at a glance. Every warrior was clad in bright armour and each held his sword in his hand. The warriors lifted up their swords and cried:

"What is your command, Archer?"

"Do battle with the host of Tsarkin Khan!" the Archer said.

And the warriors moved forward and closed with the host of Tsarkin Khan.

Then the Archer struck the ground with the thin end of his golden stick, and archers appeared without count or number, armed with bows and arrows. They lifted up their bows and said:

"What is your command, Archer?"

"I command you to do battle with the host of Tsarkin Khan!" the Archer said.

And the archers moved in and gave support to the horsemen.

Tsarkin Khan's host wavered and fell back under the onslaught, and the Archer's host pressed on, smiting and slaying. The battle had begun in the morning, and by evening there was no one left to fight against. The Archer's warriors were about to seize Tsarkin Khan himself, but he leaped to the ground from his horse and with all the strength he had in him dashed for the Archer's palace, shouting:

"Mercy! Mercy! Spare me!"

Said the Archer to his men:

"Do not kill him, but bring him to me alive. I wish to speak to him."

The warriors seized Tsarkin Khan by his arms and legs and dragged him to the Archer, and Tsarkin Khan prostrated himself before him—in his fright he failed to recognise him—and begged him to have mercy on him and to spare his life.

The Archer burst out laughing.

"Never fear," said he, "I will not kill you. You wanted to fight, and I fought. Now I desire you to join me at table. Come, Murza, we are hungry, give us food and drink!"

At once the yellow-flowered cloth unfolded, the wonderful foods and drinks appeared, and the Archer began to regale the Khan, offering him now one dish and now another.

Said the Archer:

"I have heard that in your realm is an archer, young, handsome and strong and the bravest of the brave. Where is he? I wish to see him."

"That is not possible," Tsarkin Khan replied.

"Not possible? But why?" the Archer asked.

"Because he is dead."

"Is that true? Yet I have heard that he is alive and well."

"He went off No-One-Knows-Where to seek Ne-One-Knows-What," Tsarkin Khan explained. "And he should have been back long ago. Since he does not come, he must be dead."

"But who sent him No-One-Knows-Where and why?" the Archer asked.

"No one did. He went off of his own free will, for what reason I do not know," replied Tsarkin Khan.

At this the Archer became very angry.

"I said that I would spare your life, but so shameless a liar deserves to die," said he. "It was you that sent away the Archer. And all because you wanted to take his wife from him. At first you pretended to be ill and told him to bring you the milk of a tigress. And when he did, you sent him No-One-Knows-Where to seek No-One-Knows-What. Look at me closely, and if you are not completely blinded by fear, you will see that I am that very archer.... I was far, far away, No-One-Knows-Where, and I have brought back that which has no shape, no form and no place. I am alive and well. You did not succeed in your evil design. Now, in all justice, I ought to kill you."

Tsarkin Khan shook with fear and fell at the Archer's feet; he crawled on his knees before him and besought him to spare his life.

The Archer thrust the Khan aside with his foot and said:

"You have done many evil deeds, but I will not kill you. Yet will I not tolerate your presence here. Be off with you at once and keep far away from this realm, so that no one will ever see you more."

"I thank you for this favour," said Tsarkin Khan, and taking his family with him, left the land never to return.

As for the brave Archer, he and his young wife made their home in the selfsame nomad camp, and they lived for ever after in love and happiness.

A MOUNTAIN OF GEMS

A Turkmen Fairy-Tale

In a certain village there once lived an old widow who had one son, Mirali by name. They were very poor. The old woman combed wool and took in washing and in this way managed to earn enough to feed herself and her son.

When Mirali grew up, his mother said to him:

"I haven't the strength to work any more, my son. You must find yourself work of some kind to do, and so earn your keep."

"Very well," said Mirali, and off he went in search of a living. He went here, and he went there, but nowhere could he find anything to do.

After a time he came to the house of a certain *bai*.*

"Do you need a workman, *bai*?" Mirali asked.

"I do," the *bai* replied.

And he hired Mirali on the spot.

A day passed, and the *bai* did not ask his new workman to do anything at all. Another day passed, and the *bai* gave him no orders of any kind. A third day passed, and the *bai* seemed not so much as to notice him.

All this seemed very strange to Mirali who began to wonder why the *bai* had hired him.

So he went to him and asked:

"Shall I be getting any work to do, master?"

"Yes, yes," the *bai* replied, "tomorrow you will come with me."

The following day the *bai* ordered Mirali to slaughter a bull and to skin it, and this being done, to bring four large sacks and prepare two camels for a journey.

The bull's hide and the sacks were put on one of the camels, the *bai* climbed on to the other, and they started off on their way.

When they got to the foot of a distant mountain, the *bai* stopped the camels and ordered Mirali to take down the sacks and the bull's hide. Mirali did so, and the *bai* then told him to turn the bull's hide inside out and lie down on it. Mirali could not understand what this was for, but he dared not disobey and did as his master told him.

The *bai* rolled up the hide into a bundle, with Mirali inside it, strapped it tight and hid himself behind a rock.

* *Bai*—a rich, sometimes titled man in old Turkmenia.—*Tr.*

By and by two large birds of prey flew up, seized in their beaks the hide which had the fresh smell of meat about it and carried it off with them to the summit of an inaccessible mountain.

Here the birds began to peck and claw at the hide and to pull it in different directions. The hide tore, Mirali rolled out, and the birds, seeing him, were frightened and flew away, bearing the hide away with them.

Mirali got to his feet and began looking about him.

The *bai* saw him from below and shouted:

"What are you standing there for? Throw down to me the coloured stones that are lying at your feet!"

Mirali looked, and he saw that indeed a great number of precious stones were strewn about everywhere: there were diamonds and rubies and sapphires and emeralds and lumps of turquoise.... The gems were large and beautiful, and they sparkled in the sun.

Mirali began gathering the gems and throwing them down to the *bai*, who picked them up as fast as they fell and filled his two large sacks with them.

Mirali kept on working until a thought struck him that turned his blood cold.

"How shall I get down from here, master?" he called to the *bai*.

"Throw me more of the stones," the *bai* called back, "and I shall tell you how to get down from the mountain afterwards."

Mirali believed him and went on throwing down the gems.

When the sacks were filled to the top, the *bai* hoisted them on to the camels' backs.

"Ho there, my son!" called he with a laugh to Mirali. "Now you understand the kind of work I give my workmen to do. See how many of them are up there, on the mountain!"

And saying this, the *bai* rode away.

Mirali was left on the mountain all alone. He began looking for a way to climb down, but there were abysses and precipices on all sides and men's bones lay about everywhere. They were the bones of those who, like Mirali, had been the *bai*'s workmen.

Mirali was terrified.

Suddenly there came a rush of wings overhead, and before he could turn round, a huge eagle had pounced upon him. He was about to tear Mirali to pieces, but Mirali did not lose his presence of mind, and grasping the eagle's legs with both hands, held them in a tight grip. The eagle let out a cry, rose up into the air and began flying round and round, trying to shake off Mirali. At last, exhausted, it dropped to the ground, and when Mirali released his hold, flew away.

In this manner Mirali was saved from a terrible death.

He went to the market and began looking for work again. Suddenly he saw the *bai*, his former master, coming toward him.

"Do you need a workman, *bai*?" Mirali asked him.

Now it did not enter the *bai*'s head that any workman of his could have remained alive—it had never happened before —and mistaking Mirali for another, he hired him and took him home with him.

Soon after, the *bai* ordered Mirali to slaughter a bull and skin it, and this being done, told him to get ready two camels and bring four sacks.

They made their way to the foot of the same mountain, and, just as before, the *bai* told Mirali to lie down on the bull's hide and wrap himself up in it.

"Show me how it is done, for it is not quite clear to me," said Mirali.

"What is there to understand? Here is the way it's done," the *bai* replied, and he stretched himself out on the hide which had been turned inside out.

Mirali at once rolled the hide up into a bundle, with the *bai* inside it, strapped it tight and stepped away.

"Wait, my son," the *bai* cried. "What have you done to me!"

But at that moment two birds of prey flew up, seized the bull's hide and flew off with it to the mountain top. Once there, they began to tear at it with their beaks and claws, but seeing the *bai*, were frightened and flew away. The *bai* scrambled to his feet.

"Come, *bai*, do not waste time, throw down the gems to me, just as I did to you," Mirali called from below.

Only then did the *bai* recognise him, and be began trembling with fear and rage.

"How did you get down from the mountain?" he called to Mirali. "Answer me quickly!"

"Throw down more of the gems, and when I have enough, I'll tell you how to get down from the mountain," Mirali replied.

The *bai* then began throwing down the gems, and Mirali picked them up as fast as they fell. When the sacks were full, Mirali hoisted them on to the camels' backs.

"Come, *bai*, look around you," he called to him. "The bones of the men whom you drove to their death are strewn about everywhere. Why do you not ask them how to get down from the mountain? As for me, I am going home."

And turning the camels round, Mirali set off for his mother's house.

The *bai* rushed about on the mountain top, shouting threats and pleas, but all in vain, for who was there to hear him?!

THE CLEVER BROTHERS

An Uzbek Fairy-Tale

There once lived a poor man who had three sons. He would often say to his sons:

"My children! We have no herds and no gold, we have nothing. Therefore you must try to amass treasures of another kind: you must learn to understand more and to know more. Let nothing escape your notice. Instead of large herds you will have a keen mind, and instead of gold—quick wits. With such riches you will never be at a loss and will be no worse off than others."

A long time passed by and a little time, and the old man died. The brothers got together, talked things over and then said:

"There is nothing for us to do here. Let us travel and see the world. If need be, we can always hire ourselves out as shepherds or farm hands. We shan't starve, no matter where we are."

So they got ready and set off on their way.

They crossed desolate valleys and passed over tall mountains, and they walked for forty long days.

They had now eaten all they had with them and were tired and footsore, and still the end of the road was not in sight. They stopped to rest and then moved on again.

At last, ahead there loomed up trees, towers and houses—a large town lay before them.

The brothers were overjoyed and walked faster.

"The worst lies behind, and the best ahead of us," said they.

They were nearing the town when the eldest brother suddenly stopped, looked at the ground and said:

"A large camel passed here a short time ago."

They walked on a little way, and the middle brother stopped, and looking to both sides of the road, said:

"The camel was blind in one eye."

They walked on further, and the younger brother said:

"A woman and a little child were riding on the camel."

"True," said the two elder brothers, and the three moved on again.

After a time they were overtaken by a man on horseback. The eldest of the brothers looked at him and asked:

"Aren't you looking for something you have lost, horseman?"

The horseman reined in his horse.

"Yes, I am," he replied.

"Is it a camel you have lost?" the eldest brother asked.

"Yes, it is."

"A large camel?"

"Yes."

"And blind in the left eye?" put in the middle brother.

"Yes."

"And was not a woman with a little child riding on it?" the youngest brother asked.

The horseman looked at the brothers suspiciously and said:

"Ah, so it's you that have my camel! Speak up and tell me what you have done with it."

"We have never even seen your camel," the brothers replied.

"How do you know so much about it, then?"

"We know how to use our eyes and to put two and two together," the brothers replied. "Make haste and ride in that direction, and you will find your camel."

"No," said the owner of the camel, "I will not go in that direction. You have my camel, and you must give it back to me."

"We have not so much as laid eyes on your camel," the brothers exclaimed.

But the horseman would not listen to them. He pulled out his sword, and brandishing it wildly, ordered the brothers to walk ahead of him. In this way he marched them straight to the palace of the Padishah, the ruler of the land. He put the brothers in the charge of guards and himself went straight to the Padishah.

"I was driving my herds to the mountains," said he, "and my wife and little son followed me on a large camel which is blind in one eye. Somehow they dropped behind, missed the road and lost their way. I went to look for them and overtook three men who were travelling on foot. I am convinced that these men stole my camel, and I greatly fear that they have killed my wife and son."

"What makes you think so?" asked the Padishah, when the man had finished speaking.

"Well, these men told me, without my saying a word about it, that the camel was large and blind in one eye and that a woman with a child was riding on it."

The Padishah thought for a moment.

"If, as you say, you told them nothing, and yet they were able to describe your camel so well," said he, "then they must indeed have stolen it. Go bring the thieves here."

The owner of the camel went out and presently returned with the three brothers.

"Answer me, thieves!" cried the Padishah in threatening tones. "Answer me! What have you done with this man's camel?"

"We are not thieves and have never seen his camel," the brothers replied.

Said the Padishah:

"You described his camel to him without its owner telling you anything about it. How dare you deny you stole it!"

"There is nothing surprising about that, O Padishah!" the brothers replied. "We are accustomed from childhood to let nothing escape our notice. We spent much time learning to observe and meditate. That is why we could tell what the camel was like without ever having seen it."

The Padishah laughed.

"Is it possible to know so much about something one has never seen?" he asked.

"It is," the brothers replied.

"Well, well, we shall see if you are telling the truth."

And the Padishah called his vizier and whispered something in his ear.

The vizier at once left the palace, but was soon back again with two servants bearing a large chest on a barrow.

Carefully putting down the chest at the door where the Padishah could see it, they moved aside. The brothers stood watching them from a distance. They took careful note of where the chest had been brought from, the manner in which it was carried and the way it was set down on the floor.

"Come, thieves, tell us what is in that chest," demanded the Padishah.

"We have already told you, O Padishah, that we are not thieves," said the eldest brother. "But I can tell you what is in that chest, if you wish. The chest contains a small round object."

"A pomegranate," the middle brother put in.

"Yes, and it is not quite ripe," the youngest brother added.

Hearing them, the Padishah ordered the chest to be brought nearer, which the servants did not fail immediately to do. The Padishah then commanded them to open the chest, and this being done, he looked inside it. What was his surprise when he saw lying in the chest one unripe pomegranate! Amazed, the Padishah took out the pomegranate and showed it to all who were present. Then, turning to the owner of the lost camel, he said:

"These men have proved that they are not thieves. They are indeed clever. Go and look for your camel elsewhere."

All who were with the Padishah marvelled at the brothers' cleverness, but none more than the Padishah himself. He commanded delicacies of all kinds to be brought in and began regaling the brothers.

"No blame attaches to you," said he. "You are free to go where you will. But first you must tell me about everything in the order it happened. How did you know that the man had lost his camel and how could you tell what the camel was like?"

Said the eldest brother:

"The large tracks it left in the dust told me that a very big camel had passed there. When I saw that the man who overtook us on the road kept looking on all sides of him, I knew at once what he was searching for."

"Well done!" said the Padishah. "Now which of you told the man that the camel was blind in its left eye?"

The middle brother rose to his feet.

"I did," said he.

"How did you know that the camel was blind in its left eye? Blindness does not leave tracks on the road."

"I gathered it was so because the grass had all been nibbled on the right side of the road, but untouched on the left side," the middle brother replied.

"Good for you!" said the Padishah. "And which of you guessed that a woman and a child were riding on the camel?"

"I did," the youngest brother replied. "I observed a spot where the camel had got down on its knees, and I saw the mark of a woman's boots on the sand close by. Other, smaller tracks told me that the woman had a child with her."

"That is well and you have spoken truly," said the Padishah. "But how did you find out that the chest contained one unripe pomegranate? That is something I cannot understand at all."

Said the eldest brother:

"It was evident from the way the two servants carried in the chest that it was not at all heavy. As they were putting it down on the floor I heard inside it a clattering sound as of some round object, not very large, rolling from one end to the other."

Said the middle brother:

"And I surmised that since the chest had been brought in from the garden and contained a small round object, that object must be a pomegranate. For there are many pomegranate trees growing by your palace."

"Well done!" said the Padishah, and he turned to the youngest brother.

"But how could you tell that the pomegranate was not ripe?" he asked him.

"Now is the time of year," the youngest brother replied, "when all the pomegranates are still green. You can see that for yourself."

And he pointed to the open window.

The Padishah looked out and saw that the pomegranate trees in his garden were covered with green fruit.

The Padishah could not but marvel at the brothers' unusual powers of observation and their quick wits.

"You may not be rich in money and worldly goods, but you are indeed rich in wisdom!" exclaimed he.

THE GREEDY *KAZI**

A Tajik Fairy-Tale

Believe it or not, there once lived a poor man who worked very, very hard, yet remained just as poor as ever he was. So he decided to leave his native parts and go to a distant town to earn his living. He said good-bye to his family and set off.

Whether he was long on his way or not no one knows, but at last he reached the town he was bound for and at once began going from house to house, looking for work. He did anything that came his way, never refusing any kind of work, however hard. Whatever the work offered, he would set about it willingly, and always did everything thoroughly and well.

* *Kazi*–judge.–*Tr.*

As for the money he earned, he spent only as much as he needed to buy food, and he put away the rest in a small bag, saying to himself:

"I will work a little more, save up more money and then go back to my family."

In this way he toiled unsparingly for several years and was able to put aside a whole thousand *tanga*. And since that, for a poor man, is a large sum of money, he began brooding about it and worrying, saying to himself:

"What if through some mischance my money is lost? . . . To carry it on me is folly, for I may lose it; also, a thief may learn about it and will then kill and rob me. Nor will it do to hide the money at my lodgings, for there, too, it may disappear. Someone may see me hiding it, there are many sly and evil people in the world; I shall be deprived of my money and shall have to return empty-handed to my family. . . ."

Thus his thoughts ran and he did not know what to do. But at last he decided to give his thousand *tanga* to the *kazi* to keep for him

"They say he is an honest, pious man," said he to himself. "My money will be safe with him. I will take it back when I decide to go home to my people."

Thus the poor man reasoned, and it was with this in mind that he went to see the *kazi*. The *kazi* received him and asked him what he wanted.

"I should like to give you my money to keep for me, O most honourable *kazi*; I cannot think of a safer place. Please keep it for me while I am living and working in this town."

The *kazi* took the bag of money and said gravely:

"I shall do as you ask with the greatest pleasure. You have

spoken truly. You could not have found a safer place to keep your money."

The poor man left, and the *kazi* counted the money and put it away in a large chest.

Some time passed, and the owner of the money prepared to go back to his family. He came to the *kazi* and said to him:

"Give me back my money, most honourable *kazi*, for tomorrow I am leaving this town."

The *kazi* looked at him.

"What money do you mean?" he asked.

"The thousand *tanga* that I gave you to keep for me, most honourable *kazi*."

"You must be mad!" the *kazi* shouted. "When did you ever give me any money? What an idea, indeed! One thousand *tanga*! Why, seven generations of your ancestors never even laid eyes on so much as a hundred *tanga*! Where would you get a whole thousand?"

The poor man tried to remind the *kazi* when it was he had brought him the money and what had been said between them. But the *kazi* would not listen to him. He stamped his feet and called for his servants.

"This man is a swindler!" he shouted. "Beat him, kick him, turn him out of my house!"

The *kazi*'s servants fell upon the poor man, beat him cruelly and threw him out of the house.

The poor man stumbled off down the street with tears and lamentations.

"All my hard work has been in vain! My money is lost!" he kept repeating sorrowfully. "The greedy *kazi* has taken it all!"

Just then a woman passed by. Hearing the poor man's lamentations, she said to him reproachfully:

"What has happened, my brother? Why are you, a grown-up man with a beard and a turban, crying like a child?"

Said the poor man sadly:

"O my sister, if only you knew how I have been tricked! I have been working beyond my strength for years, I never ate my fill or had enough sleep, and with the greatest difficulty I managed to save a thousand *tanga.* Now I have lost them. If you knew how it happened, you would not reproach me."

"Tell me about it," said the woman.

The poor man told her how he had been robbed of the money.

"And people say that the *kazi* is honest and pious!" he added bitterly.

The woman listened to his story with sympathy.

"Do not be sad, not all is lost," said she. "Come with me, I will think of something."

They went to her house, and the woman took a large box that stood there and said to her little son:

"I am going to the *kazi* with this man. Follow us at a distance but do not keep too close. Try not to be seen by anyone. When we reach the *kazi*'s house, hide and wait until the *kazi* gives this man his money. When you see the *kazi* stretch out his hands to take this box, run up and say: 'Father has come back with his camels and goods.'"

"Very well, I will do as you say," said the boy.

The woman placed the box on her head, and she and the poor man went to the *kazi*'s house, the woman's son following them at a distance.

They reached the *kazi*'s house, and the woman said to the poor man:

"I will go in first, and you come in after me."

She entered the house, and the *kazi* looked at her and at the large box on her head and said:

"What business brings you here, my sister?"

Said the woman:

"Perhaps you have heard of me, O most honourable *kazi*? I am the wife of Rahim, the rich merchant. My husband has taken his caravan to distant lands, and no one knows when he will return. For many nights now I have been unable to sleep peacefully. Thieves are prowling round our house, and I am sure they plan to rob us. This box contains all the money we have, as well as all our gold and precious stones. It was with difficulty that I carried it here, it is so heavy. I should like you to keep it safe for me. When my husband returns, he will come for it himself."

The *kazi* lifted the box and when he felt how heavy it was his hands shook with greed.

"There are at least forty or fifty thousand *tanga* in money in this box," he thought, "and many precious stones besides. I have heard this Rahim is a very rich merchant...." And turning to the woman he said: "Very well, my sister, I shall keep your treasures for you. They will be safe with me, you may be sure. And you will get everything back, to the last *tanga*."

But the woman took the box from the *kazi*'s hands.

"Will I truly get all of it back?" said she.

"Do not doubt it, my sister!" the *kazi* exclaimed. "All the the people in the town know of my honesty and piety."

At that moment the poor man came in. The *kazi* saw him and was overjoyed.

"Heaven itself has brought this man here," said he to himself. "There could be no better opportunity of proving my honesty to this woman. I shall give back to that beggar his thousand *tanga* and get a box full of money and jewels in return. It is worth it, ha-ha!"

And the *kazi* turned to the woman, saying:

"I repeat to you, my sister, that there is no more safe or dependable place than the house of the *kazi*. Your box will be far safer here than if you keep it in your own house. At any time, when your husband returns or whenever you yourself want it, you may have your box back."

The *kazi*'s servants and all who were present in his reception room nodded their heads as if to say that the *kazi* was indeed speaking the truth and that his every word could be trusted.

And the *kazi*, pretending to have only just noticed the poor man's presence, exclaimed:

"Why, here is the man who gave me all his savings, one thousand *tanga,* to keep! He came to me this morning and demanded his money. But I did not recognise him, I mistook him for a thief and refused to give it back. If someone who knows him will vouch for him I shall give him his money at once."

Said the woman:

"O most honourable *kazi*, we have known this poor man for almost two years. He came to this town from afar and he has been working very hard ever since. He worked at our house, too, for a time. Believe me when I tell you that he has more than earned his money, for never was there a more hard-working man. It is not for nothing that his hands are calloused."

The *kazi* exclaimed with the blandest of smiles:

"What, you know this man! Then, there's no need for delay. Come to me, my brother, and take your thousand *tanga*. Take them at once."

And the *kazi* reached into his chest, took out some money, and counting out a thousand *tanga*, presented them ceremoniously to their owner.

"Well, my sister, now you have seen for yourself how safe other people's money is with me and that I can be trusted to return it to its owners," said the *kazi* hurriedly. "Leave your box here and go home in peace."

And he stretched out his hands for the box.

At that moment the woman's son ran in from the street.

"Mother!" he called. "Come home quickly! Father has come back with his camels and goods and is waiting for you."

"There! Since my husband has returned, I need no longer fear thieves," said the woman with a laugh. "He will be able to look after our treasures without the help of the honourable *kazi*."

And with these words the woman took her box, placed it on her head and left the *kazi*'s house in the company of the poor man.

"One must never despair, my brother," said she. "Remember that there is no swindler or knave alive whose scurvy tricks work every time. Go back to your family and live in peace. You have wandered in alien parts long enough. Spend your hard-earned money and enjoy it."

And taking leave of one another, they parted.

As for the *kazi*, now that he was left alone, he flew into a terrible rage. He tugged at his beard, stamped his feet and was so annoyed and distressed that he did not know what to do with himself.

"Unhappy man that I am!" he said repeatedly in grievous tones. "What a terrible disaster! May the merchant Rahim be cursed! Why couldn't he have arrived an hour later, just one little hour! It would all have been over and done with by then, the box of treasures would have been mine. My riches would have multiplied. My large chest would have been filled to the top. I shall never get over it, never! Woe is me! Woe is me!"

BOROLDOI-MERGEN AND HIS BRAVE SON

A Fairy-Tale from the Altai

In olden days, in times gone by, there lived in the blue Altai Mountains a man-eating ogre named Almys.

Almys had long black whiskers which he wore thrown over his shoulders, like reins. His beard reached down to his knees. His eyes were bloodshot. His teeth were large and sharp. Instead of nails he had sharp claws on his fingers. And his whole body was covered with thick hair.

Almys was fierce, bloodthirsty and merciless. He attacked the hunters in the forest and the women in the villages, and he spared neither the old people nor the little children. He would pounce upon his victims and eat them up.

So strong and so cunning was Almys that no one dared to fight him. As soon as they saw Almys the people ran off and tried to hide. They did not know what else to do.

"Almys is stronger and more cunning than we," said they. "No one can get the better of him, no one can outwit him. We must learn to endure and keep silent."

And so they endured and were silent.

In one of the villages there lived a hunter, Boroldoi-Mergen by name. He was strong, he was brave and he was clever. Some people might go out hunting and return empty-handed. Not so Boroldoi-Mergen. He would always come back with a full bag: he would bring foxes and sables and ermines and squirrels. He had roamed all the forests and all the mountains. No beast ever touched him, nor did he ever come to harm, for he had a keen mind, a sharp eye and a strong arm.

One day Almys came down from the mountains to Boroldoi-Mergen's village. The terrified people began rushing hither and thither, not knowing where to hide. And Almys caught one of the children and went back to the mountains.

While he was near, the villagers dared not speak except in a whisper. But when he had gone they began talking and weeping loudly.

"Whose child will the ogre carry off next?" the mothers cried, sobbing, while the children whimpered and the men frowned and were silent.

Then Boroldoi-Mergen spoke up and said:

"It is useless to shed tears or to try to hide. We must kill Almys, then only shall we live without fear."

And the men replied:

"How can we worst Almys or rid ourselves of him? We are not birds to soar up to the sky, nor are we fish to hide in the water. We are doomed to die from the accursed ogre's claws and fangs."

Boroldoi-Mergen felt bitterly sad and sick at heart. He looked at his son, and he said to himself:

"My son did not come into this world in order that Almys might tear him with his sharp teeth. Nor was it for that that all the other children were born. Almys must be killed and the mothers' grief ended."

But how was this to be done?

To challenge Almys to battle was out of the question: Almys was strong enough to destroy them all, to say nothing of one man. Besides, the villagers would refuse to fight him. Almys had frightened and cowed them, he had deprived them of courage and spirit. To outwit Almys, too, was impossible: he was always wary of danger, always quick to see if something was amiss.

Boroldoi-Mergen gave himself no peace for thinking about how to rid the people of Almys. He thought and thought, he thought a long, long time until at last he knew what to do.

But what that was he told no one.

He took his strongest bow and his sharpest arrows, and he asked of his son:

"Have you courage in your heart?"

"I have!" the boy replied.

"And have you pity for the people in your heart?"

"I have!"

"Then come with me. Our way will be long, and our errand fearful. But go we must. Is there anything you wish to ask me?"

But the boy shook his head, and the hunter and his son set off silently together, making for the mountains which were known to be the haunt of Almys.

They passed through a dense forest, climbed rocky slopes, walked on without so much as a footpath to guide them and at last reached an open glade.

A tall tree-stump stood there and beside it grew some bushes and trees. Not a beast, not a bird was anywhere in sight.

Boroldoi-Mergen stopped, took off his hunting garb and dressed the tree-stump in it. His son watched him in silence and asked no questions. The father made up a fire near the stump, and still the boy watched and said nothing.

Said the hunter to his son:

"Sit here, by the fire, and no matter what happens, do not run away."

"I won't."

"That which will occur will strike terror into you."

"It won't."

"Well, then, sit down and wait."

The boy sat down by the fire, and the father took his bow and arrows and hid himself in the bushes. Except for the two of them, there was no one about, and it was quiet and still.

Thus they sat for a long time.

Suddenly there came a crackle of branches and a snapping of twigs, and Almys himself stepped out from the trees. His black whiskers hung over his shoulders, his eyes were bloodshot, and he was gnashing his sharp teeth. When he saw the boy by the fire, he roared out in glee:

"I was on my way to the village for meat, and here is the meat waiting for me!"

Then he glanced at the tree-stump, and taking it for a hunter, said with a laugh:

"Well, hunter, watch me eat up your son! You won't dare to defend him."

And with these words Almys rushed to the fire.

His beard streamed in the wind as he ran, and the flaps of his long fur coat flew open. Almys tried to seize the boy, but the boy ran behind the stump. He ran after him, but the boy kept running round and round the stump, and the ogre could not catch him.

Now Boroldoi-Mergen took aim, he shot an arrow and it hit Almys in the middle of the chest. Almys roared out in pain. So loud were his cries that the trees bent from the noise, and the rocks cracked and rolled down the mountains.

And Boroldoi-Mergen kept shooting one arrow after another at the monster.

Almys flew into a rage and rushed at the tree-stump which was dressed in the hunter's garb. He began gnawing and biting at it, but all of a sudden down he crashed to the ground. Boroldoi-Mergen went up to him and saw that Almys was dead.

Boroldoi-Mergen did not ask his son whether he had been frightened or not. Only one word did he say to him:

"Come!"

And then the two set off for their village.

When they reached the village, Boroldoi-Mergen said to the people:

"Our children will grow up in peace. Their mothers will live without fear. Almys is dead, he has been killed."

"Who killed him?" the people asked.

"I did."

"Why did you take your little son with you?"

"He served as bait for Almys."

"But could not Almys have torn him to bits?"

"That he could."

And without another word Boroldoi-Mergen entered his house.

So it was that the people of the blue Altai Mountains were freed from their old and cruel enemy.

WHICH IS THE BIGGEST?

A Kirghiz Fairy-Tale

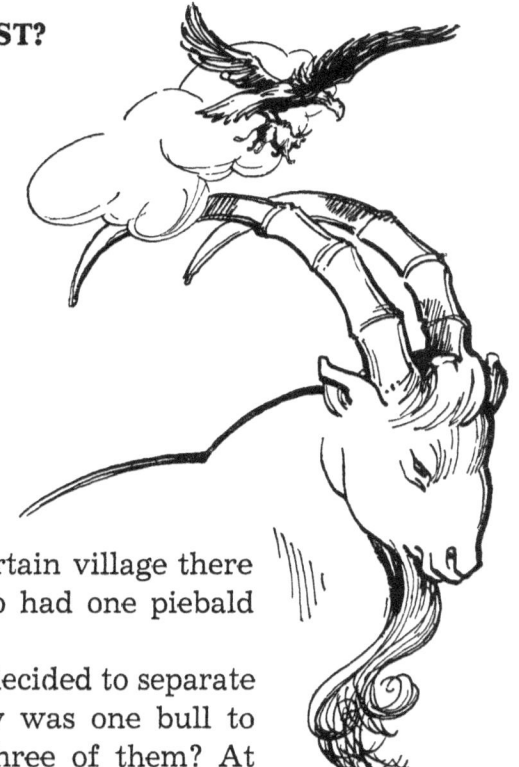

Long, long ago in a certain village there lived three brothers who had one piebald bull between them.

One day the brothers decided to separate and live apart. But how was one bull to be divided among the three of them? At first they thought of selling him, but found no one in the neighbourhood rich enough to buy him. Then they thought of slaughtering the bull and dividing the meat, but this they could not do, for they were sorry for the bull. And as to his being given to one of them—they could not agree to that.

And so they decided to go to a wise man that he might settle the matter for them.

"As the wise man decrees, so shall we do," said they, and they set off with the bull for the wise man's village. The eldest brother walked by the bull's head, the middle brother by the bull's side, and the youngest brother came behind the bull, driving him on with a stick.

At dawn they were overtaken by a man on horseback who greeted the youngest brother and asked him where he was driving the bull. The youngest brother told him all about everything, saying:

"We are taking the bull to a wise man who is going to settle the matter for us. We shall follow his advice."

And he added, as he bade the horseman good-bye:

"You will soon overtake my middle brother. He is walking by the bull's side. Give him my regards and tell him to make sure and urge on the bull. We want to get to the wise man's village before nightfall."

"Very well," said the horseman, and putting his horse into a trot, he rode away.

At noon he caught up with the middle brother who was walking by the side of the piebald bull.

He greeted him and said:

"Your younger brother sends you his best regards and asks you to make sure and urge on the bull if you want to get to where you are going before dark."

The middle brother thanked the horseman and said:

"When you ride up to the bull's head, give my regards to my elder brother and ask him to urge the bull on. We want to reach the wise man's village as soon as we can."

The horseman rode on, and it was evening by the time he reached the bull's head and passed on to the eldest brother the greetings and requests of the two younger brothers.

"There is nothing I can do," said the eldest brother. "It is already dusk. We'll have to stop driving the bull and spend the night by the wayside."

And he slowed his steps.

But the horseman did not stop and rode on.

The brothers spent the night in the steppe, and on the following morning started out again, driving their bull on. Then, suddenly, the most terrible thing happened. A huge eagle swooped down from the sky, seized the bull in its claws, lifted him up to the clouds and flew away.

The brothers grieved and sorrowed for a time, and then returned home, empty-handed.

Meanwhile the eagle flew on in the sky with the bull in its claws. Soon it spied, on a pasture below, a flock of goats and among them one which had the longest of long horns. The eagle swooped down, perched on the goat's horns and began pecking at the bull and strewing his bones all round it.

All of a sudden it began raining hard, and the goatherd and his flock of goats took shelter from the rain underneath the selfsame goat's beard.

Suddenly the goatherd felt a sharp pain in his left eye.

"A mote must have got into my eye," he thought.

Towards evening the goatherd drove his flock to the village. The pain in his eye had grown worse, and he cried out in pleading tones:

"Call in the doctors, villagers! Let them sail in my eye in forty boats and find the mote. Not a moment of peace does it give me."

And the villagers went and found forty doctors and said to them:

"Set you sail in the eye of our goatherd. Find the mote and put an end to his pain. Only see that you don't injure the eye."

The forty doctors in their forty boats set sail in the goatherd's eye, and they found the mote which was not really a mote, but the bull's bladebone; it had entered the goatherd's eye while he was sheltering from the rain under the goat's beard.

After that the goatherd's eye stopped hurting him, the doctors all went home, and the bull's bladebone was taken far out beyond the village and thrown away.

Soon after, some nomads were passing the place where the bladebone lay. Night was approaching, and the elders spoke among themselves and decided to make a halt and build a fire.

"This salt-marsh is the best and safest place we can find to spend the night," said they.

But when they were all settled and making ready for sleep, suddenly the ground began trembling and quaking. The nomads were frightened, and hurriedly piling their belongings on to their carts, hitched up their horses and moved off in haste.

Only when morning came did they recover from their fright and set up their camp. After that the elders sent forty horsemen to the site of the earthquake to discover what had happened there.

The forty horsemen soon arrived, and they saw that what at night they had taken for a salt-marsh was really a huge bone—the bladebone of a bull—at which a fox was gnawing even as they watched.

"So that is what made the earth tremble!" the horsemen cried. They took aim, shot their arrows and killed the fox.

After that they fell to and skinned it. But they only succeeded in skinning one side and had to leave the other unflayed, for hard as they tried, they could not turn the fox over.

The horsemen returned to their camp and told the elders all about it, and the elders began thinking what to do.

Just then a young woman came up to them and said:

"Please give me the piece of foxskin your horsemen have brought, to make a cap for my new-born baby."

"Very well," the elders said, "you can have it."

The woman measured her baby's head and began cutting a cap for him out of the foxskin. But she soon saw that there was only enough fur to make half a cap. So she went to the elders again and asked them to give her the second half of the foxskin.

Then the forty horsemen confessed that they had not been able to turn the fox over and skin its other side.

"If you can't make your baby a cap from one half of the foxskin," said they to the woman, "then you had better go and skin the fox's other side yourself."

The woman took her baby and went to where they had left the fox. With no effort at all, she turned the fox over, skinned its other side and made her baby a cap from the two halves of the skin.

Now here is something we wish to ask you: which, do you think, was the biggest—

Was it the bull?

Don't forget it took a man on horseback a whole day to ride from its tail to its head.

Was it the eagle?

Don't forget that it carried the bull with it to the sky.

Was it the goat?

Don't forget that it was on its horns that the eagle perched and pecked at the bull.

Was it the goatherd?

Don't forget that in his eye forty doctors sailed in forty boats.

Was it the fox?

Don't forget that it started an earthquake by gnawing at the bull's bladebone.

Was it the baby?

Don't forget that it was as much as could be done to make it a cap from the whole of the fox's skin.

Or was it the woman who had such a giant for a baby?

Think now, think hard, and, perhaps, you will be able to tell us.

ALDAR-KOSE AND SHIGAI-BAI

A Kazakh Fairy-Tale

In times gone by there lived in the steppeland a poor man named Aldar-Kose. Except for one horse, he had nothing to his name, but he was very clever and always had a whole store of tricks and jokes up his sleeve.

Now in the very same steppe there also lived a rich man by the name of Shigai-bai. Shigai-bai was very stingy. In fact, he was even more stingy than he was wealthy. Such was his niggardliness that he would not offer a guest so much as a slice of bread or a drink of water.

One day the clever, cunning Aldar-Kose decided to teach this same Shigai-bai a lesson.

He mounted his horse and went to pay Shigai-bai a visit. When his friends and neighbours learned where Aldar-Kose was going, they burst out laughing.

"Just you wait, Aldar-Kose," said they, "Shigai-bai will feast you royally. You will have your fill of fat mutton and of the choicest *airan**."

* *Airan*–a drink made of fermented milk.*–Tr.*

"Never you mind," Aldar-Kose replied, "we shall see."

He rode over the steppe for many days, looking for Shigai-bai's *yurta*, but wherever he went he was told:

"Do not look for Shigai-bai here. He has gone far off somewhere, away from the rest of us."

There was nothing to be done but for Aldar-Kose to ride on and on. At long last he saw a solitary *yurta* standing in the steppe, thick rushes growing all round it.

"It is not for nothing that Shigai-bai has settled amid the rushes," Aldar-Kose told himself.

And, in truth, he was right; for this was done in order that the master of the house and his family might know beforehand if a stranger were near. The rustling of the rushes warned them of anyone's approach, and then they would try to hide all the food in the house so as not to treat the visitor.

This ruse was at once divined by the quick-witted Aldar-Kose, and he began to think of a way of passing noiselessly through the rushes and getting to Shigai-bai's *yurta* without being heard.

But think as he would, he could think of no such way. Then he hit on a cunning plan.

Leading his horse aside, he began collecting small stones and pebbles, and did not stop until he had a good many. After that he waited till it grew dark and then began throwing the stones one at a time into the growth of rushes.

He threw one stone, and the rushes swayed and rustled. Shigai-bai rushed out of the *yurta*. He looked round him and listened for a moment.

"Who is there?" he called.

No one answered, and Shigai-bai went back into his *yurta*.

Then Aldar-Kose threw another stone. The rushes rustled as before, and Shigai-bai darted out of the *yurta* again. He looked to all sides of him, but saw no one.

"It must be the wind swaying the rushes," said Shigai-bai to himself, and he stopped running out of the *yurta*.

That was what Aldar-Kose was waiting for. He took his horse by the reins and began making his way stealthily through the rushes to the miser's *yurta*. He would take a step and stop and wait a while, take another and then stop and wait again.

In this way he succeeded in reaching the door of the *yurta*.

He lifted the hanging of thick felt and looked in. The *yurta* was crammed with all sorts of things: everywhere were rugs, and cushions, and heavy plated chests piled one on top of another. And in the middle of the floor, by the fire, sat Shigai-bai with his family. Mutton was boiling in a large pot hanging over the fire and Shigai-bai was watching it and tasting it now and again to see if it was cooked. At the same time he was stuffing a skin with minced meat, preparing a sausage. Shigai-bai's wife was kneading dough, his daughter was plucking a goose, and his workman was singeing a sheep's head over the fire.

At that moment Aldar-Kose suddenly entered.

"Good evening," he said.

The same instant Shigai-bai banged shut the lid of the pot and plumped down on top of the sausage, his wife seated herself on the dough, his daughter covered the goose with the hem of her skirt, and his workman hid the singed sheep's head behind his back.

Shigai-bai greeted Aldar-Kose and then he said to him:

"Well, what is the news from the steppe?"

Said Aldar-Kose:

"There is so much that is interesting and so much that is curious in the steppe that it would take too long to tell you about it."

"If you cannot tell me everything, at least tell me something."

"Well, as I was riding to your *yurta* I saw a great, fat snake crawling along; indeed, it was even bigger than the sausage you sat down on when I entered."

Shigai-bai made a wry face, but said nothing, and Aldar-Kose went on.

"Will you believe me, bai," he said, "if I tell you that this snake had a head as large and black as the sheep's head that your workman was just now singeing over the fire and hid behind his back?"

Shigai-bai made a wry face again, but said nothing, and the cunning Aldar-Kose went on with his story:

"This snake was crawling along and hissing like the pot in which your mutton is cooking. I jumped off my horse, seized a heavy stone and struck at the snake with all my strength. Its head was squashed and it looked like the rolled dough on which your wife is sitting. Such are the wonders I saw in the steppe. If I have lied may I meet the same fate as the goose your daughter has just plucked."

Shigai-bai winced, so vexed was he, but not a word did he say, nor did he offer any of the food to Aldar-Kose.

Aldar-Kose and Shigai-bai sat talking till late, and the mutton kept boiling and sizzling in the pot, a delicious odour filling the *yurta*.

Aldar-Kose had been long on the way, he was hungry, and he kept glancing at the pot, his mouth watering. Shigai-bai noticed it and said:

"Boil, my pot, boil for half a year!"

At this, Aldar-Kose quickly took off his boots, lay down, yawned and said:

"Rest, my boots, rest for two years!"

Shigai-bai, seeing that his guest did not intend to leave, decided to go to bed himself without his supper.

Everyone now stretched himself out on his rug, leaving the pot of mutton on the tripod.

"As soon as Aldar-Kose falls asleep," Shigai-bai told himself, "I'll wake up the family, and we'll have some mutton."

"As soon as that miser Shigai-bai falls asleep," Aldar-Kose told himself, "I'll eat my fill. Why should I go hungry when the mutton in the pot is all cooked!"

Shigai-bai was the first of the two to fall asleep. He lay there for a time, and then his eyes closed, and his snores filled the *yurta*.

Aldar-Kose rose, took the mutton out of the pot, ate it up and then threw Shigai-bai's old boots into the pot. After that he closed the pot, lay down again and waited to see what would happen.

After a time Shigai-bai woke up, listened a moment, looked at Aldar-Kose, and believing him to be asleep, began cautiously to wake his wife and daughter.

"Wake up, wake up now!" he said. "We shall have some mutton while Aldar-Kose sleeps."

Shigai-bai removed the lid, took out his boots and cut them

up with his knife. They began to eat, they chewed and chewed, but they could not bite through the pieces. What was wrong, why was the meat so tough?

"It's all that good-for-nothing Aldar-Kose's fault," said Shigai-bai to his wife. "It's because of him that the mutton's grown so tough. But never mind. When he clears out of here, we'll cook it till it becomes soft and then eat it. And now take the pieces and put them back in the pot."

Shigai-bai's wife gathered up the pieces of leather and put them in the pot. After that Shigai-bai ordered her to make up the fire and bake him some flat-cakes out of yesterday's dough.

When the flat-cakes were baked, Shigai-bai thrust them hurriedly into his robes without waiting for them to cool and went out into the steppe to take a look at his herds.

No sooner had the miser left the *yurta* than he was followed by Aldar-Kose who ran up to him and said:

"Ah, Shigai-bai, what a good thing it is that I woke up, or I would have had to leave without saying good-bye to you. I am going home today."

He threw his arms around Shigai-bai and pressed him close, and the hot flat-cakes burned the miser badly.

Shigai-bai bore the pain at first, but then, unable to stand it any longer, cried:

"Oh! Oh! They're burning me! They're burning me!"

And snatching them from his robes, cried:

"Let the dogs eat them!"

"How now, Shigai-bai," said Aldar-Kose, "why should you feed your dogs with hot flat-cakes! Why not treat me to some of them!"

And he seized the flat-cakes and ate them.

"Your wife makes fine flat-cakes, Shigai-bai," said Aldar-Kose. "I've eaten none so good for a long time."

Shigai-bai made no answer, and hungry though he was, rode off to the steppe.

He returned home in the evening, and lo! there was Aldar-Kose sitting in his *yurta*.

"Did you not say good-bye to me? I thought you were leaving," said Shigai-bai.

"I was going to, but I thought better of it," Aldar-Kose replied. "I like it here in your *yurta*."

Shigai-bai frowned in vexation, but there was nothing to be done; he could not very well turn his guest out.

The following morning Shigai-bai again prepared to go out to the steppe, and he said to his wife:

"Give me a flask of *airan* to take with me, but mind that Aldar-Kose does not see you."

Shigai-bai's wife filled a large leather flask with *airan* and gave it to him, and Shigai-bai hid the flask under the flap of his robe and left the *yurta*.

"All will be well this time," said he to himself.

But this was not to be. For Aldar-Kose at once ran out and threw his arms around him. So close did he clasp Shigai-bai that the flask of *airan* overturned, and the *airan* ran down Shigai-bai's robe.

Mad with rage, Shigai-bai seized the flask, thrust it in Aldar-Kose's hands and cried:

"Drink! Drink!"

"And so I shall, since you ask me to," Aldar-Kose replied. "I would not like to offend you by refusing."

And he drank up all of the *airan*.

Once again Shigai-bai rode hungry into the steppe, and the cunning Aldar-Kose came into the *yurta* and began chatting with his wife and daughter.

Aldar-Kose stayed at the miser's house for many days. No matter what cunning Shigai-bai used or what tricks he thought of, he could not outwit his guest. Willy-nilly, he was obliged to feed Aldar-Kose.

From morning till night Shigai-bai kept thinking of a way of turning his guest out of his *yurta* and of revenging himself upon him. He thought and he thought till at last he knew what to do.

Aldar-Kose had come to him on a horse with a white star on its head, and Shigai-bai now decided to kill the horse. He looked at the horse intently every time he chanced to pass by, and there was a look of malice in his eye.

Aldar-Kose took note of this, and that same evening he took some soot and smeared it over the white star on his horse's head, at the same time dabbing some white clay on the head of Shigai-bai's best stallion.

He then went into the *yurta* and to bed.

During the night, Shigai-bai stole out of the *yurta*, picked from his horses the one with the white star on its head, killed it and began shouting loudly:

"Oh, oh, you have fallen on evil days, Aldar-Kose! Something terrible has happened to your horse!"

But Aldar-Kose did not even come out of the *yurta*.

"Do not take it so hard, Shigai-bai," said he, "do not shout. It matters but little. Cut up the horse, and you and I will have plenty of meat to eat."

At this, Shigai-bai laughed in glee, so pleased was he that he had at last revenged himself on his hated guest.

Only in the morning did he see that he had slaughtered his best stallion.

Shigai-bai nearly burst with fury, but there was no help for it, and he had to cook the meat and share it with Aldar-Kose.

But at last Aldar-Kose himself grew weary of staying with Shigai-bai. He decided to go back to his own village and to carry off with him Shigai-bai's daughter.

"Far better for her if I make her my wife," he told himself. "Living as she does in the house of a father like Shigai-bai, she is sure to become as stingy as he."

Now Shigai-bai's daughter was named Biz-Bulduk, and at the first sight of him she had liked the gay and carefree Aldar-Kose and kept stealing glances at him.

One morning, when Shigai-bai was about to ride off to the steppe, as usual, and had already mounted his horse, Aldar-Kose said to him:

"Well, Shigai-bai, I have been your guest long enough. It is time I went home. When you return at night there will be room enough and to spare in your *yurta*."

Shigai-bai listened, and he could hardly believe his ears.

"Only give me your *biz**," Aldar-Kose went on. "I want to repair my boots before I set off."

"Very well, very well," said Shigai-bai. "Take the *biz*, repair your boots and be off with you. It's high time!"

And with these words he made off for the steppe.

* *Biz*—awl.—*Tr.*

As for Aldar-Kose, he came into the *yurta* and he said to Shigai-bai's wife:

"Well, my good woman, get Biz-Bulduk ready, she is coming with me."

"Are you out of your mind?" exclaimed Shigai-bai's wife. "Do you think that Shigai-bai will ever let a beggar like you have our Biz?"

"He has given her to me already. If you don't believe me, ask him yourself."

Shigai-bai's wife ran out of the *yurta* and called to her husband:

"Shigai-bai! Shigai-bai! Is it true that you promised to give your Biz to Aldar-Kose?"

"It is, it is!" Shigai-bai called back. "Give him my *biz*, and let him get out of the house!"

And with these words, Shigai-bai whipped up his horse and rode off to the steppe.

Shigai-bai's wife dared not disobey him. She got her daughter ready and led her out of the *yurta*. Aldar-Kose put the girl on the horse with the white star on its head, and away they rode, leaving Shigai-bai's *yurta* far behind them.

As they were riding together, Aldar-Kose said to the girl:

"You will live among good people and become good yourself."

In the evening Shigai-bai returned to his *yurta*. Learning about what had taken place in his absence, he turned red with rage, leapt on his horse's back and galloped off in pursuit. He rode all over the steppe, but he could not find Aldar-Kose anywhere and had to come back empty-handed.

THE FERN GIRL
A Yakut Fairy-Tale

They say that one morning a little old woman, mistress of five cows, rose and went out to the field.

In the field, which was big and wide, she saw a horsetail, a fern with five shoots. She pulled it out without breaking the root or any of the shoots, brought it to her *yurta* and put it on her pillow. Then she went out again and sat down to milk her cows.

She sat there, and all of a sudden she heard the jingle-jingling of bells in the *yurta*. The old woman dropped her milk pail, spilling the milk in her haste. She ran into the *yurta* and looked round her, but everything was as it had been: there lay the horsetail on the pillow, a fern like any other. The old woman went out once more and she sat down to milk her cows, when suddenly she heard the jingle-jingling of bells again. Spilling the milk in her haste, she ran into the *yurta* and whom did she see sitting on her bed but a girl of rare beauty. The girl's eyes sparkled like precious stones and her brows were like two black sables. The fern had turned into a girl!

The little old woman was overjoyed.

Said she to the girl:

"Stay with me and be a daughter to me."

And so the two started living in the *yurta* together.

One day a young hunter named Kharzhit-Bergen went to the taiga to hunt. He saw a grey squirrel and he shot an arrow. He kept on shooting arrows from early morning till sunset, but never once did he hit the squirrel.

The squirrel bounded up a spruce-tree, leapt from the spruce-tree to a birch-tree and then on to a larch-tree, and reaching the little old woman's *yurta*, settled in a pine-tree.

Kharzhit-Bergen ran up to the pine-tree and shot another arrow, but the squirrel darted away again, and the arrow fell into the smoke hole of the little old woman's *yurta*.

"I want my arrow, old woman, give it back to me!" Kharzhit-Bergen shouted, but the little old woman did not come out and made no reply.

Kharzhit-Bergen was very angry, he flushed with rage and he ran into the *yurta*.

There, before him, sat a beautiful girl. Such was her beauty that it took his breath away and made his head swim. Without a word, he ran out, jumped on his horse and galloped home.

"O my parents," said he, "the little old woman, mistress of five cows, has a most beautiful girl in her *yurta*. Send matchmakers there, for I want her for my wife."

Kharzhit-Bergen's father at once sent nine men mounted on nine horses for the girl.

The matchmakers came to the little old woman's *yurta*, they saw the girl, and such was her beauty that it took their breath away. Then, coming to their senses, they all left the *yurta*, all but one, the oldest and most respected among them.

"Little old woman," said he, "will you not give this young girl to Kharzhit-Bergen to be his wife?"

"That I will," the little old woman replied.

Then they asked the girl if she was willing, and the girl said that she was.

"You will have to pay a big ransom for the bride," said the little old woman. "You must give me as many cows and horses as my field will hold."

The cows and horses were soon driven to the little old woman's field, and so many were they that one lost count of them.

Then they dressed the girl in fine new clothes, they dressed her quickly and well. They brought a dappled horse, they bridled him with a silver bridle, they saddled him with a silver saddle and they hung a silver whip at his side. Kharzhit-Bergen took his bride by the hand, led her out, put her on the dappled horse and rode home with her.

They were riding along when suddenly Kharzhit-Bergen saw a fox on the road.

Said Kharzhit-Bergen, for he could not help himself:

"I am going to ride after the fox, but will soon be back. And you must follow this road till you reach the place where it branches off in two directions. On the eastern side a sableskin will hang, on the western side—the hide of a bear with a white throat. Do not turn down the western road. Follow the road where you see the sableskin."

And with these words, he galloped away.

The girl rode on alone, and in due time she reached the fork in the road. But no sooner was she there than she forgot Kharzhit-Bergen's behest. She turned down the road where the bearskin was hanging and soon came to a large iron *yurta*.

Out of the *yurta*, dressed in clothes of iron, there stepped the eighth devil's daughter. She had one leg, and that was crooked, one arm, as crooked as the leg, one hideous, dead eye in the very middle of her forehead, and a long, black tongue that hung down to her breast.

The devil's daughter seized the girl, dragged her off her horse, stripped the skin from off her face and stretched it over her own; then she pulled off all of the girl's fine clothes, and dressing herself in them, threw the girl over the *yurta*. After that she mounted the dappled horse and rode eastwards.

Kharzhit-Bergen caught up with her when she was nearing his father's *yurta*. But he saw nothing and guessed nothing.

All Kharzhit-Bergen's kin gathered to welcome the bride. Nine handsome young men and eight girls came out to the tethering post to meet her.

The girls spoke amongst themselves, and they said:

"The bride has only to open her mouth and speak one word, and the prettiest beads will drop out and roll over the ground."

And they brought thread so as to string the beads.

The young men spoke amongst themselves, and they said:

"The bride has only to take one step, and wherever she passes, black sables will follow in her footsteps."

And they got their bows and arrows ready so as to shoot the sables.

But when the bride started to speak, frogs dropped from her mouth, and when she took one step, mangy stoats ran after her.

All who had come to meet the bride stood aghast and grew sad at heart.

But they spread a carpet of green grass from the tethering post to the bridegroom's *yurta*, and taking the bride by the hand, led her there.

The bride went into the *yurta*, and using the crowns of three young larches, made up a fire in the hearth.

After that there was a wedding feast, and everyone ate and drank, and played games and made merry. No one guessed that this was not the real bride at all.

Soon after this the little old woman came to her field to milk her cows. She looked, and she saw that a new horsetail with five shoots had grown up in the selfsame spot, and it was even more slender and straight than the first one.

The little old woman dug up the horsetail together with the root, took it to her *yurta* and put it on her pillow. Then she went back to the field and began milking her cows. Suddenly she heard the jingle-jingling of bells in the *yurta*. She went inside, and whom did she see there but the very same girl, looking more beautiful than ever.

"How is it that you are here, why have you come back?" the little old woman asked.

"O my mother," the girl replied, "when Kharzhit-Bergen and I were on our way to his *yurta*, he told me that he was going to ride after a fox and that I was to follow the road where a sableskin was hanging and in no wise to turn down the road where a bear's hide had been hung. But I forgot his warning, took the wrong road and soon came to an iron *yurta*. The eighth devil's daughter met me, she clawed the skin from off my face and stretched it over her own. Then she pulled off all my fine clothes, and dressing herself in them, threw me over her iron *yurta*. After that she mounted my dappled horse and rode away. Some grey dogs seized me in their jaws and dragged me to the wide field near your *yurta*, and I came to life again in the guise of a horsetail. Ah, mother, will I ever see Kharzhit-Bergen again?"

The little old woman heard her story, and then began trying to comfort her.

"Do not be troubled, you will see him," said she. "And in the meantime, stay with me as before and be my daughter."

And so the fern girl began living in the little old woman's *yurta* again

The dappled horse learned that the fern girl had come to life, and he spoke to Kharzhit-Bergen's father in a human voice and said:

"Know that Kharzhit-Bergen left his bride alone as he was bringing her here, and she had to ride on by herself. When she reached the fork in the road she turned down the path where the bear's hide was hanging and came to an iron *yurta*. The eighth devil's daughter rushed out, tore the skin from off her face and stretched it over her own, pulled off her fine clothes and dressed herself in them, and then she threw her over the iron *yurta*. Now the devil's daughter lives in your *yurta* and you have her for your daughter-in-law. And as for my true mistress, she has come to life again. You must bring her back to your *yurta* and give her to your son in marriage, else things will go hard with you. The devil's daughter will pull down your hearth and your *yurta*, she will make your life a misery and will put you all to death."

Hearing this, the old man ran into the *yurta*.

"Where did you bring your wife from, my son?" asked he of Kharzhit-Bergen. "Who is she?"

"She is the daughter of the little old woman, mistress of five cows," Kharzhit-Bergen replied.

Said the father:

"The dappled horse has been complaining to me. He says that you left your bride alone as you were bringing her here and that when she reached the fork in the road she took the path that brought her to the iron *yurta*. The eighth devil's daughter dragged her from the horse's back, clawed the skin from off her face and stretched it over her own, and she put on all her fine clothes. The devil's daughter has deceived us all, she has made her home here by a wily trick. . . . Go to the little old woman and beg your bride to return to us. Bring her here. As for the devil's daughter, tie her to the tail of a wild horse and drive the horse out to the open field. Let it strew her bones over the field! Else she will put us all to death—the men and the herds."

The devil's daughter heard him, and she turned black with fear and rage.

Kharzhit-Bergen heard him, and he grew red with anger.

He seized the devil's daughter, dragged her out by her leg from the *yurta* and tied her to the tail of a wild horse.

The horse galloped off to the wide field, it kicked and it trampled the devil's daughter, and her black body turned into a mass of worms and snakes, and these Kharzhit-Bergen and his father gathered and burned.

After that Kharzhit-Bergen set off on horseback for the little old woman's *yurta*. He leapt from his horse by the tethering post, and the little old woman saw him and hurried out of her *yurta*. She was very happy, just as if someone thought lost had been found again or as if someone who had died had come back to life. From the tethering post to the *yurta* she spread a carpet of green grass and she slaughtered her best and fattest cow and her best and fleshiest horse and began preparing the wedding feast.

As for the fern girl, she looked at Kharzhit-Bergen and she burst out crying.

"Why have you come to me?" she asked him. "You let the daughter of the eighth devil spill my blood and tear my fine skin, and you gave my body to the grey dogs. How can you come here now? There are more maids in the world than there are perches, there are more women in the world than there are pikes. Go and seek for a wife among them. I will not marry you!"

"I never gave you to the daughter of the eighth devil," said Kharzhit-Bergen. "I never gave you to the grey dogs. When I rode off to the taiga after the fox I showed you the road you had to take. I did not tell you to go and meet your death."

The little old woman brushed the tears from her right eye, she brushed the tears from her left eye and she seated herself between the fern girl and Kharzhit-Bergen.

Said the little old woman:

"How is it that you who died and then came back to life, you who were lost and then found, how is it that you do not rejoice? You must love each other as before, you must live in friendship and peace. Heed my words, both of you, and do as I say."

The girl obeyed, and she said softly:

"Very well, I will do as you say, I will forgive and forget."

At this Kharzhit-Bergen jumped to his feet and began dancing and capering about and embracing and kissing the fern girl.

Then they saddled the dappled horse with a silver saddle and they bridled him with a silver bridle; they covered him with a silver horse-cloth and they hung a silver whip at his side. And the fern girl they dressed in the best of finery, and she and Kharzhit-Bergen set off on their way.

They rode a long, long time. Winter they knew by the snow that fell, summer they knew by the rain that poured, autumn they knew by the fog that hung over the fields. On and on they rode, and at last they came to the *yurta* of Kharzhit-Bergen's father.

All Kharzhit-Bergen's kin, all his nine brothers came out to meet the bride. From the tethering post to the *yurta* they spread a carpet of green grass.

"When the bride comes," said they to themselves, "she will take a step and then another, and wherever she walks, sables will leap from out of her footprints."

And with this in mind, they began making bows and arrows and worked so hard that the skin peeled from the palms of their hands.

And Kharzhit-Bergen's eight sisters began spinning thread, and they too worked so hard that the skin came off their fingers. They waited for the bride and they said to themselves:

"When she comes, she will speak up in silvery tones, and precious red beads will drop from her mouth."

Then Kharzhit-Bergen arrived with his bride, and two of his sisters tied their horses to the tethering post. They caught the bride in their arms and they let her down to the ground. The bride spoke up in silvery tones, and red beads dropped from her mouth, and the girls began gathering the beads and threading them on a string. The bride walked to the *yurta*, and black sables ran from her footprints, and the young men took their bows and arrows and began shooting at the sables.

The bride came into the *yurta*, and using the crowns of three young larches, made up a fire in the hearth.

A gay wedding feast was held. Guests gathered from all the villages. There were singers among them, and dancers. story-tellers and wrestlers, and tumblers too.

For three days the feast went on and then it was over, and the guests went home, on foot and on horseback.

And Kharzhit-Bergen and his wife set up house together. They lived in friendship and in peace, they lived happily and they lived long, and it is said that their grandchildren are living still.

THE GOLDEN CUP

A Buryat Fairy-Tale

It is said that long, long ago, in olden times, there lived a mighty Khan named Sanad.

One day he decided to remove himself and all his people to new lands where the camping sites were better and the pastures richer. But the way to those lands was long and hard.

Before leaving, Sanad Khan ordered all the old people to be killed.

"The old people will be a burden to us on the way," he said. "Not one old man or woman must we have with us, not one must be left alive. He who does not carry out my command will be severely punished."

It was a cruel order, and the people's hearts were heavy. But there was nothing for it, they had to do as the Khan willed. For they all feared the Khan and dared not disobey him.

One only of Sanad Khan's subjects, a young man named Tsyren, vowed that he would not kill his old father.

The son and father agreed that Tsyren would hide the old man in a large leather sack, and in secret from Sanad Khan and everyone else, carry him to the new lands. And as for what might happen later, well, they would take their chances. . . .

Sanad Khan left the old camping site and together with his people and herds set out for the far-off lands in the north. And with them, in a large leather sack slung across his horse's back, went Tsyren's old father. Unknown to the others, Tsyren gave his father food and drink, and whenever they made camp, he would wait until it was quite dark, untie the sack and let out the old man that he might rest and stretch his aching limbs.

So they rode for a long time till they reached the shores of a great sea.

Sanad Khan ordered his people to halt and camp for the night.

One of the Khan's attendants went down to the water's edge and noticed at the bottom of the sea something that sparkled and gleamed. He took a closer look and saw that it was a large golden cup of very unusual shape. Returning at once to the Khan, he told him that a precious golden cup was lying under the sea close to the shore.

Sanad Khan, without thinking twice, ordered the cup to be delivered to him at once. But since no one dared or was willing to dive into the sea, the Khan gave orders that they draw lots.

The lot fell upon one of the Khan's own men. The man dived in, but he never came up again.

They cast lots again, and the man upon whom the lot fell

leapt into the sea from the top of a steep cliff, but he, too, was never seen again.

In this way many of Sanad Khan's people lost their lives.

But the merciless Khan did not for a moment think of giving up his venture. On his orders, his subjects, one after another, dived, unprotesting, into the sea and perished.

At last came the turn of Tsyren to dive in after the cup. Before doing so, Tsyren went to the place where he had hidden his father to bid him good-bye.

"Farewell, Father," said Tsyren. "We are going to die, both of us, you and I."

"What has happened? Why must you die?" the old man asked.

Tsyren then explained that the lot had fallen upon him to dive to the bottom of the sea after the cup.

"But not one of those who dived in came up again," said he. "And so I am to perish in the sea by the Khan's orders, and you will be found here and killed by his servants."

The old man heard him to the end and said:

"If this goes on, you will all be drowned in the sea without ever getting the golden cup. The cup is not at the bottom of the sea at all. Do you see that mountain, not far from the sea? Well, the golden cup is standing at the top of it. What you take to be the cup is only its reflection. How is it that none of you thought of it?"

"What shall I do?" Tsyren asked.

"Climb the mountan, find the cup and deliver it to the Khan. It should not be difficult to find it. The cup sparkles so that it can be seen from afar. However, it may be that the cup stands on a cliff too steep for you to climb. In that case, this is what you must do: wait until some roes appear on the cliff and find a way of startling them. The roes will rush away and push down the cup in their haste. Waste no time then, but snatch it up quickly, or else it will fall into a deep, dark ravine and be lost to you for ever."

Tsyren thanked his father and at once made for the mountain.

It was not easy to climb to the top of the mountain. Tsyren clutched at shrubs, trees and sharp rocks, and he scratched his face and hands till the blood appeared, and tore his clothing. At last, when he had all but reached the top, Tsyren saw the golden cup. It was very beautiful. It stood on a high and inaccessible cliff, and it sparkled and shone.

Tsyren saw that he would never be able to climb the cliff. So, heeding his father's words, he waited for the roes to appear.

He had not long to wait. Several roes soon made their appearance on the cliff. They stood there calmly gazing down. Tsyren gave a loud shout. The roes were startled and began rushing to and fro on the cliff, and they pushed down the golden cup. The cup came rolling down, and Tsyren caught it nimbly as it fell.

Pleased and happy, he made his way down the mountain with the cup in his hands, went up to Sanad Khan and placed it before him.

"How did you get this cup from the bottom of the sea?" the Khan asked him.

"It was not there that I found it," Tsyren replied, "but on the top of yonder mountain. What we saw in the sea was only the cup's reflection."

"Who told you that?" asked the Khan.

"I thought of it myself," Tsyren replied.

The Khan asked him nothing more and let him go.

The following day, Sanad Khan and his people moved on.

They journeyed a long time, and at last they reached a great desert. Here the sun had baked the earth and had burnt up all the grass. There was no river anywhere about, nor even a stream. The men and the cattle began to suffer from a terrible thirst. Sanad Khan sent horsemen in all directions in search of water, but try as they would, no water could they find, for all around was dry, scorched land. The people were in despair. They did not know what to do or where to go.

Tsyren secretly made his way to where he had left his father.

"What are we to do, Father, tell me?" he asked. "We are all dying of thirst, and so are the cattle."

Said the old man:

"Let a three-year-old cow go free and watch it closely. Wherever it stops and starts sniffing at the ground, there begin digging."

Tsyren ran and let loose a three-year-old cow, and the cow hung its head low and began wandering from place to place. At last it stopped and began sniffing at the hot earth, drawing in the air noisily.

"Dig here," said Tsyren.

The people began digging, and they soon reached a large underground spring. Cool, clear water gushed out, flowing over the ground. Everyone drank his fill and was cheered and heartened.

Sanad Khan called Tsyren to his side and asked him:

"How is it that you were able to find an underground spring in this dry spot?"

"I knew certain signs that told me where it was," Tsyren replied.

The people drank some more, rested and moved on again. They journeyed for many days, and then they halted and pitched camp. Unexpectedly it began to rain hard in the night, and the campfire was put out. Hard as they tried, the people could not make up the fire again. They were chilled to the bone and wet, and they did not know what to do.

Then someone noticed what seemed to be the light of a campfire on the top of a distant mountain.

Sanad Khan at once gave orders that the fire be brought down from the mountain.

The people rushed to fulfil the Khan's orders. First one, then another, then a third climbed the mountain. They all found the fire which flamed beneath the thick branches of a large spruce-tree, and also a hunter who was warming himself by the fire. They all took away with them a burning log, but no one succeeded in carrying it as far as the camp, for the heavy rain put out the flame.

Sanad Khan was very angry, and he gave orders for all who went to get the fire but returned without it to be put to death.

When the turn of Tsyren came to go to fetch the fire, he crept to where he had hidden his father and asked him:

"What is to be done, Father? How is the fire to be carried from the mountain to the camp?"

Said the old man:

"Do not take the burning logs—they'll smoulder on the way and be put out by the rain. Take a large pot with you and fill it full of burning coals. Only in this way will you be able to bring the fire to the camp."

Tsyren did as his father told him, and he brought down from the mountain a potful of live coals. The people made up fires, dried and warmed themselves and cooked their food.

When Sanad Khan learned who it was that had brought them the fire, he ordered Tsyren to come to him.

Tsyren came, and the Khan began shouting at him angrily.

"How is it that you who knew how to bring the fire kept silent about it?" he raged. "Why did you not speak up at once?"

"Because I did not know how to do it myself," Tsyren told him.

"Yet you were able to do it. How was it so?" the Khan insisted.

And so persistently did he ply him with questions that Tsyren finally confessed that he had only been able to carry out the Khan's commands because of his father's wise counsels.

"Where is your father?" the Khan asked.

Said Tsyren:

"I carried him all the way in a large leather sack."

Then Sanad Khan commanded the old man to be brought before him, and he said to him:

"I rescind my order. Old people are no burden to the young. Age has wisdom. You need hide no longer, you may ride freely with the rest."

KOTURA, LORD OF THE WINDS

A Nenets Fairy-Tale

In a nomad camp there once lived an old man with his three daughters. The youngest was the kindest and cleverest of the three.

The old man was very poor. His *choom,* his tent of skins, was worn and full of holes. There was little warm clothing to wear. When the frost was very fierce the old man would huddle by the fire with his three daughters and try to keep warm. At night, before going to bed, they would put out the fire, and then they would shiver from the cold until morning.

Once, in the middle of winter, a terrible snow-storm came down on the tundra. The wind blew for a day, it blew for a second day, and it blew for a third day, and it seemed as if all the *chooms* would be blown quite away. The people dared not show their faces outside and sat in the *chooms,* hungry and cold.

So, too, the old man and his three daughters. They sat in the *choom* and listened to the storm raging, and the old man said:

"We'll never be able to sit out this blizzard. It was sent by Kotura, Lord of the Winds. He must be angry, he must be waiting for us to send him a good wife. You, my eldest daughter, must go to Kotura or else our whole people will perish. You must go and beg him to stop the blizzard."

"How can I go?" the girl asked. "I don't know the way."

"I will give you a little sledge. Place it so that it faces the wind, give it a push and follow it. The wind will untie the strings on your coat, but you must not stop to tie them. The snow will get into your shoes, but you must not stop to shake it out. Never pause till you reach a tall mountain. Climb it, and when you get to the top, then only can you stop to shake out the snow from your shoes and tie the strings on your coat. By and by a little bird will fly up to you and perch on your shoulder. Do not chase it away, be kind to it and fondle it gently. Then get into your sledge and coast down the mountain. The sledge will bring you straight to the door of Kotura's *choom*. Enter the *choom*, but touch nothing, just sit there and wait. When Kotura comes, do all he tells you to do."

Eldest Daughter donned her furs, placed the sledge her father gave her so that it faced the wind, and with a push sent it gliding along.

She walked after it a little way, and the strings on her coat came undone, the snow got into her shoes and she was very, very cold. She did not do as her father bade her to do, but stopped and began to tie the strings on her coat and to shake the snow out of her shoes. After that she moved on, in the face of the wind. She walked a long time till at last she saw a tall mountain. No sooner had she climbed it than a little bird flew up to her and was about to perch on her shoulder. But Eldest Daughter waved her hands to chase it off, and the bird circled over her for a little while and then flew away.

Eldest Daughter got into her sledge and coasted down the mountainside, and the sledge stopped by a large *choom*.

The girl went inside, and looked about her, and the first thing she saw was a large piece of roasted venison. She made up a fire, warmed herself and began to tear pieces of fat off the meat. She would tear off a piece and eat it, and then tear off another and eat it too, and she had eaten her fill when all of a sudden she heard someone coming up to the *choom*. The skin that hung over the entrance was lifted, and a young giant entered. This was Kotura himself. He looked at Eldest Daughter and said:

"Where do you come from, woman, and what do you want here?"

"My father sent me to you," answered Eldest Daughter.

"Why did he send you?"

"So that you would take me to wife."

"I was out hunting and I have brought back some meat. Stand up now and cook it for me," Kotura said.

Eldest Daughter did as she was told, and when the meat was ready, Kotura told her to take it out of the pot and divide it in two parts.

"You and I will eat one half of the meat," he said. "Put the other in a wooden dish and take it to the neighbouring *choom*. Do not go into the *choom* yourself, but wait at the entrance. An old woman will come out to you. Give her the meat and wait till she brings back the empty dish."

Eldest Daughter took the meat and went outside. The wind was howling, and the snow falling, and it was quite dark. How could one find anything in such a storm!... Eldest Daughter walked off a little way, stopped, thought a while and then threw the meat in the snow. After that she came back to Kotura with the empty dish.

Kotura glanced at her and said:

"Have you given the neighbours the meat?"

"Yes, I have," Eldest Daughter replied.

"Show me the dish, I want to see what they gave you in return for the meat," he told her.

Eldest Daughter showed him the empty dish, but Kotura said nothing. He ate his share of the meat and went to bed.

In the morning he rose, brought some untanned deerskins into the *choom* and said:

"While I am out hunting, dress these skins and make me a new coat from them, new shoes and new mittens. I will put them on when I come back and see if you are clever with your hands or not."

And with these words, Kotura went off to hunt in the tundra, and Eldest Daughter set to work. Suddenly the hanging of skin over the entrance lifted, and a grey-haired old woman came in.

"Something has got into my eye, child," said she. "See if you can take it out."

"I have no time to bother with you," answered Eldest Daughter, "I am busy working."

The old woman said nothing but turned away and left the *choom*. Eldest Daughter was left alone. She dressed the skins hastily and began cutting them with a knife, hurrying to get her work done by evening. Indeed, in such a hurry was she that she did not try to make the clothes nicely, but only to get them finished as quickly as possible. She had no needle to sew with, and only one day to do the work in, and it was all she could do to get anything done at all.

In the evening Kotura came back from his hunting.

"Are my new clothes ready?" he asked her.

"They are," replied Eldest Daughter.

Kotura took the clothes, and he ran his hands over them, and the skins felt rough to his touch, so badly were they dressed. He looked, and he saw that the garments were poorly cut, sewn together carelessly and much too small for him.

At this he became very angry, and he threw Eldest Daughter out of the *choom*. He threw her far, far out, and she fell into a drift of snow and lay there till she froze to death.

And the howling of the wind became fiercer than ever.

The old man sat in his *choom* and he listened to the wind howling and the storm raging day in and day out, and said:

"Eldest Daughter did not heed my words, she did not do as I bade her. That is why the wind does not stop howling. Kotura is angry. You must go to him, Second Daughter."

The old man made a little sledge, he told Second Daughter just what he had told Eldest Daughter, and he sent her off to Kotura. And himself he remained in the *choom* with his youngest daughter, and waited for the blizzard to stop.

Second Daughter placed the sledge so that it faced the wind, and giving it a push, went along after it. The strings of her coat came undone as she walked and the snow got into her shoes. She was very cold, and forgetting her father's behest, shook the snow out of her shoes and tied the strings of her coat sooner than he had told her to.

She came to the mountain and climbed it, and seeing the little bird, waved her hands and chased it away. Then she got into her sledge and coasted down the mountainside straight up to Kotura's *choom*.

She entered the *choom*, made up a fire, had her fill of venison and sat down to wait for Kotura.

Kotura came back from his hunting, he saw Second Daughter and asked her:

"Why have you come to me?"

"My father sent me to you," replied Second Daughter.

"Why did he send you?"

"So that you would take me to wife."

"Why do you sit there then? I am hungry, be quick and cook me some meat."

When the meat was ready, Kotura ordered Second Daughter to take it out of the pot and cut it in two parts.

"You and I will eat one half of the meat," Kotura said. "As for the other, put it in that wooden dish yonder and take it to the neighbouring *choom*. Do not enter the *choom* yourself, but stand near it and wait for your dish to be brought out to you."

Second Daughter took the meat and went outside. The wind was howling and the snow whirling and it was hard to make out anything. So, not liking to go any farther, she threw the meat in the snow, stood there a while and then went back to Kotura.

"Have you given them the meat?" Kotura asked.

"Yes, I have," Second Daughter replied.

"You have come back very soon. Show me the dish, I want to see what they gave you in return for the meat."

Second Daughter did as she was told, and Kotura glanced at the empty dish, but said not a word and went to bed. In the morning he brought in some untanned deerskins and told Second Daughter, just as he had her sister, to make him some new clothes by evening.

"Set to work," he said. "In the evening I will see how well you can sew."

With these words Kotura went off to hunt and Second Daughter set to work. She was in a great hurry, for somehow she had to get everything done by evening. Suddenly a grey-haired old woman came into the *choom*.

"A mote has got into my eye, child," she said. "Take it out, do. I cannot manage it myself."

"I am too busy to bother with your old mote!" Second Daughter replied. "Go away and let me work."

And the old woman made no reply and went away without another word. When night fell Kotura came back from his hunting.

"Are my new clothes ready?" he asked.

"Yes, they are," Second Daughter replied.

"Let me try them on then."

Kotura put on the clothes, and he saw that they were badly cut and much too small, and the seams ran all askew. Kotura flew into a rage, he threw Second Daughter where he had thrown her sister, and she too froze to death.

And the old man sat in his *choom* with his youngest daughter and waited in vain for the storm to calm down. The wind was fiercer than ever, and it seemed as if the *choom* would be blown away any minute.

"My daughters did not heed my words," the old man said. "They have made things worse, they have angered Kotura. You are my last remaining daughter, but still I must send you to Kotura in the hope that he will take you to wife. If I don't, our whole people will perish from hunger. So get ready, daughter, and go."

And he told her where to go and what to do.

Youngest Daughter came out of the *choom*, she placed the sledge so that it faced the wind and, with a push, sent it gliding along. The wind was howling and roaring, trying to throw Youngest Daughter off her feet, and the snow blinded her eyes so that she could see nothing.

But Youngest Daughter plodded on through the blizzard, never forgetting a word of her father's behest and doing everything just as he had bade her. The strings of her coat came undone, but she did not stop to tie them. The snow got into her shoes, but she did not stop to shake it out. It was very cold, and the wind was very strong, but she did not pause and went on and on. It was only when she came to the mountain and climbed it that she stopped and began shaking the snow from her shoes and tying the strings of her coat. Then a little bird flew up to her and perched on her shoulder. But Youngest Daughter did not chase the bird away. Instead, she fondled and stroked it tenderly. When the bird flew away Youngest Daughter got into her sledge and coasted down the mountainside straight up to Kotura's *choom*.

She went into the *choom* and waited. Suddenly the skin over the entrance was lifted and the young giant came in. When he saw Youngest Daughter he laughed and said:

"Why have you come to me?"

"My father sent me," answered Youngest Daughter.

"Why did he send you?"

"To beg you to stop the storm, for if you don't, all our people will perish."

"Why do you sit there? Why don't you make up a fire and cook some meat?" Kotura said. "I am hungry, and so must you be too, for I see you have eaten nothing since you came."

Youngest Daughter cooked the meat quickly, took it out of the pot and gave it to Kotura, and Kotura ate some of it and then told her to take one half of the meat to the neighbouring *choom*.

Youngest Daughter took the dish of meat and went outside. The wind was roaring loudly and the snow whirling and spinning. Where was she to go? Where was the *choom* of the neighbours to be found? She stood there a while, thinking, and then she started out through the storm, not knowing herself where she was going.

Suddenly there appeared before her the very same little bird that had flown up to her on the mountain. Now it began darting about near her face. Youngest Daughter decided to follow the bird's lead. Whichever way the bird flew, there she went. On and on she walked, and at last, off to one side, a little distance away, she saw what looked like a spark flashing. Youngest Daughter was overjoyed, and she went in that direction, thinking that the *choom* was there. But when she drew near, she found that what she had thought to be a *choom* was a large mound with smoke curling up from it. Youngest Daughter walked round the mound and she prodded it with her foot, and suddenly there was a door before her. A grey-haired old woman looked out of the door and said:

"Who are you? Why have you come?"

"I have brought you some meat, grandmother," Youngest Daughter replied. "Kotura asked me to give it to you."

"Kotura, you say? Very well, then, let me have it. And you wait here, outside."

Youngest Daughter stood by the mound and waited. She waited a long time. At last the door opened again, the old woman looked out and handed her the wooden dish. There was something heaped on it, but the girl could not make out what it was. She took the dish and returned with it to Kotura.

"Why were you away so long?" Kotura asked. "Did you find the *choom*?"

"Yes, I did."

"Did you give them the meat?"

"Yes."

"Let me have the dish, I want to see what is in it."

Kotura looked, and he saw that there were several knives in the dish and steel needles and scrapers and brakes for dressing skins. Kotura laughed aloud and said:

"You have received many fine things that will be very useful to you."

In the morning Kotura rose and he brought some deerskins into the *choom* and ordered Youngest Daughter to make him a new coat, shoes and mittens by evening.

"If you make them well," he said, "I will take you to wife."

Kotura went away, and Youngest Daughter set to work. The old woman's present proved very useful. Youngest Daughter had everything she needed to make the clothes with. But how much could one do in a single day? . . . Youngest Daughter spent no time thinking about it, but tried to do as much as she could. She dressed the skins and she scraped them, she cut and she sewed. All of a sudden the skin over the entrance lifted, and a grey-haired old woman came in. Youngest Daughter knew her at once: it was the same old woman to whom she had taken the meat.

"Help me, my child," the old woman said. "There's a mote in my eye. Please take it out for me, I cannot do it myself."

Youngest Daughter did not refuse. She put aside her work and soon had the mote out of the old woman's eye.

"Good," said the old woman, "my eye does not hurt any more. Now look in my right ear."

Youngest Daughter looked in the old woman's ear and started.

"What do you see there?" the old woman asked.

"There is a girl sitting in your ear," Youngest Daughter replied.

"Why don't you call her? She will help you to make Kotura's clothes for him."

Youngest Daughter was overjoyed, and she called to the girl. At her call, not one, but four young girls jumped out of the old woman's ear, and all four set to work. They dressed the skins and they scraped them, they cut and they sewed. The garments were soon ready. After that the old woman hid the four girls in her ear again and went away.

In the evening Kotura returned from his hunting.

"Have you done all that I told you to do?" he asked.

"Yes, I have," Youngest Daughter replied.

"Let me see my new clothes, I will try them on."

Youngest Daughter gave him the clothes, and Kotura took them and passed his hand over them: the skins were soft and pleasant to the touch. He put on the garments, and they were neither too small nor too large, but fitted him well and were made to last. Kotura smiled and said:

327

"I like you, Youngest Daughter, and my mother and four sisters like you too. You work well, and you have courage. You braved a terribe storm in order that your people might not perish. Be my wife, stay with me in my *choom*."

No sooner were the words out of his mouth than the storm in the tundra was stilled. No longer did the people try to hide from the wind, no longer did they freeze. One and all, they came out of their *chooms* into the light of day!

THE GIRL AND THE MOON MAN

A Chukchi Fairy-Tale

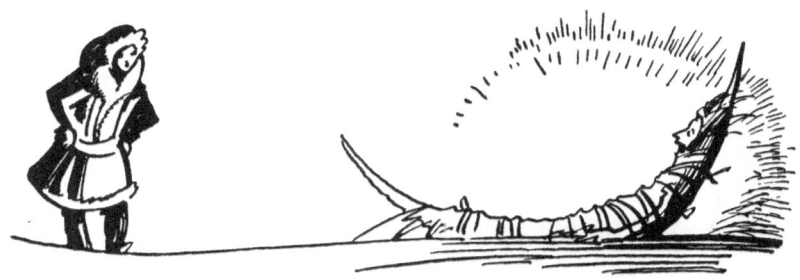

There once lived among the Chukchi a man who had only one child, a daughter. The girl was her father's best help-mate. She spent every summer far away from the camping grounds, watching over her father's herd of deer, and every winter she would take the herd even farther. Only once in a while would she return on her draught-deer to the camp for food.

One night, as they were riding to the camp, the draught-deer lifted his head and glanced up at the sky.

"Look! Look!" he cried.

The girl looked up and saw the Moon Man coming down the sky on a sledge drawn by two reindeer.

"Where is he going and why?" the girl asked.

"He wants to carry you away," the deer replied.

The girl was much alarmed.

"What am I to do? He might really carry me off with him!" she cried.

Without a word the draught-deer began raking away the snow with his hoof until he had scooped out a hole.

"Come, get into this hole, quick!" he said.

The girl got into the hole, and the deer began kicking snow over her. Very soon the girl had vanished, and there was only a mound of snow to show where she had been.

The Moon Man came down from the sky, stopped his reindeer and got out of his sledge. He walked all around, looking about him and searching for the girl. But he could not find her. He even went up to the mound and looked at the top of it, but he never guessed what it was.

"How very strange!" said the Moon Man. "Where could the girl have got to? I cannot find her. I think I'll go away now and come down again later. I'll be sure to find her then and carry her away with me."

With this, he got into his sledge, and his deer bore him off into the sky.

As soon as he had gone, the draught-deer scraped the snow away, and the girl came out of the hole.

"Let us go to the camp quickly!" she said. "Or else the Moon Man will see me and come down again. I shall not be able to hide from him a second time."

She got into her sledge and the draught-deer whisked her away as quick as lightning. They soon reached the camp, and the girl ran into her father's *choom*. But her father was out. Who would help her now?

Said the draught-deer:

"You must hide, for the Moon Man will be after us."

"Where shall I hide?" the girl asked.

"I will turn you into something—a block of stone, perhaps," said the deer.

"No, it won't do, he will discover me."

"A hammer."

"That won't do, either."

"A pole."

"No."

"A hair of the hide hanging over the door."

"No, no."

"What then? I know, I'll turn you into a lamp."

"All right."

"Well, then, crouch down."

The girl crouched down. The deer struck the ground with his hoof and the girl was turned into a lamp which burned so brightly that it lit up the whole *choom*.

Meanwhile the Moon Man had been searching for the girl among her deer, and he now came tearing on the camping site.

He tied his own deer to a post, entered the *choom* and began looking for her again. He looked everywhere, but he could not find her. He searched in between the poles that supported the top of the *choom*, he examined every utensil, every hair on the skins, every twig under the beds, every bit of earth on the floor, but the girl was nowhere to be found.

As for the lamp, he did not notice it, for though it shone brightly, the Moon Man was just as bright.

"Strange," said the Moon Man. "Where can she be? I shall have to go back to the sky."

He went out of the *choom* and began untying the deer. He had climbed into his sledge and was about to ride away when the girl ran up to the skin flap over the door, and leaning out as far as her waist, let out a peal of merry laughter.

"Here I am! Here I am!" she called to the Moon Man.

The Moon Man left his deer and rushed into the *choom*. But the girl had again turned into a lamp.

The Moon Man began to search for her. He looked over every twig and every leaf, every hair on the skins and every bit of earth, but find the girl he could not.

How very strange this was! Where could she be? Where had she disappeared to? It looked as though he would have to go back without her.

But no sooner had he left the *choom* and begun untying the deer than the girl leaned out from under the flap.

"Here I am! Here I am!" she called with a laugh.

The Moon Man rushed into the *choom* and began to look for her again. He searched for a long time, he rummaged through and turned over everything, but find her he could not.

He was so weary from the search that he became thin and weak. He could barely move his legs or lift his arms.

Now the girl was no longer afraid of him. She took on her proper shape, bounded out of the *choom*, threw the Moon Man on to his back and bound his hands and feet with a rope.

"O-oh!" groaned the Moon Man. "You will kill me, I know! Kill me, then! All right, I deserve it, it is all my own fault. I wanted to carry you off from the Earth. But before I die, cover me with skins and let me get warm, I am so chilled...."

The girl was very much surprised.

"You—chilled?" she said "Why, you live out in the open, you are homeless, you have no *choom*, you belong in the open, and that is where you must stay. What need have you of my skins!"

Then the Moon Man began to plead with the girl, and he spoke to her in this wise:

"Since I am homeless and doomed to be so for ever, let me go free to roam the sky. I will be something for your people to watch, something to give them pleasure. Let me go free, and I will serve as a beacon for your people and guide them across the tundra. Let me go free, and I will turn night into day! Let me go free, and I will measure the year for your people. First I will be the Moon of the Old Bull, then the Moon of the Birth of the Calves, then the Moon of the Waters, then the Moon of the Leaves, then the Moon of Warmth, then the Moon of the Shedding of Antlers, then the Moon of Love among the Wild Deer, then the Moon of the First Winter, and then the Moon of the Shortening Days."

"And if I let you go free and you become strong again and your hands and feet grow strong—will you not come down from the sky to carry me off with you?"

"Oh, no, never! I shall try to forget the very way to you. You are far too clever. I shall never come down from the sky again. Only let me go free, and I will light up sky and earth!"

So the girl let the Moon Man go free, and he rose up into the sky and flooded the earth with light.